*"Wh... ...ear from...*

he asked in a low voice. "How beautiful I think you are? How I haven't been able to touch another woman since you left me? How I still want you so badly I ache?"

Slowly, her movements wary, she turned to face him. "I didn't mean—"

"To goad me?" he cut in roughly, before automatically biting back his sudden surge of temper. When he was in control again, all that remained was a residue of frustration, a feeling that was becoming all too familiar since he'd agreed to be her bodyguard. At least that feeling he could handle.

Why this woman? he wondered. Why did Kate have the power no other woman possessed to rob him of his reason and steal his soul?

Dear Reader,

It's summertime. The mercury's rising, and so is the excitement level here at Silhouette Intimate Moments. Whatever you're looking for—a family story, suspense and intrigue, or love with a ranchin' man—we've got it for you in our lineup this month.

Beverly Barton starts things off with another installment in her fabulous miniseries THE PROTECTORS. *Keeping Annie Safe* will *not* cool you off, I'm afraid! Merline Lovelace is back with *A Man of His Word,* part of her MEN OF THE BAR H miniseries, while award winner Ingrid Weaver checks in with *What the Baby Knew.* If it's edge-of-your-seat suspense you're looking for, pick up the latest from Sally Tyler Hayes, *Spies, Lies and Lovers.* *The Rancher's Surrender* is the latest from fresh new talent Jill Shalvis, while Shelley Cooper makes her second appearance with *Guardian Groom.*

You won't want to miss a single one of these fabulous novels, or any of the books we'll be bringing you in months to come. For guaranteed great reading, come to Silhouette Intimate Moments, where passion and excitement go hand in hand.

Enjoy!

Yours,

Leslie J. Wainger
Executive Senior Editor

Please address questions and book requests to:
Silhouette Reader Service
U.S.: 3010 Walden Ave., P.O. Box 1325, Buffalo, NY 14269
Canadian: P.O. Box 609, Fort Erie, Ont. L2A 5X3

# GUARDIAN GROOM

## SHELLEY COOPER

Published by Silhouette Books

**America's Publisher of Contemporary Romance**

To my mother, Gail Fleisher,
for instilling in me a love of books

To my father, Dale Wray, for showing, by example, that
tenderness and strength go hand in hand

And to their spouses, Joyce Wray and Norman Fleisher,
for embracing a most difficult role—that of stepparent—
and for doing it with grace, dignity and love

 SILHOUETTE BOOKS

ISBN 0-373-07942-7

GUARDIAN GROOM

Copyright © 1999 by Shelley Cooper

Visit us at www.romance.net

Printed in U.S.A.

**Books by Shelley Cooper**

Silhouette Intimate Moments

*Major Dad* #876
*Guardian Groom* #942

---

## SHELLEY COOPER

first experienced the power of words when she was in the eighth grade and wrote a paragraph about the circus for a class assignment. Her teacher returned it with an A and seven pluses scrawled across the top of the paper, along with a note thanking her for rekindling so vividly some cherished childhood memories. Since Shelley had never been to the circus, and had relied solely on her imagination to compose the paragraph, the teacher's remarks were a revelation. Since then, Shelley has relied on her imagination to help her sell dozens of short stories and to write her first novel, *Major Dad,* a 1997 Romance Writers of America Golden Heart finalist in Best Long Contemporary. She hopes her books will be as moving to her readers as her circus paragraph was to that long-ago English teacher.

# Chapter 1

Kate Garibaldi never dreamed she would rile someone to the point where he'd try to kill her.

True, her job was to generate controversy, and she took pride in doing it well. As the author of *Straight Talk*, a nationally syndicated newspaper column, she aired her opinions daily on a wide variety of topics ranging from the current woeful state of politics to the latest craze in children's toys. No subject matter was too insignificant, no theme too untouchable to come under her scrutiny.

Her mail, which consisted of as many letters of denunciation as praise, gave her an immense sense of satisfaction. To Kate, as well as her syndicate, indifference was the kiss of death. "I'd rather anger someone any day than bore him into a catatonic stupor," she'd said during a recent radio interview. "Maybe if I anger someone enough, that person will then take action to right a wrong."

However, when she'd uttered those fateful words, her death was definitely not one of the actions she'd had in mind. In fact, on the sunny June morning that changed her life forever, the thought of death—hers, or anyone else's, for that matter—was the furthest thing from her mind.

"Howdy, Kate," greeted the head clerk when she entered the one-room post office that was nestled in the South Hills of Pittsburgh. "Terrific column today."

Kate smiled in genuine pleasure as she collected the mail from her post-office box. The column, which dealt with political ethics in general, and a well-known, popular politician with his eye on the presidency in particular, was one dear to her heart. "Thanks, Joe."

Joe's eyes twinkled with mischief. "Course, I happen to agree with you. The guy really can't be trusted. I expect, though, that box'll soon be overflowing with letters from people who think otherwise."

"I'm counting on it," she replied with a chuckle, then raised her hand in salute. "See you tomorrow."

Out on the crowded sidewalk, she moved off to one side and paused to leaf through the pile of envelopes. Since one of her nephews collected postmarks, she always made sure to check for new additions to his collection. With letters from Bismark, North Dakota and Honolulu, Hawaii, today was going to be a bonanza for Bobby.

Turning her face to the sky, Kate closed her eyes and delighted in the feel of the sun against her skin. She spent so much time staring at a computer screen that she truly relished these few odd minutes every morning when she took a break to collect her mail.

"You're dead."

The words, growled menacingly behind her, sent a chill up her spine. Her first thought was that someone was playing a trick on her. A not-so-funny trick.

"I don't think—"

Before she could turn to give the prankster a lecture on the protocol of practical joke playing, a pair of hands pressed against the middle of her back and shoved. Hard.

*Steve.*

Kate's feet left the sidewalk, and she felt the sickening

sensation of unplanned flight. Mail went soaring in a graceful arc. Palms skidded across asphalt. Knees, left bare and unprotected by her shorts, landed with a bone-jarring thud. Her head whipped forward, causing her cheek to graze against her shoulder and her front teeth to sink into her bottom lip. Through a haze of pain, she saw a Port Authority bus barreling toward her.

*Steve.*

Panic coursed through her, propelling her heart into her throat. She couldn't move. Brakes squealed a protest. The smell of burning rubber filled her nostrils. Anxious onlookers cried out in alarm.

The bus was close enough for Kate to read the look of horror on the driver's face. She squeezed her eyes shut. Holding her breath, she braced herself for the inevitable.

*Steve, Steve, Steve.*

A mixture of hot air and gasoline fumes smacked her in the face, and then…nothing. Slowly, cautiously, Kate opened her eyes. Less than an inch separated her nose from the bus's chrome bumper. The bus's unmoving chrome bumper. At the realization, her pent-up breath rushed out of her lungs, and she went limp.

A second later, the bus driver was at her side. "Are you okay?" he cried, helping her to her feet. "Did I hit you?"

Knees trembling and heart thundering, Kate stared uncomprehendingly at the mail that lay scattered in the street. She should pick it up, she knew, but at the moment she just didn't have the strength.

"N-no, you d-d-didn't h-hit me." She drew a deep, uneven breath and tried again. "I'm okay."

"Oh, thank goodness. For a minute there, I thought you were a goner."

For a minute there, she'd thought so, too.

*You're dead.* The words echoed in her brain, making her scalp prickle and raising the hair on the back of her neck. Someone had pushed her into the middle of a busy street. Even more incredible, when faced with what had seemed certain death, thoughts of her ex-husband had helped her to hang on. It was a toss-up as to which event was the more unsettling.

"Someone tried to kill me," she murmured, amazed.

"What was that?" the bus driver asked.

A white light filled her vision. The outline of the man's body blurred and divided, until she saw three of him standing before her. She blinked once, twice, but the three bus drivers refused to coalesce into one middle-aged man.

"Someone…" The world began to spin. "Excuse me, but I think I'm going to faint."

Did that high, wavering voice belong to her? Impossible. She never fainted. Fainting was reserved for women who scared easily, a trait her six older brothers had erased from her DNA when she was a child.

"Hold on." Taking her by the arm, the bus driver led her to the curb. "Put your head between your knees. Breathe deeply."

With no strength left to protest, she obeyed. Over the roaring in her ears, Kate heard him asking if anyone had seen what had happened. The replies he received all mentioned how congested the sidewalk had been, and that she'd probably fallen from the press of the crowd. No one raised the possibility that she'd been pushed.

Kate felt a surge of hope. Maybe she'd imagined the whole thing. Since she spent much of her time in the world of her imagination, the thought wasn't so far-fetched. What she knew she hadn't imagined—and couldn't ignore—was the unexpected yearning for a man she'd spent the past eighteen months trying to forget. What had that been all about?

When she raised her head a minute later, the world had righted itself once more. Only one bus driver sat at her side, and he was a kindly looking man with gray hair and bright blue eyes. The tag on his shirt read Gus Stover.

"Good." He beamed at her. "There's some color in your face. A minute ago, it was as white as your blouse."

Thanks to her Italian forebears, and depending upon her

exposure to the sun, Kate's normal skin tone hovered between a mixture of burnished copper and gold. For Gus Stover to describe her as pale was truly saying something.

"You gave me quite a scare," he went on. "I've been driving a bus for over thirty years, and nothing like this has ever happened to me before."

She had to smile. "Believe me, Mr. Stover, nothing like this has ever happened to me, either. Sorry I scared you."

"The name's Gus. And I'm just glad you're okay, Miss...?"

"Kate," she supplied.

"I'm glad you're okay, Kate. How did you end up in the middle of the street like that?"

Was she pushed? Much as she would like to deny it, her ears still rang from the rasp of a deep, malevolent voice; her back still tingled from where a pair of man's hands had pressed against her. Besides, not even in her imagination did a person go from standing three feet from the curb to crouching on all fours in the middle of a busy street. Unless, that is, she'd had help getting there. No, she was definitely pushed.

Judging by the words snarled into her ear, whoever had done the pushing had meant to do her harm. It was no prank. Her mind tried to recoil from the thought, but she wouldn't let it. Someone had tried to hurt her, maybe even kill her. The question was, who? Why? And what was she going to do about it?

For the moment, she felt too shaken and confused to come up with any concrete answers. The only thing she was certain of was that she couldn't confide her suspicions to Gus. For one thing, the poor man had had enough of a shock for one day. For another, she'd always made it a point to solve her problems on her own.

Gus probably wouldn't believe her, anyway. It was clear from the comments of the people around them that no one had witnessed her being pushed. If she started hurling accusations, Gus would most likely dismiss them as the ramblings of a woman who had just been through a traumatic experience. She wouldn't blame him for thinking that way. She was having a hard time believing it herself.

Shrugging, she said, "Just clumsy, I guess. Don't worry, I'll be a lot more careful from now on."

She'd have to be. Her life might depend on it. The thought made her blood run cold.

"Here's your mail," a woman said.

"Thanks." She answered absently, taking the pile of letters and setting it beside her on the sidewalk.

A crowd had gathered to gawk. Horns blared behind the stalled bus.

"You'd better get going," Kate told Gus.

"What about you? You should have those cuts tended to as soon as possible."

What cuts? Looking down, she saw that both of her knees were bloody. She felt a stinging in her palms and turned them over. They were scraped raw from the asphalt. Funny, before she'd been aware of her injuries, she hadn't felt a thing. Now that they'd been brought to her attention, they hurt like the dickens.

"Don't worry about me. I only live three blocks away. I'll take care of it."

Gus didn't seem so certain. "Are you sure? I could call for medical assistance on my transmitter."

The last thing she wanted was more people fussing over her. What she did want, desperately, was to go home. Once she was safely inside the four walls of her seventy-five-year-old brick house, she'd be able to think with a clear head. She'd be able to decide what to do.

"What," she joked, "drag an ambulance out for a couple of cuts and scrapes?" She nodded toward the bus. "Besides, your passengers look anxious to be on their way."

"Sure you're okay? Not going to pass out or anything?"

She summoned up what she hoped was a brilliant smile and gathered up her mail. "I'm just fine."

For the second time, Gus helped her to her feet. Then, with

obvious reluctance, he reboarded the bus. Before closing the door, he craned his head out and called, "Let's be careful out there."

Kate waved in acknowledgment, then watched as, with a hiss of hydraulics, the bus eased its way down the street. She felt suddenly alone, and terribly exposed. Was she still in danger? Was the man who had pushed her waiting to finish off the job? It was an indication of just how deeply the incident had shaken her that it had taken her this long to wonder about that possibility.

The crowd had already begun to disperse when Kate turned around to step up onto the curb. Obviously, her little "incident" was just a tiny blip on the radar screen of their lives. It might prove for some interesting discussion over lunch, but most of them would have forgotten all about it by dinner. If only she could.

She found herself peering hard at the faces of the people she did see. Had one of them pushed her? It was hard to imagine. No one looked out of place. No one appeared sinister. But then, Ted Bundy had looked normal, too.

On that comforting thought, and with her gaze trained carefully on her surroundings, Kate headed home.

Though the day was warm, the woman wore a shapeless, ill-fitting, long-sleeved dress. She was gaunt, her skin stretched tautly over hollow cheeks. Her gestures were nervous. She started at every sound, her gaze darting around the reception area of Three Rivers Security, Inc., as if she expected the boogeyman to jump out of the shadows at any moment. A pair of oversize sunglasses did little to hide the bruises on her face.

Steve Gallagher knew with absolute certainty that the long sleeves hid dozens of similar black-and-blue marks. She'd been beaten mercilessly by the man who had taken vows to cherish and protect her until death did them part. It wasn't the first time, and, if she stayed with him, it wouldn't be the last. The unavoidable truth was that, if she didn't get away from him, in all likelihood death would be parting them soon.

"I don't know how to thank you," she whispered, staring at the bus tickets he'd placed in her hand as though they were made of gold.

"You can thank me," he replied in a gruff voice, "by taking your daughter and boarding that bus to Cleveland. The shelter there is expecting you." To the bus tickets he added an envelope filled with twenty dollar bills. "You can stay there until you're back on your feet again."

Tears streamed down her hollow cheeks. "But...this is your own money, Mr. Gallagher. I can't take it. I...I'll never be able to repay you."

"You don't understand," he said gently. "You don't owe me anything. I'm the one who's repaying a debt."

"But it's so much money."

He nodded toward the frail five-year-old girl playing quietly with Liza, his receptionist, at the far end of the room. Beside the little girl sat a worn suitcase that was almost as battered as the woman herself.

"It doesn't come close to compensating either one of you for what you've been through," he said. "For her sake, I'm asking you to take the money. When you're in the position to do so, you can repay me by helping someone else in need."

She smiled wanly and nodded. "All right. I'll do that. Thank you again, Mr. Gallagher."

When the elevator doors closed on the woman and her child, Steve's smile faded. He felt drained and in need of a long nap. It was always like this after one of these encounters. That was when the enormity of the task he'd undertaken would hit him anew. There were so many women, so many children. Would it never end?

"Do you think she'll be okay?" Liza asked, breaking into his thoughts.

Wearily he turned away from the elevator. "If she uses

those tickets and goes to Cleveland. If she doesn't stop at home for one forgotten thing, and then change her mind.''

"Have I told you lately how proud I am to be working for you? I think it's a wonderful thing you're doing.''

Steve centered his attention on the younger woman. "I'm nobody's hero, Liza,'' he said roughly.

The denial of his words was clear in her eyes. "I don't see anybody else around here going out on a limb to help these poor women.''

He did it in honor of his mother, and for no other reason. He wanted no praise and no glory. His sole goal was to prevent another woman from losing her life at the hands of her abuser, the way his mother had.

In a brusque, businesslike tone he asked, "When's my next appointment?''

Ever efficient, Liza took the hint. "Fifteen minutes. A Mr. Chung is coming to discuss a long-term security contract. He owns a convenience store in the Hill District that's a popular hold-up target. After that, a Miss Bishop is scheduled. She manages a rock group called The Sour Grapes. They'll be playing at the Civic Arena in a couple of weeks, and she wants to arrange for personal protection during the performance.''

Steve nodded. "Send Mr. Chung back the minute he arrives.''

When his office door closed behind him, he stared at nothing for a long moment. His hands balled into fists at his sides as the rage he felt for what that poor woman and her child had endured engulfed him. If he could have just two minutes alone with that miserable coward, two minutes to show him how it felt....

Steve bit back the rage, ruthlessly stemming the emotion the way he'd done for years. Within seconds, he was back in control.

His glance fell on the engraved plaque proclaiming his company's motto: The Violence Stops Here. It was more than just a business maxim. It was his philosophy for living, the only way he'd be able to escape the genetic curse that haunted him. He never, for one minute, let himself forget that only a thin line, and his self-will, separated him from the SOB who had battered that poor woman almost beyond recognition.

After taking a seat, he reached for the newspaper. As he did every morning, he checked to see if the ad was there. Only once had it been missing, and he'd worried that someone who'd needed to see it had been lost. This morning, the ad was where it belonged. Though he knew the words by heart, he read it anyway.

Caught in an abusive relationship?
There is a way out. Confidentiality
guaranteed. We can help. No fee charged.

After checking that the phone number and address were printed correctly, he turned to the editorial section. To *her* column. For some reason he didn't understand, he'd been thinking about Kate all morning.

A chuckle left his throat when he read that day's offering. It was typical Kate: brash, idealistic and opinionated. She'd win no friends with this one. But then, he knew she wasn't trying to. He'd never met anyone who loved a good debate the way Kate did.

And he avoided them at all costs.

After cutting out the column and placing it in a file in his desk, Steve picked up a pen, intent on concentrating on his paperwork. But instead of seeing the words printed on the papers spread out before him, images rolled through his brain. Images of the past, in color and in vivid detail. Images of when he and Kate had been together.

For not the first time, he cursed his photographic memory. When he was a kid, it had been a source of embarrassment, something that had set him apart from his peers. Now it only served to remind him, in graphic detail, of the many times he and Kate had made love.

He remembered the little things. How she'd adored having her back rubbed after a long day spent hunched over the computer. How her brow had furrowed in concentration and she'd chewed on her lip while writing. The silky softness of her skin. The way her breath had escaped in soft little gasps whenever he'd touched her. How she'd curled contentedly to his side when she slept.

It wasn't the little things that had eroded their marriage. The big things had brought them down. Like the death of their daughter, who had lived for just a day and a half. And Kate's overwhelming need to be self-sufficient. God, she'd made him feel so useless. And then she'd walked out on him. Funny how, after the passage of eighteen months, that still hurt.

A nerve tightened in his stomach. Heartburn flared like a fiery ball in his chest. Steve reached for the antacid bottle he kept perched on the edge of his desk. Something told him it was going to be a long day.

The note was taped to her front door. Hands shaking, Kate ripped it down and read the words that were formed by letters that had been clipped from newspapers and magazines.

My Dearest Kate:
You have been corrupted by the soul of
evil and must be purified in the blood. The
time of purification is at hand. This morning
was just a warning. Know that I am watching
and waiting. Soon we will be together through
all eternity.

Your biggest fan

Well, at least now she knew who was trying to kill her, Kate thought, fighting back hysteria. Her biggest fan. Whoever that was.

After stuffing the note into her shorts pocket and scanning the empty street, she reached for the doorknob, then took a step back. What if he was inside, waiting for her? She hadn't locked the door when she'd left, hadn't deemed it necessary. She'd always felt safe in this bedroom community of older homes and friendly, working-class people. Besides, Martha was there. There had been no need to lock it.

Her hand flew to her mouth. *Martha*. Dear God, Martha was inside. Kate would never forgive herself if something had happened to her assistant.

Without care for her own safety, she dropped the mail on the porch and threw open the door. "Martha!" she screamed at the top of her lungs, racing for the rear of the house. "Martha, where are you?"

"Here. I'm here, Kate," the woman called, concern lacing her voice. "What's wrong?"

Kate rounded the corner into the room that served as both den and office. Martha was sitting at her desk, obviously alone and unharmed.

"Oh, thank goodness." Kate went weak with relief.

Martha's eyes opened wide when she got a good look at Kate. "Merciful heavens! What on earth happened to you?"

Suddenly it was all too much. Kate wasn't up to answering questions right now. What she needed was time. Time alone. Time to think. Time to reason through what had happened. Time to decide what to do next. Because, heaven help her, her brain kept conveying one message over and over—that her time was running out.

"Excuse me for a minute," she announced in a voice that was decidedly unsteady. "I need to use the bathroom. Would you do me a favor and make sure all the doors and windows are locked?" Turning, she limped from the room.

Once the bathroom door was shut firmly behind her, she leaned against the hard wood and closed her eyes. Now that she felt reasonably safe, she let reaction take hold. A shudder racked her body, and her knees buckled. She slid down the door until she sat on the floor, legs splayed out in front of her. Arms hugged tightly to her chest, she shook until her teeth chattered.

Someone was trying to kill her. A man. A man she'd never met. She had no idea whether he was tall or short, heavy or thin, blond or brunet. All she knew was that he was full of hate, and that he'd directed that emotion at her. Dear God, how did a person defend herself against that?

*Steve. I want Steve.*

This time, she understood the reason for her yearning. From the moment she'd been pushed in front of that bus, her subconscious had been telling her what she needed to do. Right now, Steve was the only one she could trust to keep her safe.

The knocking, and the vibration of the door against her back, roused her.

"Kate?" Martha called. "Kate? Are you okay?" There was a hint of panic in the older woman's voice.

Belatedly Kate realized it wasn't the first time her assistant had called out to her. "I'm fine. Be out in a minute." To her relief, her voice sounded almost normal.

Legs stiff, and feeling chilled from the air-conditioning, she rose and walked to the mirror hanging above the sink. The woman who stared back at her looked as panic-stricken as she felt. Her face was unnaturally pale, her brown eyes wide, her mouth open as if preparing to scream. A magnificent purple bruise marred her right cheek. Her bottom lip was swollen.

Kate tried to look on the bright side. She never had been a beauty, so what were a few assorted cuts and bruises? She was, essentially, in one piece. No bones were broken, no stitches required. The important thing was that she was alive.

Now all she had to do was stay that way.

After splashing her face and hands with cold water, she pulled a first-aid kit from the medicine cabinet. When she reentered her office, she gingerly settled her aching body onto the black leather sofa and placed the kit on her lap.

Martha's gaze burned into her like a laser. Kate knew it missed nothing, from her torn blouse and scraped knees and elbows, to the way her hair, normally restrained at the nape of her neck with a barrette, now fell in a tangled mass to the middle of her back.

"Is the house locked up?"

"Tighter than a drum." The older woman's eyes were narrowed and searching, her expression troubled. "By the way, I gathered the mail from the porch. Want to tell me what happened?"

Kate unscrewed the lid from a bottle of antiseptic. After soaking a cotton ball in the clear liquid, she applied it to first one knee, then the other. "I was pushed in front of a bus. Needless to say, it managed to stop in time."

Martha's hand flew to her heart. "Merciful heavens! Who pushed you?"

"My biggest fan."

The worst of her injuries tended to, Kate twisted the lid onto the antiseptic bottle and placed it back in the kit. Standing, she crossed to the floor-to-ceiling sliding window that opened onto the deck in her backyard. Her knees and elbows stung, and the bruise on her cheek throbbed. Ignoring the pain, her gaze roved from the deck to the rear of the yard. Was he out there somewhere? Was he watching her right now?

"You mean," Martha said, "the kook who cuts out letters and pastes them onto paper?"

Kate focused her gaze on a squirrel that was scampering up a tree. "That'd be the one."

The people who wrote her letters tended to fall into one of three camps: ardent support, ardent opposition and psychiatrically challenged. Since *Straight Talk* had been syndicated four years earlier, Kate had received her share of mail from the latter camp. Now that the column was published in almost every major newspaper in the country, off-the-wall letters were a daily occurrence. She'd received marriage proposals, offers to sire her children, even a letter claiming the writer was her identical twin and they'd been separated at birth. Death threats were not uncommon.

But none of the other letter writers spewed hate at her the way her biggest fan did. If, indeed, he could be called a fan. His letters had started arriving a month earlier.

Despite the threats, until today, both she and Martha, whom she'd hired a year ago to answer her fan mail and help with research, had dismissed the writer as being a harmless crank. Kate had considered his letters a part of the price she had to pay for her success.

"How do you know it's him?" Martha asked.

The squirrel disappeared into the high reaches of the tree. Squaring her shoulders, Kate faced her assistant.

"Because of this." She reached into her shorts pocket and pulled out the crumpled note. "It was taped to the front door. Did you hear anyone out there earlier?"

Martha shook her head. "Not a peep."

"You know," Kate said while Martha read, "before this morning I felt safe in the belief that he was mailing his little works of art to a post-office box. I was certain he had no idea where I lived."

Brow creased with worry, Martha looked up from the letter. "I think it's safe to assume he now knows."

"And he also knows I walk to the post office in the morning to pick up the mail. He either followed me, or waited for me there. He growled, 'You're dead,' into my ear before he shoved me into the street."

At the memory, Kate was unable to suppress the shiver of apprehension that raced up her spine. "Lord knows what else he knows about me." Her voice lowered. "Or what he has planned."

"So why," Martha demanded, "aren't you on the phone right now with the police?"

A stray lock of hair fell across Kate's eyes. She raised a not-quite-steady hand to brush it away, wincing when it grazed the bruise on her cheek. "Because I have something else to do first."

"What could be more important than calling the police?"

"Hiring a bodyguard." With a sense of purpose, Kate strode to the bookshelf located to the left of her computer work station and grabbed the Yellow Pages. "And I know just the man for the job."

She riffled through the pages until she found the listing she sought. Picking up the telephone receiver, she punched in the required numbers and listened to the ringing on the other end.

"Three Rivers Security," a bright female voice trilled into her ear.

Kate drew a deep breath, then plunged ahead. "I'd like to speak to Steve Gallagher, please."

"I'm sorry, but Mr. Gallagher is in conference."

"Is it possible to get him out of conference? This is an emergency."

"Are you calling about the newspaper ad?"

What newspaper ad? "No, this is a personal matter."

"I'm sorry," the woman repeated, "but Mr. Gallagher cannot be disturbed. Can I take a message? He'll return your call at his earliest convenience."

Frustrated, Kate bit her lip. The way she saw it, she had two alternatives. She could either stand here wasting precious time trying to persuade this woman to put her through to Steve, or she could go in person to his office. Once she was there, he would have to see her. She wouldn't take no for an answer.

"No," she said. "No message."

"You're hiring your ex-husband to protect you?" Martha asked, clearly disbelieving, as Kate slowly replaced the receiver.

Never having met Steve, for Martha to recognize his name so easily meant that Kate mentioned it far too often, a tendency she would have to rectify once this matter was settled. "Yes."

"Why?"

"Because," Kate said firmly, meeting her friend's gaze head-on, "he's the best in the business. And I believe in hiring the best."

"But won't that dredge up all sorts of things you'd rather not dredge up?"

Good question. Unfortunately, Kate didn't have the time to address it at the moment. She had other, more pressing matters to occupy her time.

"I don't see why it should. We're both adults. The divorce was a year and a half ago. Whatever we felt for each other is long dead. We've both gone on with our lives. All I know is, if anyone can figure out who my biggest fan is and keep me safe in the process, it's Steve. I have no other choice."

# Chapter 2

It took all Kate's powers of persuasion, and a promise to call the police the minute she'd spoken to Steve, to convince Martha to leave. Once the older woman's car disappeared down the street and Kate was satisfied her friend was safe, she raced upstairs.

Five minutes later, she peered both ways before slipping out the side door. It was a door she rarely used, an exit leading to a narrow sidewalk kept in perpetual shade by the bulk of the two buildings that were built on either side of it. Because of its proximity to downtown Pittsburgh, property in her town was at a premium. Homes had been built so close to one another, a person could literally reach out and touch her neighbor.

In Kate's case, the neighbor in question was Mrs. Edmund, an elderly woman with a penchant for games. When she needed a break from her writing, Kate often spent a delightful hour or two sitting across the card table from Mrs. Edmund.

At the moment, she prayed Mrs. Edmund didn't see her lurking between their two homes. Much as she adored the woman and enjoyed her company, Kate wasn't in the mood for small talk. Nor did she want to put her neighbor in danger, if danger was lying in wait.

When she saw no one suspicious, and when Mrs. Edmund remained closeted securely behind the walls of her redbrick, three-story house, Kate heaved a sigh of relief and headed for the two-car detached garage at the rear of her property. As she walked, she stuffed her hair under a Pirates cap and settled a pair of dark sunglasses on her nose.

In addition to the cap and glasses, she wore a pair of baggy, three-sizes-too-big jeans and an oversize T-shirt her niece had left behind on a recent weekend visit. Her legs teetered precariously atop a pair of wedgies with six-inch heels. A canvas bag served as a makeshift purse. Hopefully, the outfit was different enough from her normal apparel that even her own family would have to look twice in order to recognize her.

Though she would have preferred looking a bit more mature when she saw Steve, the only other disguise she'd been able to scrape up on such short notice was the Cruella de Vil costume she'd worn last Halloween to the party her oldest brother had hosted at his restaurant. While it had scored a ten on the approval scale—at least, according to the party's attendees—on the blending-in scale, the best it could hope to achieve was a dismal minus five. And the point of the exercise was not to attract unwanted attention. Hence, the outfit preferred by four out of five teenage girls. God forbid, though, she would have to run. She'd probably break her neck.

On that thought, Kate promptly tripped over the hem of the jeans and nearly fell against her car. Her car...

It suddenly occurred to her that if her biggest fan had been keeping tabs on her, he probably already knew the make and model of her car. Which meant that the minute she drove away in it, her disguise was blown. Damn!

She briefly considered taking the subway before discarding the idea. Even if her cover was blown, she felt safer behind the wheel of her dependable Subaru as opposed to crowding in next to who-knows-who on the subway. She really was no good at this cloak-and-dagger business, which was all the more reason to get to Steve. Fast.

Grimacing, she tugged at the waistband of her pants. Though she had her belt cinched as tightly as it would go, the pants still threatened to slide over hips she'd often cursed as being far too generous. How did her niece, with her slender, hipless figure, manage to keep the darn things up? Kate couldn't imagine. What she did know was that, if she wasn't careful, she'd be adding more scrapes and bruises to the ones she already had.

While she drove toward the parkway that would lead her into downtown Pittsburgh, she kept her gaze focused on the rearview mirror. Not one to waste time, she normally used her infrequent stretches behind the wheel to generate ideas for her column. An alien in a purple flying saucer could follow her, and she'd never notice.

Not today. Today, Kate made it a point to inspect every car and driver that came into view.

The sensation of being watched itched across the back of her neck. *Was* someone following her? How on earth was she supposed to tell? Her only experience with spotting tails was what she'd read in books or seen on television. She wasn't about to start weaving in and out of traffic to see if another car followed suit. The way her luck was running, if she tried that particular ploy, she'd most likely wind up ramming head-on into the concrete barrier dividing the four-lane road.

Biting her lip, Kate clenched the steering wheel. Relief coursed through her when she finally reached her destination and no one followed her down the ramp into the parking garage located beneath the skyscraper, which housed, among others, the firm of Three Rivers Security, Inc.

What did follow her during the elevator ride some thirty floors up were a whole host of doubts and reservations. In just a few minutes, she would be face-to-face with the one person she'd never thought she would see again. Steve Gallagher. Her ex-husband. The man who had shattered her heart into a million tiny little pieces.

The galling thing was, in some perverse way she didn't understand, she was actually looking forward to their meeting. What did she hope? That he'd take one look at her, get down on his knees, tell her that the past eighteen months had been empty and meaningless without her, and beg her to come back to him? A glance at her outfit had a welcome chuckle bubbling in her throat. Not even *her* vivid imagination could conjure up that scenario.

Just before the elevator reached its destination, Kate removed the baseball cap and shook out her hair. After a moment's hesitation, she decided to leave the sunglasses on. She didn't want Steve to see how scared and vulnerable she felt.

Above her head the number thirty-four lit up and the elevator doors slid open to reveal a wide lobby. Feet aching from trying to maintain her equilibrium on the wedgies, she nearly twisted her ankle when she stepped onto thick beige carpeting that covered a huge room bisected by four twelve-foot-tall columns. Awestruck, she surveyed her surroundings.

The columns were painted the same stark white as the walls, which were adorned with modern art. The few pieces of furniture scattered about were sleek, monochromatic and obviously expensive. The whole combined to give a feeling of light, airy openness.

It was as far removed from the crowded Victorian atmosphere of Kate's house as green cheese was from the moon. But then, she and Steve always had favored different things, which was probably why their marriage had been doomed from the start. She'd favored communication and time spent together, while Steve had leaned more toward the tight-lipped, workaholic school of thought.

By the looks of it, he was doing very well. Very well, indeed. Now that she thought of it, it was ironic how well they'd both done since they'd been apart.

She was glad, she told herself, as her gaze took in the

details of what appeared to be a Native American sculpture. Deep down—despite the time or two in her darkest moments, when she'd wished a plague or pestilence would descend upon him—she truly was happy for him.

"May I help you?" a pleasant voice greeted.

Kate recognized the dulcet tones of the woman she'd spoken to on the phone. Abandoning her memories of the past, she made her unsteady way to the chrome-edged desk holding court in the center of the four pillars.

There was only one word to describe the woman seated there: gorgeous. Mouth-watering, testosterone-rising gorgeous. She was everything Kate was not: large breasted, tiny waisted, ivory skinned, face a perfect oval, eyes an incredible azure blue, hair a delicate blond. The entire package was set off to advantage by a peach-colored suit.

Never in her life had Kate felt more inadequate. Her sense of inadequacy was intensified by the fact that she teetered before this stunning creature in baggy jeans and a T-shirt that had If You're Not Wasted, The Day Is stenciled across the front.

"Yes," Kate said, forcing her lips into the semblance of a smile and trying to infuse some confidence into her voice. "My name is Kate Garibaldi. I'd like to see Mr. Gallagher."

Expecting resistance, Kate was surprised by the spark of sympathy that flared in the other woman's eyes. "You're here about the ad in the paper, aren't you?"

The ad again, Kate thought, bemused. Was Steve advertising for help? If so, it wouldn't make sense for her to show up dressed as she was. Still, if that was what it took to gain entrée into his inner sanctum, she was willing to play the part.

"Yes," she lied. "I'm here about the ad."

"Just a minute."

The woman picked up a telephone receiver and spoke quietly. Then, nodding at Kate, she said, "Straight through the doors over there, last office on the right."

Second thoughts assailed Kate, and her steps grew progressively heavier as she walked down the long, narrow hallway till it felt as if she were trudging through molasses. Now that she'd had some time to think with a clearer head, she decided this wasn't such a good idea, after all. She really wasn't up to seeing Steve today. She wasn't sure she'd ever be.

Wouldn't it be easier all around to let her fingers do the walking through the listings of bodyguards in the Yellow Pages? Surely there were dozens of firms offering the same services Steve did. And all of them had the plus of coming without the emotional chains that simply walking down this hallway hung around her neck.

Unfortunately, she didn't know those faceless men and women. She didn't know their work ethic, or their degree of skill. While it might be fine to occasionally take potluck when it came to hiring a plumber or a carpenter, it wasn't fine to do so when her life was on the line.

There were worse things than hiring your ex-husband to protect you, Kate decided. Offhand, she could easily think of three. Developing an allergy to all foods but green beans. Having a root canal without benefit of anesthesia. Premature, preventable death.

Kate set her chin at a defiant angle. She needed a bodyguard, and Steve was the best. That they shared a personal history was irrelevant. Her heart was dead to him. This was business. Important business. Even though she wasn't dressed for it, she would conduct herself in a businesslike manner.

And she would feel nothing.

At the end of the hallway, she stopped in front of a closed door with a raised gold plate that announced it as the office of Steve Gallagher, President and CEO. Kate's heart beat faster, and she tried to rub some warmth into suddenly clammy hands. Before her courage entirely deserted her, she knocked once, softly.

"Come in," a familiar voice called.

Though Kate had told herself she was prepared for it, she

was powerless to halt the jolt of awareness that shot through her like an electrical current when she saw Steve standing stiffly behind a desk similar to the one in the lobby. He looked different: harder, cynical, incredibly remote. It felt strange to see him in a gray suit, white shirt and tie. He'd been an undercover cop when they were married, and she'd gotten used to seeing him in jeans and leather. Stranger still was the close-cropped blond hair that, except for one stray lock, hugged his head, accentuating intelligent blue eyes and a hawkish nose. Last time she'd seen him, his hair had been almost as long as hers and pulled back in a ponytail.

He wasn't the prototypical bodyguard. This was no hulking giant with gold chains around his neck, a bald head, barrel chest and bulging arm muscles. At six foot one, he was tall, but not overbearingly so; slender without being skinny; muscular without being brawny.

Nor was he handsome. Not in the traditional sense, anyway. His forehead was too broad, his nose too prominent, his chin too stubborn. What he was, was compelling. There was an intensity about him that demanded attention. An intensity that told the world he was not a man to be trifled with. Confident and uncaring of what other people thought of him, Steve Gallagher was a man who would not be ignored.

Kate tried to tell herself that she was totally unaffected by him, and knew immediately it was a lie. One thing she'd made a point of never doing after she'd ended her marriage was to lie to herself. She'd done enough of that for a dozen lifetimes while they were together.

Looking at him now, his features set in the hard, uncompromising lines that had grown so familiar to her over the last tense weeks before she'd left him, it was hard for Kate to believe that this was the man she'd laughed with, made love with, planned to spend the rest of her life with. It dismayed her how fresh her memories were, how easily she could recall all the pain and disappointment. During their marriage, she'd never been privy to his private thoughts or emotions. She'd never known him at all. She still didn't know him. What was he thinking? What was he feeling?

One thing was certain: she couldn't read him any better today than she could eighteen months ago. It took all her willpower not to squirm as his gaze roved slowly over her. Thank goodness she'd left the sunglasses on.

"This is a new look for you," he drawled.

She almost smiled. Leave it to Steve to ignore the formalities. Not even a "How are you?" or an "It's been a long time." He didn't extend his hand in greeting, for which she was heartily grateful. She wasn't ready for his touch.

"Look who's talking," she replied lightly, taking a seat in one of the chrome-backed chairs positioned in front of his desk. "For your information, this is a disguise."

She watched as Steve leaned back in his chair and folded his arms across his chest. What was it all the body language experts said about crossed arms? That the person doing the crossing was physically distancing himself. Closed off. Uncommunicative. It could be Steve's epitaph.

"Works for me," he said. "No one would ever guess you're—what?—twenty-nine now. In that getup you look like jailbait."

He'd said much the same thing to her the day they met, a day Kate remembered far too well for her peace of mind. It was a Garibaldi family tradition to share Thanksgiving dinner with those who would otherwise be alone. On that particular Thanksgiving day, her brother Antonio had invited a fellow police officer. Kate had taken one look at Steve and known he was the one.

She brought herself up short. Now was not the time for those memories.

The problem was, she'd never been much good at resisting him. From the moment they'd met, she'd found herself lost to the tug of a powerful physical attraction, the likes of which she'd never encountered. Before or since. Even during the most painful moments of their marriage, all he'd had to do was reach out for her, and she'd burn for him. Despite the eighteen months yawning between them, she knew that, if he touched her right now, the emotion she would feel would be far from indifference. Unbelievably, after everything that had happened, the tug was still there.

That scared her more than the thought of her biggest fan.

"The point was not to be recognized," she told him.

"I see."

Just what was proper etiquette here? Kate wondered. She could hardly say, "Hi, I know I left you, but eighteen months have passed, and we're both a little older and wiser. By the way, I think someone's trying to kill me."

Because she didn't know what to say, and because Steve didn't seem to be in any hurry to discover the reason for her visit, she took refuge in small talk. "So, you're a bodyguard."

"We prefer to call ourselves personal protection specialists."

She looked around the room. Same white walls and beige carpeting as in the lobby. Same wall hangings. Despite the expensive furnishings, the room was cold, impersonal. Like its owner.

"I was surprised when I heard you'd left the police force. You always seemed to love your work." It was the one thing she'd been certain he did love.

"The decision was a long time coming."

Since he'd resigned three weeks after she left him, it meant he'd been thinking about it during their marriage. Why hadn't he told her? She didn't know why that should amaze her. After all, he'd never let her get close. He'd never shared his deepest thoughts and feelings. The only thing he'd ever truly shared with her was his body. For a while, it had been enough.

"I never got to tell you how sorry I was about Quincy," she said.

Quincy Ellis had been Steve's best friend. They'd grown up together, joined the Pittsburgh police force together, and together had risen quickly through its ranks. But somewhere along the way, Quincy had made a wrong turn. The lure of money, the downfall of many an undercover cop, had proven too much for him. He'd become heavily involved in the drug trade. One night, a deal had gone very wrong, and an innocent child had been killed. Steve had been the major force behind the sting that nabbed his friend. Though Quincy was being held without bond, because of legal maneuvering by his lawyers the case had yet to come to trial. When it did, though, she knew Steve would have to testify.

She also knew how much Quincy's friendship had meant to Steve. It must have darn near killed him to realize Quincy had been corrupted.

"Quincy made his own bed." He spoke without a trace of emotion.

"Still, it must have been hard for you to turn him in."

He shrugged. "I was just doing my job."

Even for Steve, the comment was unfeeling. She had a sudden flash of insight. "Did your leaving the force have something to do with Quincy?"

Leaning forward in his chair, he folded his arms on his desk and leveled his gaze on her. "I don't think you came here to talk about Quincy. Or my career change."

She drew a deep breath. "No. No, I didn't."

Once again, his gaze roved over her. He had a photographic memory, she recalled. Was he cataloging the changes that had taken place since he last saw her? Was he comparing her to the sleek, beautiful woman who graced his reception area?

"Does the reason for your visit have something to do with the bruise on your cheek and your split lip?" he asked.

Kate's fingers tightened around the canvas bag. "Yes."

"Liza told me you're here because someone beat you up."

Kate started. "Liza? The woman out front?"

"Yes."

"Why would she say a thing like that?"

"You did tell her you were here in answer to the ad, didn't you?"

That blasted ad. She wished she knew what this was all about. "Yes, but that was just because I thought it would make it easier to get in to see you. What does my supposedly answering an ad have to do with your receptionist assuming I was beaten up?"

"It's not important," he sidestepped. "Want to tell me why you're here?"

Deciding to leave the question of the ad for another time, Kate plunged straight to the heart of the matter. "I need a bodyguard. Someone pushed me in front of a bus."

"You were pushed?"

For the first time she heard a hint of emotion in his voice. His lips thinned, and his jaw tightened.

"Yes."

"By whom?"

She slid the straps of the canvas bag off her shoulder and delved a hand inside. When she withdrew it, she held a pile of letters secured by a rubber band. On top, she'd placed the letter that had been taped to her front door.

"The man who sent these. He calls himself my biggest fan."

Steve reached for the packet, and she carefully handed it to him, making sure their fingers didn't touch. While he read through them, she recited every detail she could remember of the incident.

When he looked up, he asked, "Have you shown these to the police?"

"Not yet."

"Why not?"

"Until this morning, Martha and I just assumed they were written by some harmless crank."

"Martha?"

"My assistant."

Steve placed the letters aside. "If you thought they were written by a crank, why'd you keep them?"

Kate raised her arms in a dismissive gesture. "You know me. I'm a pack rat. I keep everything."

"They need to be shown to the police immediately," Steve said. "You also need to file a report about what happened in front of the post office. Despite what you heard, they might be able to find a witness. I'll make a note for whoever's assigned to act as your personal protection specialist to see to this immediately." Picking up a pen, he began scribbling on a legal pad.

The thought of someone other than Steve acting as her bodyguard sent her into a near panic. "No," she said.

His pen stilled. "No?"

"I want you to be my bodyguard, Steve."

"I'm sorry, but I no longer work in the field."

Kate bit her lip. Her fingers played restlessly with the straps of the canvas bag. "Couldn't you make an exception in my case?"

"Because we used to be married, you mean?"

"Yes."

Impassive as ever, he stared at her and said, "Tell me something, Kate. Three of your brothers are cops. Why didn't you go to them with this? Why come to me?"

How to explain what she didn't completely understand herself? All she knew was that she wouldn't feel safe with anyone but Steve. The need to have him by her side during this crisis felt as elemental as breathing.

"I live in a small town. Even though Carlo is chief of police, the force itself is too small and inexperienced to give me the protection you can. And you know how my brothers overreact when it comes to me. They'd go off half-cocked, finding crazed fans behind every tree. Sooner or later, someone would get hurt, and I'm afraid it would be one of them."

His lips curled into a sardonic half smile. "So, if anyone's going to get hurt, you'd rather it be me. Is that it?"

Thoughts of him getting hurt had never crossed her mind. Even when they were married, and he'd worked undercover, she'd never worried. She'd always thought of him as invincible.

"Isn't that your job?" she asked.

Instead of answering, he surprised her by commanding, "Take off your glasses."

"Why?"

"I want to see your eyes."

"And if I refuse?"

"Scared?" he challenged.

She hadn't backed down from a dare since she was three years old, and she wasn't about to start now. Kate slowly lowered the glasses to her lap. When her gaze locked with his, she felt more exposed than if she had removed her shirt.

"All right," she said, her voice sounding brittle. "I took them off. Satisfied?"

Blue eyes that glittered like sapphires stared into hers for what seemed an eternity. "Why'd you come to me, Kate?" he asked softly.

Unnerved by the intensity of his regard, she looked away. Several answers, all of them flippant, hovered on the tip of her tongue. She bit them back. Instinctively she knew that everything hinged on what she said next. Nothing but the truth would serve her now.

She drew a deep, shuddering breath. What good was her pride when it was standing between her and the thing she wanted most? Turning her gaze back to his, Kate no longer bothered to hide her confusion. Or her fear.

"I'm scared, Steve. Really scared. Someone tried to kill me! I don't know what to do about that. But I know that you do. Please, will you be my bodyguard? I…I need you."

To her surprise, a look of pain crossed his face. "If you only knew—" he said gruffly, then broke off.

"Knew what?" she asked.

"Nothing." He cleared his throat. "Give me a minute, will you?"

He picked up the phone, and for the next ten minutes Kate listened while he made the necessary arrangements to take a temporary leave of absence. While it was obvious he had a well-thought-out backup plan in place for just such an eventuality, she couldn't help wondering why he'd go to all that bother for her.

"Okay, Kate," he said when he hung up the phone. "I'll be your bodyguard."

All thoughts of why he was accepting her case were swept away as sweet relief coursed through her. The only thing that mattered was that Steve was going to help her. For the first time since she'd found herself on her knees in front of that bus, she felt safe.

"Thank you."

"Tell me," he asked, all business once more, "why do you automatically assume it's a man who wrote these letters? Why do you think a man pushed you?"

"The voice that growled in my ear was definitely male," she replied. "The hands that pressed against my back felt big and masculine. Besides, aren't most of these people men?"

"For the most part. There are women stalkers, however."

Stalker. She didn't like the sound of the word. She didn't like it at all. Somehow, it had seemed less threatening when she'd thought of her letter writer as a fan. A very sick fan, but a fan, nonetheless.

"So, what do we do next?"

Steve twirled the pen in his hand. "I come home with you and set up a command post. Then we figure out who this guy is and turn him over to the police."

Because it looked so out of place amid the sleek, modern furnishings of the room, the bottle of antacid on the corner of his desk caught her attention. She shook her head and bit back a wry smile. The more things changed, the more they stayed the same.

"Stomach still bothering you?" she asked.

"I eat too much spicy food."

He kept too much inside, she silently amended. That was why he suffered from heartburn. It had nothing to do with indigestion. How many times during their marriage had he walked away whenever an issue between them had escalated to the point of argument? Oh, how that had infuriated her. If he would just let go of his emotions once in a while, empty himself out, he'd probably find he no longer needed an antacid.

Steve reached into a desk drawer and removed a sheet of paper. "This is a listing of our fees. It's pretty standard for the industry."

Kate barely glanced at it. It really didn't matter what he charged, she would have agreed to any terms. "Looks good to me."

"Fine. I'll have a contract drawn up." Bracing his palms against the edge of his desk, he pushed his chair back. "Did you drive downtown or take the subway?"

"I drove."

"I'll follow you home." He removed his suit coat and draped it across the back of his chair before opening another drawer and removing a gun and holster. After checking to see that the gun was loaded, he secured the holster around his left shoulder. He strapped a second gun around his right ankle.

"Are they necessary?" Kate asked.

"They're a precautionary measure." He shrugged back into his suit coat. "You wouldn't expect a surgeon to operate without a scalpel, would you?"

"No, but..."

He turned his gaze on her. "What's wrong, Kate? You've never been squeamish about my wearing a gun before."

"I know. It's just..." It made it all seem real. Too real. "Nothing. Let's go."

When they reached his office door, Steve opened it and stood aside. "After you."

Kate waited patiently. "You know I don't stand on ceremony."

His smile, such as it was, was sardonic. "My mistake. I forgot. Except when your life's in danger, you don't take help from anyone, do you? Sufficient unto the end is Kate Garibaldi." There was an unmistakable note of bitterness in his voice.

Kate blinked. Is that how he thought of her? Sufficient unto the end? Yes, she enjoyed her independence; she'd fought long and hard for it. And yes, she liked the fact that she could stand on her own two feet. But that didn't mean she didn't need other people. She needed her family. She needed her friends. When they were married, she'd needed Steve. Too much.

Instead of challenging his words, she simply followed him out the door. All that was in the past. What good would it do to rehash it now?

What on earth was he doing? Steve wondered as he tailed Kate's forest-green Subaru. Had he completely lost his mind? He must have, because instead of dumping Kate's case on one of his employees' desks like the good administrator he was supposed to be, he'd taken it himself. Why?

Two reasons, he decided. The first was that she'd looked at him with her big, doe-brown eyes and begged for his help. How many times during their marriage had he prayed in vain that she would turn to him in need? Finally, now that it was all over, she'd done exactly that. And, when it came down to it, he could resist anything but her needing him.

The second, more important reason was that he didn't trust anyone but himself to keep her safe. Not even the six over-protective bullies she called brothers.

"You were born a century too late, pal," Quincy had been fond of teasing him. "A hundred years ago, you could pull out your six-shooter and single-handedly rid the world of all the bad guys."

Quincy.

Over the past eighteen months, Steve had tried very hard not to think of his former best friend. Almost as hard as he'd tried not to think of Kate, and the child they'd lost.

She'd said she was surprised that he'd left the police force. Little did she know how close she'd come to the truth when she'd asked if Quincy had had something to do with his decision. First, he'd lost his daughter, then his wife, and finally his best friend. After that, nothing had made much sense, especially work in a field that often seemed as riddled with corruption as the people he had a sworn duty to protect. At least now he could pick and choose who he decided to put his life on the line for. Like Kate.

The camera in his mind replayed the minute she'd walked into his office. Even in that ridiculous getup, and with a bruise on her cheek and a split lip, she'd looked beautiful. When Liza had announced that Kate was there in answer to his ad, he'd assumed the worst. All of his protective instincts had risen to the fore. Now that he knew the truth, he almost wished he was dealing with a batterer. A batterer he could easily handle. An unknown fan, however, was a different story altogether. Steve knew he had his work cut out for him.

His suspicions were confirmed when he parked in front of her house, climbed out of his car and got his first good look at his surroundings. The sight so dismayed him that he nearly groaned aloud.

With its outdated windows, many doors and close neighbors, Kate's house was a protection specialist's worst nightmare. If someone truly meant to do her harm, it would be all too easy. He'd wager the house didn't even have an alarm system. Anybody could use the stately maple tree in the front yard to gain access to the windows on the second floor. And the park across the street…a person could find a million different places to hide there.

"I see you bought the old house you always wanted," he said when she joined him.

She gazed with obvious fondness at the three-story, red-brick building that had probably been built sometime in the early twenties. "Yes. I love these old places. They have so much character."

Steve didn't feel quite as charmed by the square, architecturally-undemanding structure, but he kept his thoughts to himself. He also kept alert for any suspicious activity while she slid her key into the front door lock and turned the knob. A step behind her, he wasn't prepared when she stopped dead in her tracks. Body still in motion, he barreled headlong into her. His hands shot out and closed around her shoulders, pulling her against him as he struggled to keep them both from falling.

The heat of her skin seared him at the same time that her scent took his breath away. Anticipation tightened his stomach muscles. Lord, he'd forgotten how good she smelled. How good it felt just to hold her.

When the urge to slide his hands down her arms and nuzzle his nose in the silkiness of her hair grew overwhelming, he thrust her away from him. "Sorry," he muttered, then forgot all about his response to her when he saw the look on her face. The color had drained from her cheeks, and her eyes were wide with fear.

"What's wrong?" he demanded.

"Someone's been here."

# Chapter 3

"Get down!" Steve grabbed Kate by the arm and pulled her along behind him.

Crouching low and shielding her body with his, he took cover behind the intricately carved Victorian sofa located to the right of the front door. As he removed the gun from beneath his suit coat and disengaged the safety, he mentally berated himself for his dangerous lapse of control. It could prove deadly.

"How do you know someone's been here?" he whispered, carefully scanning what he could see of the room. Though he wasn't familiar with the layout, at first glance nothing looked odd or out of place.

"The furniture's been rearranged," she whispered back.

Damn, damn and triple damn! He wasn't in the house more than three seconds, and already his worst fears had been realized. This place was going to be a bear to secure.

"Anything missing?"

"Not that I can tell."

Which pretty much ruled out robbery. Not that any self-respecting burglar he'd ever arrested had bothered to rearrange his victim's furniture. Unless, that is, the rearranging was of the destructive sort.

"What do we do now?" Kate asked.

Good question. In a perfect world, he'd have backup, someone to watch over Kate while he checked the place out. But this wasn't a perfect world. They could do one of two things: go forward or backward. Going backward meant going outside, where they'd be sitting ducks for whoever might be lurking there. Like it or not, they were safer inside. Which meant their only viable option was to go forward.

He glanced over his shoulder. "Figure out whether or not we still have company."

"And if we do?"

"Immobilize whoever it is and call the police. Ready?"

"As I'll ever be."

Her face was a pasty white, and her voice shook. Steve felt a flash of admiration for her courage. All in all, she was having one heck of a day. He just hoped it didn't get worse.

"Keep behind me, and stay close."

"Don't worry. I plan on sticking closer than your shadow."

Cautiously, sweeping his gun in an arc in front of him, Steve inched forward to peer around the sofa. True to her word, Kate stuck to him like a burr. His gaze quickly roved the room in a counterclockwise sweep.

The only sounds were the soft ticking of a grandfather clock and the whoosh of cool air passing through the wall vents. No shadowy figure lurked in a corner, waiting to pounce. What Steve did notice were scattered indentations in the pile of the rose wall-to-wall carpeting. Indentations indicating the spots where pieces of furniture had previously rested.

"See anyone?" Kate asked.

"No." He eased the gun down to his side. The house had a feel to it, an emptiness that told his gut they were alone. When it came to his personal safety, he'd learned long ago to trust his gut. It had saved his life on more than one occasion. Still he planned on covering every inch of the place, just to be sure.

"I think whoever was here is long gone," he said.

"Why?"

Now that the immediate danger didn't seem so immediate, he grew suddenly aware that her hands had settled on his shoulders. Her breath pulsed warmly against his neck. He stood up, and she followed, her knee brushing his calf. She was too close for comfort. His comfort. If she leaned any closer, her breasts would nestle in the middle of his back. The thought made his blood race in anticipation.

He turned to face her, and her hands fell away. "Two things. Number one, if someone broke in here intending to do you bodily harm, he wouldn't warn you in advance by rearranging your furniture. Number two, we weren't exactly quiet when we came through the door. It would have been easy for anyone lying in wait to pick us off. Whoever did this is toying with you, Kate. He left his message and beat a hasty retreat. Wherever he is, he's probably getting a sick thrill out of imagining your reaction."

She digested his words in silence. He hadn't thought it possible, but her face seemed a shade paler. "My biggest fan?"

Steve supposed there was always the possibility that a phantom interior decorator was on the loose in the neighborhood, but he doubted it. It would be just too much of a coincidence for someone to break into her house the same day someone else had threatened her life. One thing he didn't believe in was coincidence. To his way of thinking, every effect had a specific and identifiable cause.

Even though her presence stirred up memories and emotions that were best forgotten, he was suddenly, fiercely glad she'd come to him. It would give him the greatest pleasure to catch this sick SOB and toss his sorry carcass behind bars.

"Anyone else have a key to the house?" he asked.

She shook her head. "Only me."

"What about your assistant? Could she have shifted things around in here?"

"Martha? Why would she? Besides, I sent her home before I left for your office."

"Any disgruntled lovers with an ax to grind?"

"No."

Did that mean she had no lovers, or that none of them were disgruntled? Just because he hadn't been able to date seriously since their divorce didn't mean she'd experienced the same difficulty. Given that she'd left him, the odds were probably against it. He couldn't see the unattached men of this town leaving a woman like Kate alone for long. Whatever, it was no longer any of his business.

"Anyone angry at you, or maybe someone with a penchant for practical jokes?"

"Just the ardent opposition."

"The ardent who?"

"Opposition. That's what Martha and I call the people who write me letters, telling me how wrong I am when they disagree with one of my columns. Then there's the psychiatrically challenged, which I don't think I need to define for you. Out of both groups, so far as I know, only one person seems to know where I live."

"Then to answer your question, yes," he said, "the evidence seems to indicate your intruder was the psychiatrically challenged man who calls himself your biggest fan. It isn't unknown for stalkers to enter their victims' homes and move the furniture around. It's almost as if they're moving in, putting their stamp on the place, so to speak."

Her mouth was a grim line. "That's what I was afraid of. Tell me more about stalkers, please."

"They're usually lonely, troubled and smart. They pursue no matter what."

"How do you know so much about them?"

"This isn't the first time I've run up against one. I've made it my business to know."

She reached out a hand toward a blown-glass figurine on

the fireplace mantel, and he shook his head at her. "Don't touch anything until the police have dusted for fingerprints."

Her hand fell to her side. "This guy can't be sane."

He knew it wouldn't make her feel any better, but she had to know what she was up against.

"Odds are, he isn't. Ninety-five percent of stalkers suffer from mental disorders. They're schizophrenics, manic-depressives, people with delusions. That said, experts agree only two percent of them are actually dangerous."

"Great," she said, her gaze focused at a point over his shoulder. "Just my luck to get one of the dangerous ones."

The confusion in her voice dragged at his heart. Damn. He still had feelings for her. He'd thought she'd killed them the day she'd walked out on him, but apparently that wasn't the case.

So he wasn't totally immune to her. Big deal. Some things in life just weren't worth pursuing. Chief among them was the small ember in his heart that refused to die out no matter how much water he tossed on it. He'd learned his lesson the first time. He didn't need it reinforced.

Nodding toward a doorway at the far end of the room, he asked, "Where's that lead?"

"The kitchen."

"Come on. We're going to check out the rest of the house."

"Why? You said we were alone."

"I said I thought we were alone. The only way to be absolutely certain is to check."

"Oh, my God!" she cried.

Steve whirled, heart thundering, gun at the ready. "What?"

Hand to her mouth, she breathed, "Fred and Wilma."

"Who the hell are Fred and Wilma?"

Without answering, she took off past him at a run. Biting back a curse, and praying that her biggest fan wasn't lying in wait around the next corner, Steve chased after her. To his relief, he found her, safe and sound, in a room at the rear of the house. Judging by the looks of it, the place doubled as both office and den. She had her back to him and was cooing to the parakeets chirping in a cage that hung over one of two computer workstations.

For a long minute he just stood there. Heart still racing, he struggled with the urge to wrap his hands around her lovely neck.

"You risked your life for a couple of dumb birds?" he finally accused.

"I wasn't risking my life." She swept an arm in front of her, encompassing the room. "No one's here. And they're not dumb. For your information, parakeets are highly intelligent."

"I don't care if they can whistle 'Dixie' while reciting the theory of relativity. They still aren't worth risking your life over."

"I wasn't risking my life," she repeated in that stubborn tone he knew so well.

Steve raised the hand holding the gun. "Then why," he said in a soft, deadly voice, "am I still carrying this?"

The sight of the weapon seemed to jolt her back to reality, and she stared at him mutinously.

No other woman could wriggle under his defenses like a rabbit under a fence. No other woman could push his temper to the point where it threatened to erupt uncontrollably. While they continued staring at each other, engaged in a silent battle of wills, Steve fought the urge to let loose the hot, angry words boiling inside him. Words that would let her know in no uncertain terms how irresponsibly she'd acted.

His terror that he might not stop with words was what ultimately enabled him to lock them deep inside by sheer force of will. Before Kate entered his life, he'd never intended to marry anyone. He'd kept his relationships short and sweet. While emotionally unsatisfying, he'd felt reasonably secure, and his dates had remained safe.

When he met Kate, he told himself it was infatuation, and he'd waited for it to fade. By the time he realized he was in love with her, she was pregnant. So, they'd married. And he'd spent the next year in mortal fear that he would harm the one person he loved above all else.

That he hadn't was testament only to the fact that his will-power had managed to override his baser instincts. Except for one never-to-be-forgotten occasion once he'd reached the age of majority, he had never lost control of his temper. He wasn't about to start now.

When he spoke, his emotions were under firm control, and his voice was measured and even. "No matter what you say, Kate, until we finish searching this house, you were risking your life by running off like that. I guess now's as good a time as any to establish some ground rules. While I'm in charge, I call the shots. Period. From now on, you don't so much as go to the bathroom before I've secured it first."

Her back went ramrod straight. "I had to know whether he'd harmed my birds."

"A fact we could have just as easily discovered by taking the proper precautions. This isn't a game, Kate. I can't do my job without your cooperation. So let me know now. Am I wasting my time here? 'Cause if I am, you can hire some-one else."

He half hoped she'd tell him to go. Then he could walk away without a backward glance. But could he really do it? Knowing that her life might be on the line, could he entrust her safety to anyone else? Damn it all, he knew he couldn't. If anything happened to her, he'd never forgive himself.

She sighed. "I'm sorry, Steve. I behaved like an idiot. I wasn't thinking. It won't happen again."

"Glad to hear it." He turned his attention to the parakeets. "What happened to Lucy and Desi?"

"They went to the great birdcage in the sky." She reached her hand into the cage and ran one long, lean finger across a bright yellow breast. "Desi went first. Lucy never was the same after. She didn't last long. I think she gave up the will to live."

There had been a time when he'd been close to giving up that will, too. He would be wise not to forget that.

"Come on," he said roughly. "Let's go search the rest of the house."

None of the doors and windows on the first floor had been tampered with. In the basement, though, they found an open window.

"So now we know how he got in," Kate murmured.

"And out," Steve said, pointing to the laundry basket that had been turned upside down and positioned beneath the window. "My guess is he'd planned to leave by your back door, until he discovered he'd need a key to unlock the dead bolt."

"It was pretty easy for him, wasn't it?"

"The only way it would have been easier is if you'd left your doors unlocked and sent him an engraved invitation."

"So what do we do now?"

"We make it a lot harder for him to get in, should he have a return visit in mind."

Steve made a mental note to call a glass specialist. Before tomorrow morning, he wanted the basement windows replaced by glass block. And that was just the top of a long list of alterations he had in mind. He hoped Kate hadn't turned into a tightwad, because if she had, the bill for what needed to be done to make this place relatively secure would be enough to give her a coronary.

The search of the second floor proved uneventful. Surprisingly Kate balked at the door leading to the third floor. "Do we have to go up there?"

He wondered why she was so leery. "Yes, we do."

"But I only use it for storage. It's hot up there. There's no ventilation." A hint of desperation edged her voice when she added, "No one in their right mind would want to hide there."

"We have to make sure, Kate."

With a resigned sigh, she followed him up stairs that creaked under their weight. The heat was oppressive. In seconds, his clothing clung uncomfortably to his skin, and perspiration matted the hair at the back of his neck. Despite his discomfort, he took the time to carefully search every nook and cranny.

"You are a pack rat," he murmured, his gaze running over a stack of cartons that had been labeled as containing memorabilia from each of her school years. Another stack gave witness to the fact that she kept all her fan mail. Beyond them stood a bookcase filled with children's books. He saw an old vanity, a big steamer trunk, and a double bed that was straight out of the fifties.

"Told you so," she replied, her voice sounding strained.

From the look of things, she'd saved nearly every item she'd ever owned. He wouldn't be surprised to find the proverbial kitchen sink.

"You didn't have all this stuff when we were married."

"That's because we lived in an apartment. It was in storage at my father's house."

When he finally threaded his way to the very back of the room, he stopped dead in his tracks. Now he knew why she hadn't wanted to come up here. In the far corner, under a protective layer of clear plastic, sat a crib, a dresser that had been painted white and stenciled with pictures of frolicking lambs, and a bassinet.

The pain washed over him, as fresh and exquisitely agonizing as if it were yesterday. At the time of their divorce, Kate had asked him what he wanted to do with the furniture, and he'd told her to get rid of it. After Molly died, he hadn't been able to bear looking at it.

Slowly he turned to face her. "You kept it all," he murmured gruffly.

Eyes looking suspiciously moist, she nodded. "I always intended to give it away to some charity, but so far I haven't been able to." Her gaze skittered from his and settled on the crib. "I had so many dreams wrapped up in that furniture."

They both had. And their daughter's death had pretty much

brought them crashing down around them. It had also brought their marriage crashing down.

The trip to the first floor was made in silence.

"How do you think he found my address?" Kate asked when they were once again in her office.

"I imagine he hired a private detective. It's a fairly easy thing to do."

She swayed on her feet, and he quickly moved to her side. Before he could reach out to her, she raised a hand and stopped him.

"I...will...not...faint," she vowed from between clenched teeth.

"Are you sure you're okay?"

Her nod was determined, although the lack of color in her cheeks put her assertion into doubt. She aimed eyes filled with anguish at him.

"Do you have any idea how it feels to know that out there, somewhere, is someone who hates you enough to want to kill you? Can you even begin to know how I'm feeling at this moment?"

If there was one thing he understood, it was how it felt to have his life threatened. When he'd worked undercover, he'd received more threats than he cared to remember. Shortly after their marriage, one of the lowlifes he was scheduled to testify against had even threatened Kate. He'd never told her about it. Instead, he and her brothers had somehow managed to have her guarded without her being aware of it. It had been a tricky job, but they'd managed to pull it off.

"Yes, Kate," he said, his gaze steady on hers. "I can."

"Then you'll understand that right now I feel like hiding under my bed and never coming out. I'm scared out of my mind, Steve."

"And you hate being scared," he murmured. Because it meant she would have to rely on someone other than herself for her safety. Because, right now, she needed him. And that need made him want to reach out to her, to comfort her. It was a risk he couldn't take.

His job was to protect, he reminded himself. He was a professional, and he had to behave professionally. That meant he couldn't be paying attention to her. He had to watch what was going on around her, to outthink this biggest fan of hers and anticipate the man's next move. It was the only way he'd be able to keep her safe.

A familiar burning sensation in his chest had him wishing for his antacid bottle. He crossed to a computer workstation and picked up the receiver of the phone he saw there.

"What are you doing?" she asked.

"Calling the police. It's way past time."

They'd just entered the living room when Kate heard a car screech to a halt outside. Running to a window, she parted the curtains and saw a familiar blue-and-white cruiser join the cars already parked out front. Her heart sank when the door flew open and her brother Carlo climbed out.

"Get away from the window!" Steve yelled.

Kate nearly jumped out of her skin. The curtain fell from suddenly nerveless fingers as she whirled to confront him. His face wore a look of supreme exasperation, a look parents reserved for the most unbelievable and idiotic stunts performed by offspring who were supposedly old enough to know better. She wondered if he was having second and third thoughts about taking this job.

"What did I do now?" she asked wearily.

"Made yourself a perfect target, that's what. Until this guy is caught, you aren't going to be looking out any more windows." Taking her by the elbow, he led her over to the fireplace. "Or standing in front of them, for that matter."

Kate tried to ignore the way the heat from his hand seared her skin. And the way the familiar scent of his aftershave wound its way sinuously up her nostrils and into her bloodstream.

"Would it make you happy if I crawled around on the floor on my hands and knees?" she asked sweetly through gritted teeth.

"If that's what it takes," he retorted. He dropped her arm abruptly, as if the touch of it offended him.

"You'll have to forgive me," she said stiffly, "but I'm a little new at this damsel-in-distress business."

She knew she was behaving badly, but she couldn't seem to stop herself. She felt as if she'd been trapped on a runaway roller coaster for hours and then, for good measure, run over by a steamroller. She knew Steve was just doing his job, but it irked her that she couldn't even move around in her own home without first obtaining permission. The tension was getting to her, and she wasn't reacting well.

Threading unsteady fingers through her hair, Kate expelled a long breath. "I'm sorry, Steve. I'm not exactly making your job easy for you, am I?"

His sigh sounded as weary as she felt. "I'm sorry, too. I don't usually lose control like that."

She wouldn't exactly describe his brief outburst as losing control. During their marriage, the only times she'd ever seen him lose the careful control he maintained over his emotions were when they were in bed together. For passion, he would let down his guard. For anger, never. How many times had she begged him to yell at her, scream at her, anything but keep so much hidden from her? And how many times had he refused and walked away?

A sudden thought occurred to her. While he was with her, guarding her, he couldn't walk away. His job wouldn't permit it.

Carlo's fist pounding against her front door interrupted further analysis. Instead of moving to answer it, Kate held her position in front of the fireplace. "I suppose you want to get that?"

"See?" he said, flashing her a brief grin and chucking her under the chin. "You're learning."

Feeling like a pupil who'd just been awarded high praise from an exacting teacher, Kate watched in bemusement as he crossed to the door.

"Hello, Carlo," she heard him drawl a minute later. "They sending the police chief out on B and E's now?"

Her bemusement vanished as she watched her brother's eyes narrow and his shoulders square as if for battle. "What are you doing here, Gallagher? Where's Kate? If you've so much as—"

"I'm right here, Carlo," she called.

Steve stood aside, and her brother bulldozed his way into the room. Physically, Carlo Garibaldi was a good two inches under the six-foot mark, which made him three inches shorter than Steve. But what her brother lacked in height, he more than made up in muscle. When he wasn't on the job, or romancing one of the endless stream of women he dated, he was pumping iron at a local gym.

"What's going on?" Carlo demanded. "I was standing next to the dispatcher when the call came in." He jerked a thumb over his shoulder. "Why's he here?"

"Because I asked him to be here," Kate said calmly. While her ex-husband had always remained an enigma, her brother she could read easier than large print. Long years of practice had taught her the best way to handle him.

"What for?"

"He's agreed to act as my bodyguard."

"Why do you need a bodyguard?"

"Maybe I should jump in here?" Steve suggested.

Kate shrugged. "Be my guest."

Steve quickly and concisely filled Carlo in on the day's events. When he finished, Carlo turned accusing eyes her way.

"Why didn't you tell me about this when the letters started arriving?"

"Because I didn't see any need to. If I came running to you with every crazy letter I receive, you'd never get any work done."

"Yet you went running to *him* the minute you discovered you were in danger." Though the look on his face was belligerent, Kate heard the hurt in his voice.

"He's the best at what he does, Carlo," she said gently. "Your little police force, good as it is, just doesn't have the manpower to give me round-the-clock protection. Nor do they have the training Steve does."

"I do. Bruno and Antonio do. One of us could have stayed here with you."

"Really? And just how would you have managed that, along with the demands of your job?"

"We could have taken turns—"

Kate held up a hand. "I've made my decision, Carlo. I intend to stand by it."

Carlo stuck his chin out. "I don't want him alone here with you."

She'd had enough of overprotective, macho men for one day. "For goodness' sake! He's not going to ravish me."

"Oh, yeah? The last time we left you alone with him, you ended up pregnant."

The pain hit her, and she sucked in a harsh breath. Carlo took one look at her face and swore.

"I'm sorry, Sis," he said, running a hand across the back of his neck. "I didn't mean that the way it sounded. I'm just trying to look out for you."

That was the problem. Every second of every day, it seemed, one of her six brothers was looking out for her. She'd wished a thousand times already that they'd all marry and start families, so she could have at least five minutes' peace. To date, though, barring her oldest brother, Roberto, they'd remained steadfastly single.

"I know you are, Carlo," she said. "You always are. But you know what? I'm twenty-nine, not twelve. Like I've been telling you for years, I'm old enough to look out for myself. And when I need it, I'm quite capable of hiring somebody to protect me. You know how good Steve is. He'll keep me safe."

"You going to call a fingerprint team to dust this place?" Steve asked, as if the subject were settled.

"I'll have them here in a minute," Carlo said stiffly.

"One more thing," Steve said.

"What's that?"

"Can you keep this out of the papers? These nuts really thrive on publicity."

"Don't worry, it won't be in the papers." Carlo nodded across the room toward Kate. "You hurt her again, Gallagher, I'll cut your heart out."

He stormed out of the room. When the front door slammed shut, it rattled in its frame.

"Your brother seems to have forgotten that you were the one to leave me," Steve remarked.

"No, Steve." She shook her head. "You left me long before I got the courage to pack my bags and walk out the door. Now, if you don't mind, I need to go to my office. I have a deadline to meet."

She turned her back on him, not caring whether he followed or not.

# *Chapter 4*

The noise made Kate's ears ring. Never had she heard such a racket. Not even as a child, when her brothers' stomping around the house had made a charging elephant sound light on its feet.

From the basement came the pounding of hammers as seventy-five-year-old windows were torn out and replaced by glass block. The whir of drills revealed the location of the locksmiths, who were updating what Steve had called "woefully inadequate and antiquated" locks with a keyless entry system.

A security specialist and his team of helpers shouted back and forth to one another while they busily installed window sensors. Along with the sensors, they mounted cameras above all exterior doors. This would establish what Steve had called "intrusion detection and perimeter control." All activity would be scrutinized on the bank of television monitors that now rested atop Martha's desk.

If possible, it was even noisier outside. A crew of men boisterously traded good-natured insults while they stationed motion-activated lights. The scream of a buzz saw split the air as another crew trimmed the branches of her lovely old maple to prevent access to the second floor. The one time Kate had gotten close enough to a window before all the curtains had been drawn, she'd seen that she was the talk of the neighborhood. Resident and visitor alike gawked at the men who swarmed over her house like bees around a hive.

To top it all off, every single one of her brothers had seen fit to pay a visit. Even Fred and Wilma hadn't been able to resist getting into the act. They chirped delightedly and flew around their cage in the throes of ecstasy, as if all the noise were a wonderful symphony they hoped would never end. Their activity caused a shower of seed casings and colorful feathers to fall onto the column Kate was trying to edit.

"At least someone is enjoying this," she muttered to herself as she brushed them away.

She glared across the room to where Steve sat at Martha's desk. His cellular phone was glued to his ear as he jotted down something into an open notebook. He'd been that way for the past two hours, since the team of policemen who'd dusted her living room and basement for prints had departed. It was obvious the noise didn't bother him the way it did her.

The speed with which he'd accomplished all this activity made Kate's head spin. He was like the Pied Piper, and the telephone was his pipe. Once he started dialing, everyone he called came running to do his bidding.

"Why is it, whenever I need a repairman, it takes hours of time on the phone setting up the appointment, and then I have to wait weeks for him to fit me into his schedule?" she groused.

Steve set the phone aside and turned to look at her. "You talking to me?"

"Yes. Don't you need to go home, get a change of clothes or something?"

His lips curved in the first genuine smile she'd seen all day. "Trying to get rid of me?"

Lord, but she'd forgotten what his smile could do to her. Kate felt the impact of it clear down to her toes. In response, her pulse rate shot up and her hand shook, causing a streak of red ink to zigzag across the page she was editing. She quickly placed her pen on the desk before she could do any further damage.

"You and everyone else," she said, grateful her voice, at least, remained steady. "I'm under deadline, and I can't work with all this noise."

As if on cue, the hammering in the basement rose to a crescendo. Kate winced. "How much longer is this going to go on?"

"An hour or two at most. I want everything in place by dark. Liza will be bringing round the things I need in a few minutes. Do you want me to ask her to pick up a pair of earplugs for you?"

Liza, the delectable receptionist, Kate thought sourly. Just what was the woman to Steve? Trusted employee? Devoted friend? Lover? All three? Not that she cared. She was simply curious.

*Liar,* her inner voice chided. "No, thanks. I'll muddle through."

Standing, Kate stretched her arms over her head and rolled her neck to get the kinks out. When she saw the way Steve was looking at her, she stopped mid-stretch. After the police had gone, she'd changed out of her niece's clothing into a pair of white shorts and a navy blue scoop-necked top. Now, with his gaze burning hotly on her, she found herself suddenly wishing she still wore the baggy jeans and oversize T-shirt. It made no sense, since he'd already seen much more than her figure-hugging outfit revealed. And touched. And— She brought her thoughts up short.

Their gazes met and clashed. For long, agonizing seconds, Kate held her breath while they stared wordlessly at each other. Steve looked away first.

"Time for a break anyway," he said abruptly. "We need to get a couple of things done."

Kate let out her breath, and her arms fell to her sides. "Such as?"

"Such as scheduling your normal routine, along with anything special you have planned over the next few weeks. And making a list of everyone you come in contact with on a daily basis."

"Why do you need to know my normal routine?"

He answered her question with one of his own. "Would you be willing to stay in this house until we discover the identity of your biggest fan?"

"Of course not. That could take weeks." The realization that the search could be a prolonged one caused her stomach to dip. Being with Steve was turning out to be a lot harder than she'd anticipated. So much for her assertion that their past was a closed and dusty book. "I'd go stir-crazy stuck inside."

"Which is why I need to know your normal routine, so we can vary it. Sort of like the way the Secret Service varies the president's jogging route. A precautionary measure to keep whoever's watching you off guard. As for anything special you have planned, like a speaking engagement, the more advance time we have to prepare for it, the better."

She nodded. It made sense. "But why a list of the people I come into contact with?"

He turned to a fresh page in the notebook and readied his pen. "To check them out, see if one of them is your biggest fan."

She felt taken aback. "You think he's someone I know?"

"I think it's a good possibility."

"Why?"

"A number of reasons, the main one being that all the letters bear a Pittsburgh postmark. They were all mailed from the post office you visit every day."

Kate's knees suddenly threatened to give out on her, and she sank down on her chair. After all the checking of postmarks for Bobby's collection, how could she have missed that one significant fact? Maybe it was because she always checked the postmark without paying any attention to how the letter was addressed. Maybe it was because, until yesterday, she'd never taken the letters from her biggest fan seriously. Or maybe it was simply denial on the part of her subconscious. Because the last thing Kate wanted to believe was that her biggest fan was someone she knew.

"I didn't notice," she said in a small voice.

They completed her schedule for the week in roughly half the time it took to fill out her list of contacts. When it was finished, Kate was surprised at its length. Over half of the names were male.

"I never realized I knew so many people," she said.

Steve shook his head. "You certainly are...busy. Just when do you get any work done?"

"This is a relatively small town," she defended. "People aren't afraid to speak to each other. Evidence to the contrary, I do spend most of my day in this chair. I'm also very productive when I sit down to write." A staccato burst of noise from the buzz saw made her grimace. "When I have peace and quiet to do it in, that is."

She moved to peer over his shoulder at the names on the list. "I still can't believe any of these people would try to hurt me. They're all so warm and friendly. A good number of them are older than my father."

"Mental illness is an equal opportunity employer," Steve replied. "It doesn't care what race, religion or age you are. You'd be surprised how much warm friendliness is just a mask for a cold hatred."

Confusion and fear balled Kate's stomach into a hard knot. Was her biggest fan someone she knew? Shivering, she wrapped her arms around her midriff.

"Do you always expect the worst from people?" she asked in a low voice.

His gaze remained fixed on the list. "Yes."

"Why?"

"So that when I get it, I'm never disappointed."

"And you think that's a good way to live?"

The tightening of his fingers around the pen he held was the only indication that her words had an impact on him. "You tell me," he said mildly, turning to look over his shoulder at her. "You're the one who left me. Think how that might have thrown me if I hadn't been prepared for it."

Kate felt her hands clench at her sides. Unable to bite back the words, she accused, "If you were so certain our relationship was doomed from the start, why'd you marry me?"

His hesitation was barely noticeable. "Because you were expecting my child."

She flinched at the open acknowledgment of what she'd always known to be true. He'd been infatuated with her. He'd desired her. But he'd never loved her.

"Hell," Steve muttered, dropping the pen and rising to his feet. He threaded a hand roughly through his hair. "I didn't mean that the way it sounded, Kate."

"No." She hardened her heart against the regret she saw in his eyes. She didn't want his pity, couldn't bear it. The only thing she'd ever wanted from him was his love. Lord, why did it still hurt so much? "Don't say any more. Please."

The ringing of the doorbell was a welcome intrusion. Steve's gaze broke away from hers to travel to the bank of television monitors. On the far right screen, the camera mounted above her front door zoomed in on the face of a young man with red hair and freckles.

"Recognize him?" he asked, all business once again. Their conversation might never have taken place.

It took Kate a couple of heartbeats to regain control of her emotions. "He's on the list. Vinnie Hirsh. He's a delivery boy for the local florist."

"Did you order flowers?"

"No."

"Stay here. I'll check this out."

Kate began following him out of the room. "You can't possibly think Vinnie's the one who's—"

Steve turned. "Until I learn otherwise, he's number one on my list. Stay here, Kate."

"But he's just a child. He's barely seventeen."

Steve's lower lip curled in contempt. "Have you listened to the news lately? Need I remind you the kind of crimes seventeen-year-olds are committing?"

His words effectively stopped her in her tracks. "Don't forget to give him a nice tip," she said. "His father's on disability. Vinnie's working to earn money for college."

She watched on the television screen as Steve cautiously opened the front door. Though she couldn't see his face, the way Vinnie's bright smile died told her that her ex-husband was at his most forbidding. At least he gave Vinnie a tip before sending him on his way.

When Steve reentered the room, he was all but obscured by a huge bouquet of red roses.

"They're beautiful," Kate breathed. "Why, there must be at least three dozen."

"Six," Steve said, placing the flowers on the coffee table. The heady scent of roses filled the air.

Kate automatically reached for the card, and Steve shot out a hand to stop her. "They might be from your biggest fan," he said in answer to the question in her eyes.

After taking a seat on her leather sofa, he wrapped a handkerchief around the tiny envelope and carefully extracted it from amid the blooms. There was an odd note in his voice when he read aloud, "'For a lovely lady. See you at seven-thirty. David.'" His glance settled on her. "I don't recall seeing a David on the list."

"That's because I thought we were concentrating on the people I see daily, here and in town."

"Looks like we'll have to amend the list." He paused. "Hot date?"

Not really. Though they'd met numerous times at the functions of a local charity they both supported, she and David had only gone out twice. They were light-years away from being serious, although Kate could tell that David's ultimate goal was to deepen the relationship. While she enjoyed his company, a part of her remained aloof whenever they were together. She never felt completely at ease with him. The sad truth was, she'd never felt completely at ease with any of the men she'd dated since the divorce.

"We're having dinner at the LeMont," she said. "With everything that's happened today, I'd forgotten."

"I want you to call and cancel," Steve said.

Squaring her shoulders, she searched his face for...what? A sign that his reluctance stemmed from jealousy? What on earth was wrong with her? He'd out and out told her that he had never loved her, and still she hoped he cared? What a fool she was.

Which was precisely why she was going to keep this date. "No. I need to see David."

Truer words had never been spoken, Kate realized. The attempt on her life had lowered her defenses where Steve was concerned. If a mere smile had the power to make her tremble, she dreaded to think what could happen if he decided to switch on his not inconsiderable charm. Despite his open acknowledgment that he'd never loved her, that he'd only married her because she was pregnant, she was feeling terribly vulnerable to him. An evening with David would provide a welcome distraction after having to keep such close company with her ex-husband.

"It's not safe, Kate. Public places are difficult to defend."

Folding her arms across her middle, she leaned against her desk. "Difficult, but not impossible. Besides, I don't think there'll be anything to defend against. We're having dinner at a popular restaurant. There will be a lot of people there. My biggest fan isn't going to try something stupid with so many witnesses hanging around."

"Oh yeah? He pushed you from a crowded sidewalk into the middle of the street," Steve reminded. "And no one saw him do it."

"Yes," she conceded, "but I wasn't paying attention. And you weren't with me. The playing board has changed."

Impatience flickered in his eyes. "Not to me, it hasn't."

"Tell me," she challenged. "When you guard a politician

on the campaign trail or a celebrity when he's on tour, do you insist they stay locked up in their rooms?''

"Of course not."

"Then why should I be any different? You yourself said you didn't expect me to stay cooped up inside twenty-four hours a day.''

Leaning forward, he placed his elbows on his knees and eyed her speculatively. "You tell me something, Kate. Is this hot date of yours so important you're willing to risk your life for it?''

She'd had time to think this through when they were married, and she'd realized there was a possibility his job could place her in danger. "I was willing to risk it for you.''

He seemed taken aback. "What do you mean?"

"You forget, I grew up in a family of cops. Even if you would never talk about it, I knew what it meant for you to work undercover. The whole time we were married, I was aware there was a chance someone might come after me to get at you. It never happened, but I knew what I was going to do if it had.''

"Which was?"

"The same thing you did. Nothing. You never let the threat get in the way of your job, and I wasn't going to let it get in the way of my life. I'm not going to let this guy drive me underground like a mole. If I do that, he wins. He's the one in control, not me.''

"He might take offense to you being out with another man, you know. This could spur him into making another attempt on your life.''

"I realize that."

"Doesn't that scare you?"

She met his gaze head-on. "It terrifies me. Look, I'm not trying to make your job difficult. I simply refuse to let fear dictate the way I live my life.''

A nerve throbbed in his cheek. "This Donald means so much to you?" he asked quietly.

"David," she said. "His name's David."

"Whatever. He means that much to you?"

It had nothing to do with David. Why couldn't Steve see that? "This date is important to me," she allowed.

He looked tired all of a sudden, and she found herself wrestling with a ridiculous urge to smooth the grooves of worry from his forehead.

"If we had a little more lead time to secure the restaurant, I'd have no problem with you keeping your date," he said. "As it is, there's barely enough time to brief the extra protection agents this expedition would entail. I'm asking you to stay home tonight, Kate. Please."

She could have resisted a demand; she had no strength to fight a plea. Besides, assertion that she wouldn't allow her fears to control her life aside, she didn't want to do anything stupid. She always walked out of movies where, knowing that her life was in danger, the ditsy heroine went ahead and investigated a strange noise and was invariably confronted by the villain. She didn't want to behave the same way.

"All right," she gave in. "I'll call David and invite him here instead."

The scowl that crossed Steve's face gave her an inordinate amount of pleasure.

Liza Cook brought Steve's things by at five o'clock, and the workmen departed just before six. At seven twenty-five, the house blessedly silent and the dinner she'd ordered from a local Chinese restaurant keeping warm in the oven, Kate descended the stairs.

Because it hid her scraped knees from view, she'd selected an ankle-length black halter dress for her dinner with David. A skillful application of makeup covered the bruise on her cheek, and an ice pack had worked wonders to reduce the swelling in her lower lip. She felt fairly confident that, other than the slinky dress, she looked her normal, everyday self.

Which was good, because she'd downplayed the day's events to David. The truth of the matter was, she hadn't told him anything about the attempt on her life, just that she'd received some threatening letters. Steve's presence was explained away as temporary and a mere precaution. No mention was made of his being her ex-husband. The omissions weren't deliberate lies; she just hadn't been up to the questions she'd have to answer if David knew of both the threat to her life and that she and Steve shared a past.

She didn't owe David an explanation about everything that went on in her life, she rationalized as she reached the landing that marked a turn in the staircase. After all, this was only their third date.

When she turned the bend in the stairs, she saw Steve awaiting her at the bottom. All thoughts of David fled as, eyes dark, glittering and mysterious, he studied her from the top of her head to the tips of the toes peeping out from black dress sandals.

Never in her life had she been more aware of the length of throat and arm exposed to view. Now she knew how Scarlett O'Hara felt that first time Rhett Butler watched her climb the stairs at Twelve Oaks. What was it she'd whispered to her companion? Something about him knowing what she looked like in her underwear.

The look in Steve's eyes told her he was remembering that, and much more. The thought of the much more made Kate's cheeks warm. Deliberately she let her unbound hair fall forward, in hopes that it would shield her face from him. And disguise the fact that she was studying him as intently as he studied her.

Hair still wet from a recent shower, he looked devastating. He'd changed out of his gray suit into a casual pair of navy blue chinos and a striped cotton shirt. Just looking at him made her heart beat faster and her mouth go dry.

And she'd thought she was in danger from her biggest fan.

"You look beautiful," he said when she drew even with him. His voice held an odd, husky quality.

"Thank you," she whispered, incapable of speaking any louder. *David,* she reminded herself. *The dress is for David, not Steve.* Why was it, though, that whenever David looked at her that way, she never felt as if the room temperature had shot up twenty degrees?

Kate cleared her throat. "Are you sure you won't join us for dinner? There's plenty of food."

Steve shook his head. "Liza brought everything I need. I'll just fix myself a sandwich and spend the evening in your office. I have a lot of paperwork to catch up on."

For some reason, along with the relief she felt, there was also a touch of guilt. Which was ridiculous. He was, after all, simply doing the job she'd hired him to do. Except it pulled at her heartstrings to think of him closeted away in her office, alone with the bank of television monitors and his sterile paperwork. She couldn't help wondering when was the last time Steve had abandoned work to enjoy himself. He'd certainly never done so when they were married, and she'd lay odds he hadn't done so since. She hadn't forgotten the antacid bottle that, no doubt, had been delivered here by the delectable Liza, and what it symbolized.

"Before your date arrives," he said, extending one hand, "there are a couple of things I want to give you."

"What's this?" Ignoring the warmth that shot through her veins at the touch of her fingers against his palm, Kate picked up an object that looked like a lipstick tube attached to a leather string.

"An alarm. Just press the top, and it emits an ear-shattering whistle that will bring you instant attention. Wear it around your neck."

Kate felt her lips curve as she glanced down at the bare expanse of chest left exposed by the square neckline of her dress. "It doesn't exactly go with my outfit."

"It's for when we're out in public. For now, tuck it under one side of your dinner plate. And tuck this under the other side."

She raised her eyebrows in question.

"Pepper spray," he supplied. "Aim for the eyes."

Her laugh was disbelieving. "You can't possibly think David is my biggest fan."

"I don't, but only because he has an alibi for this afternoon. While you were being pushed in front of that bus, he was elbow-deep in a root canal."

She narrowed her gaze at him. "How do you know that?"

"I had him checked out."

"You had him checked out?" Closing her eyes, she slowly counted to ten. "Why?"

"It's my job, Kate."

When she opened her eyes, she said, "But I already told you that David isn't the man we're looking for."

"Under the circumstances, you'll have to forgive me if I consider you less than objective about the man you're involved with. You wouldn't be the first woman taken in by a false smile and a smooth line."

She'd never been taken in by false smiles and smooth lines. Her downfall was a particular brooding workaholic who only had to look at her to make her lose all sense of perspective and common sense. Like now. But, of course, she couldn't tell him that.

"I believe in being prepared for all contingencies," he went on, "which is why I'm the best at what I do. I want you to carry the whistle and the spray with you at all times. Especially when we're away from the safety of this house."

She frowned. "But I thought you were supposed to protect me when we're away from here."

"It's just a precaution, Kate. In case, for whatever reason, we should get separated."

"Oh."

He didn't move, just stood there staring at her with his deep, blue, fathomless eyes. Unbidden, memories chased themselves around in her mind, like a kitten after a ball of twine. Memories of how it used to be between them, how he'd made her blood sing just by looking at her the way he did now. And when he'd touched her...

Kate bit her lip. To her left, in the living room, the grandfather clock ticked away seconds that seemed to pass in a haze. Slowly, almost imperceptibly, Steve's eyes darkened with desire. His glance fell hotly to her lips, and she felt them part in response as an answering desire shuddered through her.

It had always been this way between them. One look was all it took for rational thought to fly out the window. Even the bad times hadn't been able to change this most elemental of chemical reactions.

He took a step toward her, and the scent of his skin filled her nostrils and swirled through her veins. A wave of heat struck her at the look of unmistakable intention in his eyes. He was going to kiss her. No matter how unwise, she couldn't ignore the way her body suddenly craved the feel of his, how her lips yearned for his possession.

"Kate," he murmured unsteadily, the raw need in his voice causing a pulsing heat to center low in her abdomen. His head lowered and his arms reached out to encircle her. Breathlessly she awaited his touch.

The doorbell rang. Kate jumped, and Steve jerked away. He crossed to the door and peered through the newly installed peephole.

"Dilbert's here." His voice was expressionless. "That is, if he's six-one, has blond hair, blue eyes and a weak chin. Sound familiar?"

"His name's David," she said, expelling a shaky breath. "And he doesn't have a weak chin."

When Steve turned, the desire was gone from his eyes. They were once again remote, unreadable. "If you say so."

He opened the door, and Kate sent a silent prayer heavenward that her biggest fan would be found as soon as possible. She didn't know how much more of this she could take.

# Chapter 5

"So I told him," David said, "that if he didn't start flossing on a regular basis, pretty soon I'd be fitting him for false teeth."

Only half listening, Kate nodded. Careful to keep her scraped palms hidden, she took a bite of General Tso's chicken. What was wrong with her? she wondered, while David expounded on the merits of different brands of dental floss. Why was she having so much trouble concentrating on the conversation?

The atmosphere was ripe for romance. She wore her best dress. Her companion was decked out handsomely in a black suit and crisp white shirt. They sat alone together in a room softly lit by candlelight. Six dozen red roses, their heady perfume mixing pleasantly with the aroma of Chinese food, graced a mahogany table that had been set with her best china. By all rights, she should be staring starry-eyed at both her companion and the food.

Instead, the spicy food tasted like sawdust in her mouth. No matter how hard she tried, she couldn't get her mind off the earlier scene with Steve in the front hallway. So keenly did Kate feel his presence, she continually fought the urge to look over her shoulder to see if he was standing behind her. Absurd as the thought was, having dinner with another man while Steve was in her house almost made her feel as if she were cheating on him.

They were divorced. She was a single woman, free to date any man she chose. And the man she'd chosen tonight was David. Okay, so maybe she didn't find the discussion of dental floss as scintillating as he did. And maybe, until this moment, she hadn't realized how much time he spent talking about himself and his work.

Still she shouldn't be wasting her time, and his, thinking about her former husband. She most certainly shouldn't have let herself become so distracted by thoughts of Steve that she'd allowed David to pull out her chair when they sat down to eat. She, Sara Katherina Garibaldi, the woman who never stood on ceremony, had done so in spite of herself.

"I guess a lot of people are pretty lax about the care of their teeth," she said.

"You would be amazed," David agreed. "I constantly find myself scratching my head at the things people do."

Irreverently she wondered how he would react if she told him that, whenever it came time for her to buy a new toothbrush, she simply picked out a color she liked, ignoring brand and styling. Most likely, he'd be horrified.

"Tell me about some of them," she said, trying to sound enthusiastic.

He needed no further prompting. "Just the other day..."

Settling her gaze on his animated face, Kate forced a smile and tried to focus on the conversation. David was an easy, outgoing man. He exuberantly shared all his thoughts and feelings with her, and would happily debate any subject she pleased. He was everything she'd always wanted Steve to be. Why was it, then, that she still found him curiously lacking? Especially tonight, with Steve in residence.

But that was the way it had been since her divorce, she

realized with a pang. She was twenty-nine years old, and the only lover she'd ever had was her ex-husband. Prior to meeting Steve and falling hopelessly in love with him, she'd been fighting so hard to be independent of any man's influence that she'd never allowed herself to be drawn into a sexual relationship. After their divorce was final, no other man had ever been able to erase the memory of Steve's kisses, the memory of his caresses. Would she never be free of Steve Gallagher?

She recalled the early days of their relationship, when their passion for each other had seemed all-consuming. Due to malfunctioning birth control, she'd found herself pregnant and married almost before she could draw breath.

Steve had changed after they married. The man who'd claimed to prize her independent spirit had suddenly wanted to know her every move. It was then that she realized she didn't really know him. Oh, she knew a little about the past that had shaped him. She knew that his mother was dead, and that his father was in prison for killing her. She knew that his father had repeatedly beaten both Steve and his mother, and that after his mother's death he'd been raised by his maternal grandparents. When she'd tried to learn more, though, she'd found herself pressing against an invisible wall.

Although, after a few weeks of persistent demands, she'd finally gotten him to relax his claustrophobic vigil over her, she'd never been able to get him to open up to her. She'd known he was under a lot of pressure at work, but he wouldn't talk about that, either. And, no matter how hard she'd tried to provoke him, he wouldn't argue with her. While she'd regularly aroused the ire of many of her readers, the one person she'd never been able to anger was her husband.

It wasn't the arguments that killed a marriage, she'd learned. It was the silences. Her marriage to Steve had been more silent than most. Not surprisingly, at the same time that Steve was growing quieter and more withdrawn, Kate's column was becoming more and more daring. Any reaction had been preferable to none.

The only time Steve had ever seemed to relax and focus solely on her was when they'd made love. Not surprisingly, it was also the only time she'd felt close to him.

After Molly died, and he immersed himself in his work to the exclusion of all else, she'd come to the inescapable conclusion that he didn't love her, had in fact only married her because she was pregnant. That was when she left him. It had been destroying her soul to stay.

Now he was back in her life, however temporarily, and she'd just discovered that he still wanted her. Worse, she wanted him, too. Badly. What was she going to do?

"Kate?" David said. "Kate?"

"Hmm?" She blinked and looked across the table at her date.

"Are you okay?"

"I'm fine."

"You seem miles away, and you've barely touched your food. Is there more going on here than you've shared with me? Is this threat more serious than you originally indicated?"

She didn't want to get into this right now. She'd had enough attention focused her way for one day. "It just feels a little strange having someone else here with us."

A frown creased his forehead. "Speaking of this bodyguard of yours, will you be okay, alone with him, after I leave? If you'd like, I'll stay and sleep on the sofa."

His gallant offer made her smile. "Thank you, David. That's very thoughtful of you. But I'll be just fine."

"You feel safe with him here with you?"

Physically, yes. But emotionally? That was a far different question.

"I'll be just fine," she repeated. "So, tell me, what's your opinion on pacifiers?"

He shook his head and gave a rueful laugh. "Don't get me started on that one."

"Please," she urged. "I'm really interested."

As David launched into a detailed answer, Kate knew one thing with absolute certainty. Had their situations been reversed, and had Steve been the one sitting across from her at this table, he never would have offered to sleep on the sofa. He would have been in her bed. At her insistence.

With dismay, she noted that David's chin really was weak.

The sound of Kate's husky laughter floated into the room, and the pencil Steve was using snapped in half. His jaw ached from gritting his teeth, and he wiggled it back and forth, trying to relax.

He really should be in there having dinner with the two of them, but he hadn't been able to stomach the idea. If he'd had to sit there and watch Kate flirt with another man, he wasn't certain he'd be able to keep his dinner down. Or his hands from wrapping around Dimwit what's-his-name's throat.

So much for his objectivity, an absolute necessity in his line of work. He had to get a grip.

The curtains were all drawn; no one could see in. If necessary, he could be by her side in under five seconds. The images played back to him on the television monitors were of a quiet, deserted street. Outside, his men were at their appointed stations and had reported no unusual activity. She was safe enough, he rationalized. Lover Boy was certainly no threat. One look was all it had taken for Steve to see how besotted the man was. What he hadn't been able to assess were Kate's feelings.

How long had they been dating? he wondered. Though he got the sense that the relationship was still new, still tentative, he wasn't certain whether his conclusion was based on objective observation, or wishful thinking.

She'd looked beautiful in that black dress. Kate's wasn't a conventional beauty. Her face was too round, her lips too full, her hips and shoulders just a touch too broad. Put together, however, her features had combined to form a package he hadn't been able to resist. A package he still found hard to resist.

He never had liked women who looked so fragile they might break. He preferred women who had substance. Kate was definitely substantial. He'd always thought of her as a cat: sleek, independent, purring like mad when petted, and impossible to own.

Would she allow her date to spend the night? The thought of another man in her bed made Steve want to resort to the violence he could feel simmering dangerously close to the surface.

He was not jealous, he told himself firmly. Their marriage was over. He no longer had a claim on her.

So much had happened in the short, tumultuous year they were married. Much of it had been good, but most of it had not. Maybe it was better they had parted. There were too many terrible associations with their time together: the loss of their daughter; the threat to Kate's life; the realization that Quincy was a rogue cop, and that Steve would have to turn his friend in.

Then, too, there was Kate herself. Ironically, the quality he'd loved most about her—her independent spirit—had been the one thing that had driven them apart. She'd never let him do anything for her. All she'd seemed interested in was goading him into an argument, something he couldn't—wouldn't—allow. After Molly died, she'd turned to her brothers for comfort, instead of him. The only time he'd felt needed was when they were in bed together. Even then, he'd never deluded himself that he was the only man who could give her the release she sought in his arms.

He'd never told her he loved her. It wasn't that he hadn't felt the emotion. At the time, he'd loved her desperately. It just wasn't in him to spout flowery words and phrases.

He didn't put much stock in words. Along with his fists, his father had used words as a weapon to cut and wound. How many times, in an alcohol-induced rage, had the man snarled his love for his wife and child while beating them senseless? How many times, temporarily sober, had he cried and begged their forgiveness, swearing he'd never hurt them again?

Steve had learned from a young age to allow people's actions to speak for them, and to ignore their words. As much as he'd been able, he'd tried to show Kate what she meant to him. When she left him, her actions had spoken volumes. He wasn't about to let himself repeat his earlier mistake.

Kate laughed again, and he felt a familiar burning sensation in his chest. She'd laughed like that for him, too, in the early days of their relationship, he thought sourly, reaching for the antacid bottle.

He couldn't protect her properly if he was constantly distracted. For her sake, and for his own, he had to nip this in the bud. Now. He could not allow his emotions to become involved.

The birds chose that moment to raise a ruckus, and he stood and crossed to the cage.

"Know what really gets me?" he said. "She let him pull out her chair. If I'd tried that, she would have slapped me down. Fast. At least she tucked the whistle and the pepper spray beneath her plate, the way I told her to."

Disgustedly he ran a hand through his hair. He really was losing it. Now he was talking to a pair of dumb birds. What would he be talking to next? The potted tree in the corner? The stop sign at the end of the street?

A sudden thought occurred to him, and he picked up his cell phone. Jock Oldham, a friend from his police force days, answered on the third ring.

"Hey, old buddy," Jock said after Steve had identified himself. "Long time, no see. How they hangin'?"

"Fine, Jock. I've got a favor to ask."

"Name it."

"Would you check on these names for me? See if any of them are back out on the street yet?" The list consisted of the names of the men his testimony had put behind bars while he and Kate had been married. It was a long shot—especially now that they were divorced—but he had to make sure that Kate's biggest fan wasn't someone trying to get back at him through her.

"Will do," Jock said. "I'll call you soon as I find out.

Hey, did you hear O'Connor took early retirement? Seems he..."

For several minutes, Steve chatted with his old friend about the changes that had taken place in the department since his departure. To his surprise, he felt no lingering regret about his decision. When he hung up the phone, he saw Kate standing in the doorway.

"David's ready to go," she said.

Unbidden, his gaze flew to her lips to see if they were swollen from the other man's kisses. It gave him immense satisfaction to realize she didn't have a hair out of place and that her lips bore a more than fair trace of the lipstick she'd applied earlier. Whatever they'd been doing in the other room, it hadn't included a wild make-out session.

"Lover Boy not spending the night?" Damn! Why had he gone and said that?

The look she sent him told him she was well aware of the reason why. "Not tonight. He has surgery first thing in the morning."

It wasn't the answer he'd been not-so-subtly fishing for. He had yet to discover whether her relationship with the oral surgeon had moved from the hand-holding stage to something far more intimate. Still he couldn't help feeling relieved as he silently followed her out to the living room. Whatever the reason, they weren't spending this night together.

"Thanks for dinner," David said when Kate reached his side.

Hands balled into fists, Steve watched while the other man circled his arms around Kate before bending his head and brushing his lips across hers.

"Good night," she said when David released her. Steve could swear he heard a reluctance in her voice to let the man go.

At the door, David turned to Steve. "Take care of her," he said gruffly. "She's a very special lady."

It took all of Steve's self-restraint not to close the door in the other man's face. "No one will harm her while I'm around."

He watched David drive off before closing and locking the door. After checking to make sure the security system was properly activated, he joined Kate in the living room. She seemed lost in thought.

"I never thought you'd settle," he said.

Her brow furrowed in confusion. "Settle?"

"That kiss."

"What about it?"

"It was so...tepid."

A spark of anger flared in her eyes. "Tepid?"

"Yes," he repeated. "Tepid."

She settled her hands on her hips. The action pulled the fabric of her dress tightly across her breasts, and he had to forcibly focus his gaze on her face.

"Did it ever occur to you," she said in a cold voice, "that the reason David didn't sweep me into a torrid embrace was because you were standing there? That maybe we don't prefer to express our feelings in front of others?"

Steve's smile was deliberately provocative. He knew he was betraying his inner turmoil, but he didn't care. Something inside him had snapped at the sight of her in the arms of another man.

"Your pal Denton has about as much passion as a neutered sheep."

Her swiftly indrawn breath told him his barb had hit its mark. "I'll have you know, *David* is an extremely passionate man."

He raised his eyebrows. "Really? All I know is, whenever we kissed, there was enough combustion to start a fire. I didn't hear any smoke alarms going off when he kissed you."

"That's because David's kiss was gentle and reassuring. It was exactly what I needed after everything that happened today."

"If you say so. Whatever, I resent being replaced by that pale imitation of me."

She drew herself up to her full height and glared at him. "David is not a pale imitation of you."

"Isn't he?" he challenged. "Same height, same blond hair, same blue eyes. Except for that weak chin of his, I thought I was looking in a mirror."

Her eyes grew stormy with emotion. "I'm not dating David because I think he's like you. Far from it."

Something had taken hold of him, a primitive force that refused to let go until this situation had played itself out fully. "Prove it," he challenged.

"How?" was her immediate response, as he'd known it would be.

"Show me that the fire between us has burned out." His voice lowered, became soft, seductive. "Kiss me, Kate."

Her eyes went round with shock, and she took a step back. "What?"

"Kiss me. Show me you prefer my clone's meek little kisses to mine."

For countless seconds, she stared at him. Then the shock left her eyes, and she shook her head. "No."

"No?" he said disbelievingly. "The Kate I remember never backed down from a dare."

"Well, this Kate does."

"Scared?" he taunted.

Instead of taking the bait, she merely turned away. "I don't have to prove anything to you, Steve," she said with quiet dignity. "Now, if you'll excuse me, I'm tired. I'm going to bed. Good night."

Long after her last footfall had stopped echoing on the stairs, long after her bedroom door had softly closed behind her, Steve remained in the middle of the living room floor. Absolutely still, he stared at the spot she'd vacated and wondered what exactly had happened.

Because she was feeling paranoid after everything that had happened that day, once she'd donned her nightgown, Kate placed the whistle Steve had given her around her neck. She sighed when the cool metal settled reassuringly between her breasts. A feeling of not-quite security, but a first cousin to that sought-after state, settled over her.

After turning out the light, she climbed into bed, pulled the sheets up to her neck and proceeded to toss and turn for what seemed hours. Though her body had passed beyond exhaustion, her mind refused to quiet. Her brain had too much information to process to allow her to slip peacefully into oblivion.

It was all Steve's fault, she decided. For the life of her, she couldn't figure out what had gotten into him after David had gone. Why had he challenged her to prove that it was all over between them by kissing him? Was it jealousy? Or was it simply that he was a sore loser and couldn't bear to see someone else taking his place? One thing was certain. She'd never seen him act that way before.

*Be careful what you wish for.* The old adage echoed in her brain. She'd finally gotten a rise out of Steve, and it had been nothing like she'd anticipated. It surely hadn't solved anything. On the contrary, it had served only to make things more uncomfortable between them.

And what about the discomfiting assertion that she was dating David because he reminded her of Steve? Physically, she acknowledged, there was a definite resemblance; she couldn't deny it. But there, any similarity ended. Never had any two men been more unalike.

Down in the living room, the grandfather clock chimed the hour. The echo of the gong made its way faintly through her closed bedroom door. Two o'clock. With a sigh, she climbed out of bed. If she wasn't going to sleep, she might as well get some work done.

Grabbing the canister of pepper spray from her bedside table, Kate padded barefoot into the hallway. In the bathroom, she flipped the light switch and blinked at the sudden brightness. The sight greeting her when her pupils adjusted forced a groan of dismay from her throat.

Steve's belongings were all over the place. His robe swayed from the hook on the back of the door. The towel he had used cuddled next to hers on the wooden towel bar. His toiletries laid claim to the marble surface of the double sink.

One of the disadvantages of owning this old house was

that it was shy on bathrooms. No master suites with attached baths here. Unless she wanted to walk all the way to the bathroom on the first floor, she would have to share.

Her stomach rumbled. The sound echoed loudly in the small room, and she remembered she'd barely eaten anything at dinner. After splashing cold water on her face, Kate wandered silently downstairs and into the kitchen. She'd make a snack, and then get a head start on the next day's column.

When nothing inside the refrigerator appealed, she moved to the freezer, only to find it stuffed with carton after carton of Steve's favorite ice cream: rocky road. With a wry smile, she acknowledged that the two words could have been the motto for their marriage. And, probably, the days to come.

A feeling akin to desperation filled her as she stared at the offending cartons that had no doubt been delivered by Liza Cook. Steve had taken over her office, her bathroom, and now her freezer. If she wasn't careful, before she knew it, he'd once more have unrestricted ownership of her heart, as well. That, she simply couldn't allow.

Faintly at first, then growing stronger, she heard the strains of a flute from the direction of her office. Kate's heart gave a jolt of fear before thudding rapidly in her chest. Was her biggest fan lurking in there, trying to lure her into his trap by playing the radio?

"Get hold of yourself, Kate," she murmured out loud. "The president himself couldn't sneak in here without setting off an alarm. You know what a workaholic Steve is. He's probably still doing paperwork."

Cautiously she tiptoed to the doorway, making sure her fingers were at the ready to depress both the pepper spray and the whistle. Just in case.

# Chapter 6

When she peered into her office, Kate gaped at the scene that greeted her, pepper spray and whistle forgotten. As she'd imagined, Steve sat in front of the bank of television monitors. But what she'd never figured, even in her wildest imagination, was that he would be sitting there, clad only in pajama bottoms, eyes closed and his mouth pursed against the mouthpiece of a flute. The melody of "Danny Boy" filled the air.

Fascinated, Kate watched his long, beautiful fingers depress the round keys. The notes that issued from the instrument were pure, haunting and full of emotion. The sound was so beautiful it made her want to cry.

As if sensing her presence, Steve abruptly stopped playing. Opening his eyes, he lowered the flute to his lap.

"I'm sorry," she said, her gaze drinking in his naked torso. His shoulders were broad, his waist narrow, the pale hair matting his chest thick and curly. When they'd been married, she'd seen and touched that part of his body thousands of times. So why did the sight fascinate her so? "I didn't mean to disturb you."

"You didn't disturb me."

Unfortunately, she couldn't say the same about him. Because he definitely disturbed her. More than she cared to admit. "That was beautiful."

"Thank you."

She moved into the room and perched on the edge of the leather sofa. Nodding at the television monitors, she asked, "You're not staying up to keep an eye on them, are you?"

He shook his head. "No. George has his own set of monitors outside in the van. He'll keep watch until morning."

"Out of curiosity, just how many people do you have working on this case?"

"Four. Seven, actually, if you count shift changes. I'm inside with you. George is outside in the van. One man patrols the neighborhood, and another takes care of the park."

She hadn't realized her protection would be so involved. "Are all these people necessary?"

"I think so. Why?"

Why? Because it tended to make a person feel just the tiniest bit claustrophobic to know that her every movement was being monitored by one person, let alone four.

"If you're not watching the monitors, why are you down here?" she asked.

"Same reason as you, I expect. I was too wound up to sleep. Playing the flute relaxes me."

She gazed at the instrument curiously. He'd never played it when they were married. "When did you take it up?"

"When I was a kid," he surprised her by saying. "I started taking lessons when I was eight."

"How long did you take them?" To play as well as he did, she imagined he'd have to have studied for years.

"Till I was ten, when—" He broke off.

"When what?"

He looked away. "It's not important."

One of his three standard responses, when he didn't want

to open up, was "It's not important." The other two were "I don't want to talk about it" and "I'll be back when you calm down." Kate stared at him in frustration. Why did everything have to be such a big secret with him? Would it hurt him to, just once, share something with her, without her bullying him into it?

"What is it," she joked, "a state secret? Classified information, and I don't have the proper clearance?"

That made him smile. "Hardly."

"Then why won't you tell me what happened when you were ten?"

"It really is no big deal, Kate." He spoke lightly, his gaze on the flute.

"You're the one making it into a big deal, Steve, by behaving this way."

He lifted one shoulder in an indifferent shrug. "If you must know, I quit because my father wanted me to."

Surely the man had to have been aware of his son's talent. So why would he make him quit? Kate knew that money had always been a problem for the elder Gallagher. The rare times the man had held down a job for longer than a week or two, he'd drunk most of the money away.

"Were the lessons too expensive?" she asked. "Was that why he didn't want you taking them?"

"No. I took lessons at school. Except for a small instrument rental, they were free."

"Then why did he make you quit?"

After a brief hesitation, during which Kate felt sure he'd decided not to answer, he said, "My father didn't consider flute playing a proper pursuit for young boys. A real man, if he had to play an instrument at all, chose the drums, the saxophone or the trumpet. He did not play the flute."

A real man didn't batter his wife and child, Kate thought. "If he felt that way, I'm surprised he allowed you to take lessons in the first place."

Steve turned the instrument over in his hands. "He didn't. I took them in secret. My mother arranged everything."

Kate felt the prickling sensation of déjà vu as an awful suspicion began forming in her brain. "But he found out," she guessed.

Steve nodded. "He came home unexpectedly one day and caught me practicing. I...didn't take any more lessons after that."

With Steve, a person had to learn to read between the lines. She was eighteen months' rusty, but, given his history with his father, it didn't take a genius to figure out what had happened.

"He beat both of you, didn't he?"

Jaw tight, spine rigid, Steve stared straight ahead of him. "I don't want to talk about it."

"I'm sorry," she whispered.

The tension left his body, and he lifted his head to gaze at her. "Why? You didn't do anything. If anyone should apologize, it's me, for dumping all of this on you. Anyway, a few months ago I was feeling at loose ends, so I took it up again. I'm taking lessons at the university."

How like Steve to apologize for unburdening himself. That was the way he was. He never lost his temper. He never fought. He never showed any weakness. Except for that brief, astonishing challenge earlier that evening, he never showed any reaction whatsoever. And he never burdened another person with his problems. Not even when the person in question was the one person in the world he should feel free unburdening himself to: his wife.

If anything should serve to underscore how little she knew him—how little they knew each other—it was this revelation. How could she have been married to the man and not known how much he loved music, how beautifully he played?

She couldn't help picturing him as the ten-year-old he'd been; couldn't help imagining the fear he must have felt, and the pain, when his secret was discovered. Reading between the lines again, she was convinced he would have tried to lessen the impact of the beating on his mother. The frail, skinny ten-year-old she'd seen in the one pitifully thin photo album he possessed would have absorbed the brunt of the brutality.

The mental image made her want to go to him now and offer comfort for all his past hurts. What, she wondered, would he do if she did? Would he turn her away? Or would he accept her solace?

And if he did accept it, for a while, like when they were first married, things would probably go well between them. For a time, the passion that always blazed when they were together would mask any subconscious feelings of emptiness and dissatisfaction. And then, one morning, she'd wake up and realize she was living with a stranger. That, by his choice, he'd always be a stranger. She'd be right back where she started.

That was one place she most definitely did not want to revisit. "You play wonderfully," she said.

His smile made her heart flip-flop. "Thank you." The smile faded. "About earlier, Kate, when I dared you to kiss me. I'm sorry. I don't know what got into me."

Memories, she thought. Memories had gotten into him, the way they had her. And they were warping their judgment and common sense. "That's okay. It's been a long, trying day for both of us."

"Yes, it has. Tomorrow will be better."

"It certainly couldn't be worse." She stifled a yawn.

"You should get some sleep," he said.

The look in his eyes made her remember she was clad only in her nightgown. She glanced over at her computer, then turned away. Never had the idea of work held less appeal. Not with her dressed the way she was, feeling as vulnerable as she did, and with Steve sitting half-naked across the room.

Unbidden, another yawn made its way past her throat. Suddenly, sleep no longer seemed an impossibility. She'd toddle off to bed, get some rest, and in the morning this unwanted attraction to her ex-husband would be history.

"I think I will go upstairs. You should get some sleep, too."

"I'll be up shortly."

In the doorway, she turned back. "How long do you think it will take to catch this guy?"

"I don't know." He shrugged. "A day. A week. Maybe a month. It won't be long, Kate. Sooner or later, he'll make a mistake. They always do. And when he does, we'll be ready for him."

"I hope so." The sooner the better. "Good night."

"Good night, Kate." He raised the flute to his mouth and began playing.

The haunting notes followed her all the way to her room. He really was the Pied Piper, she thought. And if she wasn't careful, she'd find herself led into deep waters from which she couldn't swim.

"What time do you normally pick up the mail?" Steve asked.

Kate put down her pen and swiveled in her chair to face him. This morning, he'd traded in his gray suit for one of navy blue. His shirt was still white and crisply pressed, his tie sober and cinched tightly at his neck. His close-cropped hair was slicked back from his forehead. There were no bags under his eyes, no telltale signs to indicate he'd sat in that very seat, playing his flute, until nearly four in the morning. A fact Kate knew all too well, since she'd lain awake that long, listening to him. In short, he was perfectly put together, not a stray hair or wrinkle to be found. He looked as refreshed and as awake as if he'd received a full eight hours of sleep.

And she was so tired she could barely see straight.

He couldn't be comfortable, Kate decided, yawning as she glanced down at her ancient yellow T-shirt and jeans that could hardly be called blue anymore. Her right kneecap poked through where the fabric had worn away from countless washings. Her feet were bare. Her hair was clasped into a barrette at the base of her neck to keep it out of her way while she worked. She wore no makeup.

There was no way she'd be able to be creative if she spent her days straitjacketed in formal wear the way Steve did. It would be too confining. Too stultifying. Too uncomfortable.

Trouble was, he didn't look confined. He didn't look at all stultified. And he most assuredly didn't look uncomfortable. What he looked was...expectant, as if waiting for her to say something.

"Kate?" he prompted.

Blinking, she mentally shook her head to clear it. Contrary to her prediction the night before, she was as aware of him as ever. Whether terrified for her safety, or tired and cranky, it seemed she just wasn't going to be able to ignore him. Fine. So be it. She accepted the fact that he still had the power to draw her, probably always would. He was that type of man. But just because he possessed the power, it didn't mean she had to bow before it.

"I'm sorry," she said. "I lost my train of thought. Did you ask me something?"

"I was wondering what time you normally picked up the mail."

A glance at her watch told her it was nearing ten o'clock. "Anytime between now and noon. Whenever I feel like taking a break. Why?"

"Because we're going to vary your routine a little today. I want Martha to walk to the post office and pick it up."

Her reaction was immediate. "No."

"You don't think I'm going to send you, do you?" he said, arching an eyebrow.

She gave him a patient look. "Of course not. I just don't think Martha should go."

The woman under discussion looked up from the card table that was serving as a temporary work space because Steve had appropriated her desk for the surveillance equipment. Martha's eyes gleamed brightly with questions. Questions that had started forming an hour earlier, when she'd first arrived and met Steve. Kate knew her assistant was dying to get her alone so she could begin voicing some of them. With any luck, that would be a long time coming.

"Why shouldn't I go?" Martha said. "I think it's a great idea."

"Because it's not safe," Kate pointed out. "I don't think we should take any unnecessary chances."

"Of course it's safe," Martha replied. "Your biggest fan is gunning for you, not me."

Kate winced at her friend's choice of words.

"To be fair," Steve conceded, his attention on Martha, "Kate does have a point. There's a chance it could be dangerous. For the reason you pointed out, however, I think the chance is a remote one. Obviously, Kate disagrees. That's why one of my men will follow you at a discreet distance. Kent will make sure you get there and back without incident."

Kate stared at him in mounting frustration. Was she the only one thinking sanely this morning? Obviously lack of sleep had muddled Steve's thought processes. Otherwise, she was certain, he would see the inherent danger in what he was proposing.

"Why don't you just send Kent? After all, he's trained for that sort of thing."

"Because," Steve said, "if your biggest fan doesn't already know you've hired protection, I don't want to tip him off to it."

"How could he not know, after all the racket you raised around here yesterday?"

Reaching beneath the desk, Steve pulled out his briefcase and set it on his lap. "I think it's a safe bet he made himself scarce after he broke in. He didn't want to be caught anywhere near here. None of my men saw anyone suspicious hanging around yesterday."

She stuck out her chin. "I still don't think Martha should go."

"Has she picked up your mail before?"

"Yes," Kate was forced to admit.

"When?"

"When I'm too rushed to get it myself."

"Is that a frequent occurrence?"

"Fairly."

"Has she picked it up recently?"

Kate sighed heavily. "Yes."

"More than once in a week?"

"A couple of weeks ago I picked it up three days in a row," Martha volunteered, much to Kate's dismay.

Steve's eyes flashed with triumph, and Kate found herself gritting her teeth.

"Then it's settled," he said. "If your biggest fan sees Martha picking up your mail, he probably won't think anything's out of the ordinary. But if he sees a strange man opening your post-office box, he'll know we're waiting for him. We'll have lost our element of surprise."

He turned to Martha. "I have another favor to ask of you while you're out."

"Name it, and I'm there."

After crossing to the leather sofa and taking a seat, Steve placed his briefcase on top of the coffee table and opened it. Both Kate and Martha craned their necks to see what was inside.

Kate never would have guessed that the staid, mature mother of six grown children nursed a private passion for adventure. But when Martha saw the dozen or so gizmos and gadgets that looked as if they'd come straight out of the "Get Smart" reruns Kate had adored as a child, the older woman's eyes went wide with wonder.

"What do you want to do?" she asked, her excitement obvious. "Wire me for sound?"

Steve's lips twitched. "Nothing quite so dramatic, I'm afraid." He picked up an ordinary-looking quartz watch. "I want you to wear this."

Though Martha looked disappointed, she strapped the watch around her wrist. "What's it do?"

"It's a camera," Steve explained, and the woman immediately brightened. "You aim the watch face at the person you want to photograph and push that button there. It's quite simple and unobtrusive. No one will know what you're doing. I want you to take a picture of everyone you see in and around the post office. Maybe we'll get lucky and capture this nut on film."

"Since you have no idea what he looks like," Kate said, "how do you expect to identify him, even if we do manage to get his picture?"

"That's our job to figure out. Once the film's developed, we'll try to identify everyone. I know it sounds like a long shot, but I'm looking for patterns, Kate. If the same guy shows up, day after day, and he doesn't have a valid reason for being there, we just might have our man."

"You mean you want Martha to pick up the mail every day?" Her voice rose.

"If she's willing."

"I'm willing."

Something told Kate it wasn't going to be so easy. And the look on Martha's face told her that her friend wouldn't be dissuaded from the task she'd so eagerly undertaken.

Steve closed his briefcase and spoke into the mouthpiece of what appeared to be a headphone, but which was in actuality, Kate knew, a walkie-talkie that allowed him to maintain contact with the men he had placed outside.

"Kent is waiting for you out front," he told Martha. "Don't acknowledge his presence in any way. Try to act as normally as possible. And don't forget to take as many pictures as you can."

"You can count on me." A wide grin on her face, Martha left the room.

After watching her friend's exit on the television monitors, Kate turned back to her writing. Worry made it impossible for her to concentrate. Five minutes later, she pushed back her chair and began pacing the floor.

"She'll be just fine," Steve said from Martha's desk.

Kate rounded on him. "Really? Are you willing to give me a written, money-back guarantee?"

"We've taken every reasonable precaution, Kate."

Instinctively her hand went to the whistle that hung around her neck. "And what if this guy does something unreasonable? I'll never forgive myself if something happens to Martha."

"She wanted to do this," he reminded her. "I didn't exactly twist her arm."

"I don't care." Kate flopped down onto the sofa, pulled her knees up to her chin and glared at him as she wrapped her arms around her legs. "It's one thing for you and me to be at risk. I have no choice, and you're getting paid to assume the danger. As is Kent. But Martha is a friend. A dear friend. And an employee. The only reason she's working right now is because she insisted. I wanted her to stay away until this whole mess was resolved. So you can understand why I feel a responsibility toward her. I think it was highly irresponsible to let her go for the mail."

"He's never harmed her before when she's gone to pick it up," Steve pointed out. "I think it's safe to assume he won't do so now."

"Before yesterday," she retorted, "he hadn't harmed me, either."

"She'll be just fine, Kate. Kent won't let anything happen to her."

"For his sake, he'd better not."

She stared at him mutinously until he looked away. An uneasy silence filled the room. When his cell phone sounded, Steve picked it up. A second later, he was deep in conversation.

Unable to sit still, Kate resumed her pacing. After a few minutes, she stopped in front of the curtains that had been drawn across the sliding glass doors. In her current restless mood, the closed curtains seemed an affront.

"Could we at least open the drapes?" she snapped. "I'm going stir-crazy. It feels like the walls are closing in on me."

Steve concluded his conversation and placed the phone on the desk. Ever patient, he spoke in a soothing voice. "You know we can't, Kate. It would make you a prime target. Look, let's talk about something. It'll help take your mind off your worries."

She folded her arms across her middle. "As I recall, you and I never were much good at small talk."

"No, I suppose we weren't," he said with a wry smile. "We usually had...other things on our minds."

Kate felt her cheeks warm. She wished he hadn't said that. While it effectively distracted her from her worries, it also brought to mind things she'd rather not remember. Like the taste of his mouth on hers. The feel of his hard arms wrapped around her. The glory of his possession.

"So," she said quickly, "what do you want to talk about?"

"You choose."

She thought a minute. "Do you always wear a suit and tie to work?"

"Yes."

"Why?"

"Most of my clients serve in a professional capacity. It's the required uniform."

She glanced down at her jeans and T-shirt. "As you can see, the uniform around here is a lot more casual. You can dress down, if you'd like."

"I'll take it under advisement."

"Good."

Silence filled the room. So much for that line of conversation, Kate thought. Tapping her foot, she looked at Steve expectantly. *Your turn,* she silently willed him.

"How's your father?" he asked.

"Well. He retired to Florida six months ago. He has a new lady friend. I think it's serious."

"I'm happy for him."

"So am I."

Silence again. The ball was squarely back in her court. Several minutes passed while Kate twiddled her thumbs behind her back and looked at the walls, the ceiling, the floor. Anything but Steve. There had to be something they could discuss that would consume more than thirty seconds. Surely they weren't that abysmal at small talk.

A thought occurred to her, and she grasped at it like a lifeline. "How are your grandparents?"

Steve had gone to live with them when he was thirteen, after his mother's death. Kate had met them only once, shortly after she and Steve had married. They hadn't said much, had been in fact coolly polite and distant. She'd left their home with the distinct impression that they didn't approve of either her or the marriage.

"Dead," he stated baldly.

Kate started, and her gaze flew to his face. He was staring down at the desk, his features impassive.

"When?"

"Shortly after our divorce. My grandfather died first. Heart attack. My grandmother went in her sleep a few months later."

That explained the plushness of his office, she realized. As sole heir to his grandparents' considerable estate, he could easily afford to present the image his prospective clients desired. Not that inheriting money detracted from his ability to provide top-notch protective services. Before long, Steve would be able to maintain those offices on his own, without aid from his grandparents' estate. It just would have been surprising for him to achieve that level of success in such a short period of time. After all, it was only in the past year, three long years after she'd been picked up by her syndicate, that her column had really taken off.

"I'm sorry," she stammered, wishing she'd never broached the subject. "I didn't know."

"Don't be," he said. "I'm not."

Her uneasiness forgotten, she stared at him in disbelief. "How can you be so unfeeling?"

When he raised his head, she saw that his eyes were anything but unfeeling. On the contrary, they blazed with a hatred that made him look harder than diamonds. A hatred that snatched her breath from her throat.

While she'd always known that he locked away his most deeply felt emotions safely inside him where no one could reach them, she still wasn't prepared for their intensity, now that she'd unwittingly stumbled across the combination that unleashed them. How could any one person harbor so much hatred?

"How can I be so unfeeling?" he said, his lower lip curling. "Easy, Kate. You can't believe how easy. I learned from the masters. There was no love lost between my grandparents and me. Surely you knew that."

She hadn't, not really. Yes, at the time, when he'd taken her to see them, it had felt like a duty visit. Still, she'd never suspected the depth of his antipathy. And, since he'd never told her in so many words or shared with her any details of his relationship with them, how was she supposed to know?

Kate tried to think what it would take for her to feel the same way about her own family. After her mother's death, when she was ten, her brothers had taken it upon themselves to shield her from life's harsh realities. Since then, they'd nagged her incessantly, interfered in her life even more, and coddled her to death. She'd had to put up one heck of a fight to win her independence from their loving tyranny. But, when all was said and done, she knew she'd be lost without them.

While on one level, it appalled her that Steve could feel this way toward his family, on another she felt a sense of elation, a spark of hope. This was the closest she'd ever seen him come to revealing what he hid from the rest of the world. They were approaching a bridge they had never crossed before. And if they crossed it? Would it make things magically okay between them again?

She wasn't so naive as to believe that. The twenty-six-year-old who had trusted in the power of love, and the happily ever after of marriage, had died right along with the expiration of said marriage. Still, if Steve did open up, if he allowed himself to express what he was feeling, it would be a positive step. It would give her hope that, one day, he could totally let go of the past that held such a grip on him.

"What did they do to you to make you feel this way?" she asked, holding her breath and crossing her fingers.

"I really don't want to talk about it."

She sagged in defeat. "Standard response number two," she muttered.

"What?"

"It's what you always say when you want to run away from a conversation," she said tiredly.

"As you can see, I'm still sitting here. I'm not running anywhere."

Not physically, anyway. "Prove it," she challenged, echoing the words he'd uttered the night before. "Tell me what your grandparents did to you to make you feel this way."

The air around them seemed to crackle with the fury that sparkled in his eyes. A nerve throbbed in his temple as, body rigid, Steve clenched and unclenched the hands that rested on the desktop. Then, before her eyes, his anger disappeared as suddenly as the blip of a falling plane from a radar screen. His body relaxed. His fingers went slack. The nerve in his temple quieted, and his eyes went blank.

As a triumph of will over instinct, the transformation was truly awe inspiring to witness. Like the first time she'd watched the wonders of computer-enhanced imagery on the movie screen, all Kate could do was stare in wonder. And fight the urge to cry.

She should have known it wouldn't be so easy. After all, if the intimacies of marriage hadn't been able to break down the barriers he'd built between him and the rest of the world, what made her think their nonintimate, enforced togetherness would?

Steve took a drink from his antacid bottle, then drew a deep, shuddering breath.

"You want to know what they did, Kate?" he said mildly. "They turned their backs on my mother when she married my father. They never lifted a finger to help her when she went to them after my father started beating her. They had a ton of money, but they couldn't be bothered to spare a small portion of it so she could take me and get away from him. And all because she was young and foolish enough to marry a man they didn't approve of. They never forgave her for that, not even after she died."

"They did take you in," Kate felt compelled to point out.

He nodded. "Because of all the publicity surrounding my mother's death. They were worried what people would say if they didn't. Believe me, if there hadn't been so much media attention, they would have been more than happy to let me rot in foster care. They never once showed me an ounce of affection while they were alive. Don't expect me to grieve for them now that they're gone."

*And don't expect me to care, about anyone or anything,* he might as well have said.

Didn't he have any close, emotional ties with anyone? Kate wondered. Outside of herself and Quincy, if there was anyone else he'd been close to, she'd certainly never been aware of it. And now she and Quincy were no longer a part of his life. How lonely he must be.

But then, maybe he wasn't lonely at all. Surely there was at least one woman out there who would be more than willing to share his bed without asking for more.

Kate tried to look at him with a critical eye, to observe him as a stranger would. A stranger of the female persuasion. What she saw was a forceful, attractive, compelling man. She didn't kid herself that he could turn quite a few heads. He'd turned her own nearly three hundred and sixty degrees the day they met.

In all probability, there was a long line of women who would gladly stick around without constantly griping because he didn't share more than his body with them. At the head of the line, in Kate's mind anyway, stood Liza Cook. The woman seemed devoted to Steve. After all, she had not only delivered a suitcase full of clothing that she'd presumably packed, but his antacid bottle and favorite ice cream, as well. How many employees would go that extra mile for a man who was merely her boss? Kate's stomach turned at the thought.

She bit her lip. It was one thing to realize that she was still attracted to her ex-husband. It was another thing entirely to feel a stab of jealousy at the thought of some other woman being held in his arms. Being jealous meant that she wanted to be held there, too. And she didn't. Not unless he could offer her real intimacy, along with the physical.

Twice, in a matter of hours, he'd managed to take her by surprise. First, the story of his secret flute lessons and their horrific aftermath, and now this. She'd learned more about him in one day than she had the entire time they were married. What, she wondered, was the difference between now and then?

The difference, she decided, was that while he was guarding her, he couldn't walk away. He couldn't spend hours away from her, immersed in his work, because she was his work. He couldn't dismiss her or what she had to say with one of his three standard responses. He couldn't distract her by taking her in his arms and kissing her until she was a mindless mass of carnal need. Whether he liked it or not, he had to stay put and deal with her.

She supposed she should feel heartened that he'd actually spoken about two of the events that had shaped him into the man he was today. But she wasn't. If anything, she was disheartened. By suppressing the emotion evoked by his recollections, he was distancing himself from his own past. And, in so doing, he was distancing himself from anything or anybody who could possibly cause him further pain.

"My turn to ask a question, I believe," Steve said, intruding on her thoughts. "What about you and Dagwood? How serious is it between you two?"

# Chapter 7

Kate rolled her eyes. "His name's David."

"Ah, yes," Steve drawled, "Davin." Leaning back in the leather chair, he swiveled it around so that he was looking at her head-on, instead of from the side. "Are you two, as they say, an item?"

She had just about reached the end of her proverbial rope. Steve had a photographic memory; he knew darn well what David's name was. And this gag was growing old fast.

"It's David," she snapped, resisting the childish urge to stomp her foot. "David, David, David. Stop pretending you can't remember, when we both know better. And, no, we're not an item. We barely know each other."

"From what I observed, Dirk—" At her warning look, he cleared his throat. "Er, David would like to change that. The question is, would you?"

She wasn't about to discuss her current relationship with her former husband. "What about you and Liza?" she countered.

He blinked. "Liza and me? What about us?"

She borrowed his phrasing. "Are the two of you an item?"

"Liza's married, Kate. She's very much in love with her husband."

"But she doesn't wear a wedding ring," Kate blurted, then bit her lip in consternation at what she had revealed. Equally distressing was the relief she felt, now that she knew Steve wasn't involved with his beautiful receptionist.

Steve's gaze narrowed on her. "You checked to see if Liza was wearing a wedding ring?"

Unable to sustain the intensity of his regard, she looked away. "It's an automatic reflex," she explained, trying not to sound defensive. "Women always check. Don't men?"

"Not other men. And we only check out a woman when we're interested. Even then, some of us don't bother."

"Oh," she said weakly.

"The reason Liza isn't wearing a wedding ring is because it's at the jeweler's. They're adding the diamond her husband gave her for their first anniversary."

Kate was beginning to wish she'd never brought up the subject. "He sounds like a devoted husband."

"He is. They're very happy."

She heard Steve push back his chair. A second later, the outline of his shadow fell directly across hers, and the heat from his body reached out to encircle her. Kate looked up into blue eyes that brimmed with curiosity, and something else. Something that made her heart pound.

"Why did you think Liza and I were involved?" he asked softly.

Her shoulders lifted and fell in what Kate hoped was a nonchalant shrug. "She's a beautiful woman. She seemed to anticipate your every need before you said a word. She stocked my freezer with rocky road ice cream. I just assumed…"

"That it meant we had an intimate relationship," he supplied.

She nodded.

"Liza is an extremely efficient receptionist, which makes her worth her weight in gold."

"I hope that's reflected in her paycheck," was all Kate could think of to say.

"It is."

"Good."

"Did it bother you?" he asked, his gaze still on hers.

"Did what bother me?"

"The thought of Liza and me together."

Kate swallowed. If only he knew. "Why should it bother me?" Even to her own ears, her voice sounded strained.

He took a step closer, entered her personal space, and Kate had to tilt her head up a notch to maintain eye contact. She fought the urge to take a step back. Not for the world would she let him see exactly how much his closeness affected her.

"Maybe," he said, "it bothers you for the same reason that the thought of you and David together makes me sick to my stomach."

This was not going at all the way she had anticipated, Kate thought desperately. She had to find a way to defuse the situation, before she did something silly, like throw herself at him.

"We used to be married, Steve. It's only logical we should feel a lingering sense of...protectiveness toward each other."

"Is that what we're feeling? Protective?"

His eyes glittered with a familiar promise, and her mouth went dry. He smelled good, too, like her soap and his aftershave. The thought of him using the same bar of soap that she had shot Kate's pulse rate up.

"What else could it be?" she squeaked.

He leaned in closer. "I was thinking that, maybe, it might have something to do with the fact that you still turn me on."

Kate's heart thundered. Oh, boy. This was definitely not good. She was starting to feel the way she had in their early days together, when all he had to do was look at her for her to be lost. "I...I do?"

"You know you do. And I still turn you on, too." His gaze bored into hers, making it difficult for her to breathe. "The question is, what do you want to do about it?"

What did she want to do? She wanted to jump him, that's what. But she couldn't go back to what they'd had before. It hadn't been enough then, and it wouldn't be enough now.

Kate drew a deep, bracing breath. "Nothing."

"Nothing?"

"What would be the point? It won't change anything, Steve. It certainly won't change the past. Besides, just because there's still a leftover...something...between us, it doesn't mean anything. I understand it's quite common in divorced couples, given their earlier, er, intimacy. It certainly doesn't mean we can't fall in love with someone else and build a lasting relationship."

"Someone like David, you mean."

"Yes."

Steve's eyes went suddenly blank, and he stepped away. Kate nearly sagged in relief.

"It'll never work, you know," he said.

"What won't?"

"You and David." When she looked at his face, she saw that he was once again the distant, cynical man he'd been in his office yesterday. "The two of you together would be disastrous."

Kate welcomed the anger that flared at his audacity. How dare he? And why, even in his most infuriating moments, did she still find him so damnably attractive? Why did she still ache for him with every fiber of her being?

"So what you're telling me," she said, "is that, on top of your photographic memory, you can also see into the future? Okay, Karnac, I'll bite. Why won't it work?"

"Because he's put you on a pedestal. He'll give in to your every whim and wait on you hand and foot. In short, he'll worship the ground you walk on, treat you like a queen."

Surprised laughter bubbled from her throat. "And this is a bad thing?"

Steve nodded. "For you it is. Trust me, Kate. You'll be bored to tears in no time. Not to mention claustrophobic. Because, on top of worshiping at your altar, David will also want to know every little move you make."

He was right, darn him, but she wasn't about to tell him so. Nor was she about to admit that she'd already decided not to see David again. The decision had come to her the night before, while lying awake in bed, listening to Steve play his flute.

Truth was, she'd known the minute David kissed her last night that there was no hope. With all her heart she'd wanted to feel something when his lips had touched hers, had willed herself to feel at least a twinge of promise for what was to come once they had some time alone together. But there had been nothing. The kiss had been merely pleasant, and nothing more. She'd felt no twinge. Zip. Zilch. Nada. Her pulse rate had remained steady, darn it all.

It wasn't that she wanted Steve back. She wasn't a glutton for punishment. But surely, somewhere, there had to be at least one man who could make her feel the way Steve did just by looking at her. One man who would share with her his hopes, dreams and thoughts without compromising her need for space. Or was she wishing for the moon?

"That's just your opinion," she said.

"You're right," he replied. "It is. So, are you going to answer my earlier question? Are you falling for him, Kate?"

She didn't have the energy for any further prevarication, particularly when that prevarication inevitably landed her in a pot that was hotter than the one she was already in. "It's too soon to tell. Frankly, after what I went through when our marriage failed, I'm in no hurry to fall for anyone."

For the briefest of seconds, she thought she saw relief flash in his eyes. Before she could be sure, the emotion, whatever it had been, was replaced with his normal cool detachment. One eyebrow arched in query. "You sound bitter."

"Is that so surprising? After everything that happened?"

"Frankly, yes, seeing as you were the one who walked out

on me. If anyone should be bitter, I would think it would be me.''

Which he obviously wasn't. She wondered how long it had taken him to erase her presence from his apartment, to forget she'd ever been there. She wondered if he'd ever lain awake night after endless night, body and soul aching, because his other half was missing. Looking at him now, his eyes alight with cynical amusement, it was impossible to imagine.

''As I said before, you left me long before I left you.''

He inclined his head in acknowledgment. ''Yes, I do seem to recall you saying something like that.''

She waited for him to ask her to elaborate, but he offered nothing more. Which was vintage Steve. When she'd announced that she wanted a divorce, he hadn't asked her to elaborate then, either. Instead, he'd merely nodded, told her to have her lawyer call his, donned his coat and walked out the door, leaving her to shed rivers of tears while gathering up what few possessions she'd wanted to take with her.

He glanced at his watch. ''Martha should be back any minute. Anything else you want to discuss before she arrives?''

Kate rubbed a hand over the tight muscle at the back of her neck and longed for a few hours of deep, comalike sleep. She couldn't think clearly anymore. Being so close to the source of her agitation wasn't helping any.

''Actually,'' she replied, ''there is. Two things, really.'' One had nagged at her since yesterday afternoon. The other had badgered her since the demise of their marriage. ''About the ad Liza thought I came to your office to answer?''

''Yes?'' He sounded cautious.

''What was it for?''

There was a long pause. When he spoke, the tension in his shoulders, as well as his voice, told Kate that he was uncomfortable with the subject.

''My company keeps a running ad in the newspaper. We help battered women escape their abusers.''

Because of his mother. How like Steve, she thought, to do

something so wonderful. And not to want to take any credit for it, saying his company kept the ad in the newspaper, when *he* was the company. Kate wished she hadn't asked. Now that she knew, it was going to make him even more difficult to resist.

"So, Liza thought I'd come about the ad because of my injuries?"

He nodded.

"It must be very rewarding to help others like that."

His response was immediate. "I don't do it to be rewarded. I do it because the job needs to be done." The words were clipped, dismissive. "What was the second thing you wanted to know?"

Kate knew it was useless to press any further. Besides, her other question was far more important. "When we were married, why would you never argue with me?"

The tension left him, and he gave a faint smile. Obviously this subject didn't begin to bother him the way speaking about the ad did.

"The same reason I won't now. Like I told you then, Kate, I don't argue."

She recalled the conversation well. Equally well, she remembered how she'd brushed off his statement as being unimportant. At the time, she'd been so starry-eyed in love, she hadn't been able to ever envision them arguing. Little had she known that a day would arrive when she'd yearn for just one word spoken in the heat of the moment.

"That still doesn't tell me why."

"I thought it was obvious. I grew up in a home where it was rare not to hear voices raised in anger. When I grew old enough to realize that most people don't live that way, I decided I wouldn't, either."

Coming from a family where opinions were openly and vocally aired, Kate just couldn't accept his decision. How dull life would be if everyone in the world agreed with everyone else.

"Well, I don't think there's anything more therapeutic than a spirited debate. It's invigorating."

"I disagree," he retorted. "There's nothing invigorating about force-feeding your will down someone else's throat."

She knew he was referring to his father, and her heart ached for the pain he had endured. "Everyone doesn't fight dirty, Steve. Not all people use their fists to make a point."

"I certainly don't."

No, he didn't. There was something else, she knew. Something he wasn't telling her. Something she couldn't see, lying just beneath the surface, that made him swallow his pain and anger every time it threatened to erupt. There had to be for him to be so ruthlessly militant about maintaining his self-control. She wished she knew what it was, but she didn't hold out any hope that he would eventually share it with her.

"Martha and Kent are back," he announced.

Kate heaved a silent sigh of relief when the security cameras revealed Martha, safe and sound from her cloak-and-dagger escapade, coming up the front walk. Thank goodness. She didn't know what made her more grateful: that no harm had come to her friend, or that she would no longer be alone with Steve.

"Got it," the older woman proclaimed triumphantly a moment later when she swept into the room. The sparkle in her eyes spoke of how much she'd enjoyed her adventure. Holding an envelope out to Steve, she dumped the rest of the mail onto the card table. "It's from him."

Steve took the envelope, and Kate moved to stand by his side. Careful not to disturb any fingerprints, he extracted the letter and unfolded it. Peering over his shoulder, Kate read along with him.

My dearest Kate,
I am disappointed in you. Why are you trying to keep us apart? Be assured that he cannot save you. We are destined to be together. Until that glorious day when we are united through eternity, I remain faithfully yours.
Your biggest fan

Kate shivered and turned away. Wrapping her arms around her shoulders, she crossed to the birdcage, where Fred and Wilma sat grooming each other. She was cold, so cold. Why was he doing this to her? Why had he singled her out? Why wouldn't he leave her alone?

"I think he knows about you, Steve," Martha murmured.

"So much for our element of surprise," Kate added. She felt relief on one level, at least. There was no further need for Martha to collect the mail. Kent could do the job. Now if she could only talk her friend into taking a paid leave of absence.

"Did you get the pictures?" Steve asked.

Martha nodded and unfastened the watchband.

"If you'll excuse me," he said, "I'll take this out to one of my men to have the film developed."

Kate sat down at her computer. When she glanced across the room, she saw that Martha's color remained high and that her eyes still sparkled with excitement.

"Had a good time, did you?"

Martha's laugh was pure joy. "A blast. When I was a little girl, my father used to entertain us with stories of my uncle who was a resistance fighter in France during World War II. Today, while I was taking all those pictures of people without their knowing it, I felt like a resistance fighter myself."

"A lot of those resistance fighters didn't live to see the end of the war," Kate retorted, an edge to her voice.

Some of the pleasure left Martha's eyes. "Did I do something wrong? You seem angry."

Kate suddenly felt like a bully who had kicked a defenseless puppy. It wasn't Martha's fault that the stress was stretching her nerves to their limit.

"I'm sorry. It's just…I was worried about you."

Martha immediately looked contrite, which only made Kate feel worse.

"How thoughtless of me. Of course you were. And here I was, having a grand old time. But you needn't have worried, Kate. I had every confidence in Steve. I knew he'd keep me safe."

Kate poised her fingers over the keyboard and squared her shoulders, willing herself to attend to her work. "When I married him, I had every confidence in him, too," she muttered to herself. "Look how that turned out."

She'd obviously spoken louder than she'd intended, because Martha asked, "Are you saying he let you down? Is that why you divorced him?"

Kate didn't know what she was saying anymore. Her fear over what her biggest fan might do next was all mixed up with her confusion over her unexpected attraction to her ex-husband. Only one certainty remained. If she didn't fax this column to her editor by three o'clock this afternoon, she was going to miss her deadline.

"We let each other down, Martha. Now, if you don't mind, I have to get back to work."

For several minutes, the only sound in the room was the clacking of her keyboard and the chatter of the birds. Kate paused in thought over a turn of phrase and heard Martha clear her throat.

"Kate?"

"Hmm?" she said, thinking her assistant was going to ask a research question.

"You never told me he was so…male."

Dismayed, Kate peered over her shoulder at the older woman. "Aren't you the one who told me you haven't looked at a man since your husband died, because no one could possibly measure up to him?"

"I wasn't looking at him for me," Martha explained. "I was looking at him for you."

"Been there. Done that. No thanks."

She saw the speculation in Martha's eyes. Since Kate had

hired the older woman a year earlier, they'd grown close and often shared confidences. Even though she chafed against similar treatment from her brothers, Kate allowed Martha to nurture and nudge her as if she were one of the woman's own children. Had she been into self-analysis, she most likely would have said it was because she'd lost her own mother, and that Martha's interest filled that void. Whatever the reason, she had told Martha things she'd told no one else.

The one thing they had never discussed, however, was her marriage to Steve. While she'd disclosed the fact that she had been married, and with whom that marriage had been—far too often, if Martha's ready recognition of Steve's name yesterday was any indication—she'd never divulged any details. Until now, Martha hadn't pressed.

With a sigh, Kate's hands fell to her lap and she swivelled around in her chair. "You want to know why I left him, don't you?"

"Only if you want to tell me."

She didn't. The last thing she wanted to talk about was Steve, or their marriage. But after what Martha had risked by going for the mail, Kate would have felt churlish refusing. Besides, she didn't want to make everything a deep, dark secret, the way Steve did.

"We met, fell in immediate lust, and before we could get to know each other, found ourselves facing impending parenthood. A civil ceremony followed. Predictably, the marriage lasted a little more than a year."

"You were pregnant?"

Throat tight, Kate nodded. Though the sharp edge of the pain had dulled somewhat, there was an emptiness inside her that she knew would always be with her.

"Did you miscarry?"

"No. I…we had a beautiful baby girl. She…she died."

"Oh, Kate." Martha's eyes filled with sorrow. "How awful for you, for the both of you. I'm sorry I brought up such a painful subject. You have enough to deal with right now."

"Don't be sorry," Kate said, surprising herself. "I want

to talk about it. I haven't spoken of Molly in such a long time. My family always avoids the subject. I know they're trying to spare me pain, but it sometimes makes me wonder if they wish the whole thing had never happened. That she'd never been born.''

"I'm sure they don't feel that way.''

"Deep down, so am I, but I wish they wouldn't be so protective of me." She gave Martha a lopsided smile. "That's been the story of my life, hasn't it?''

"There are worse fates," the older woman pointed out.

Like being shut out by the man you love. "Yes, I suppose you're right.''

"Was she sick?''

"No." Kate traced the pattern of the sculptured carpet with her foot. "She was just perfect. According to my obstetrician, what happened the night she was born was just one of those things. Totally unpredictable and unpreventable.''

"What happened?''

"A week before my due date, my umbilical cord ruptured. I hemorrhaged. Steve was working late that night. By the time I got to the hospital, Molly had been without oxygen for almost eight minutes." Kate expelled a shuddering breath. "She lived for thirty-six hours.''

Tears shimmered in the corners of her friend's eyes. "So much tragedy for one so young.''

Answering tears burned Kate's eyes, and she blinked them away. "Steve took it as hard as I did. Harder even. For weeks afterwards he barely spoke. I tried, but I wasn't able to comfort him. We separated five months later.''

Martha nodded. "I've heard it happens that way. The tragedy of losing a child often tears a marriage apart.''

"It wasn't just that. We had other problems. Molly's death was just the final straw.''

"He seems like a good man, Kate.''

"He is a good man," she said softly.

"He's certainly not hard to look at.''

Kate felt her lips curve. "No, not hard at all.''

"How about in the bedroom? He do okay there?"

Had any other person asked her that very question, Kate would have wasted no time putting her firmly in her place. But Martha, she knew, was not asking out of idle curiosity.

"I had no complaints."

"You still find him attractive." The words were a statement, not a question.

Kate started. "Is it that obvious?"

"Only because you can't keep your eyes off him. If it's any consolation, he can't keep his eyes off you, either."

That was what made him so dangerous. "And your point is?"

"You're going to be spending a lot of time together. This is a unique opportunity, one most couples never get. If you're lucky, maybe the two of you will be able to work things out."

The part of Kate that was romantic enough to yearn for a happily-ever-after ending wished that it could be so. But her practical, realistic side told her not to fool herself.

"It's not that easy, Martha. You see, he was an abused child. When he was thirteen, his father beat his mother to death. He doesn't share his thoughts and feelings. He puts up walls. Unscalable ones."

Ironically, his reticence about sharing himself was one of the things that had most attracted her when they first met. In the beginning, he was all lighthearted laughter and fun. Where her family was boisterous, combative and, above all, nosy when it came to personal matters, Steve played things close to the chest and didn't press for any meaningful revelations from her. Kate had fought long and hard for her independence and was relishing her newfound sense of freedom when they met. It had thrilled her that, except for those few brief weeks when they were first married, Steve never seemed to want to put any restrictions on her, never wanted to be so close that she couldn't breathe. It was the first relationship with a man where she hadn't felt claustrophobic.

Only when it was too late did she realize that she needed more from him than he could give.

"Oh, the poor thing," Martha crooned. "Of course he puts up walls. That doesn't mean they can't come down. They tore down the Berlin Wall, remember?"

"Yes, but take it from someone who's bashed herself against Steve's walls many a time, and has the bruises to prove it. The Berlin Wall was flimsy. It was only made of concrete. Steve's walls are made of much stronger stuff. I don't know that the explosive has been invented that could blast through them."

"You'll never know if you don't try."

"I have tried, Martha. So many times. All I got was heartache. I just don't have the strength to go through it all over again."

The echo of footfalls on the bare wood of the hallway floor heralded Steve's approach, and the two women lapsed into silence. Kate watched Martha begin sorting the mail before turning her attention to the flickering cursor on her computer screen.

To Kate, the silence had a furtive feel to it. A feel Steve obviously picked up on, because he'd barely taken his own seat when he asked, "Am I interrupting something?"

"Nothing important." Kate picked up the insulated cup of ice water she kept by her computer and took a sip.

Her face the picture of innocence, Martha looked up from the mail. "We were just talking about explosives," she offered blithely.

Kate choked on the liquid in her throat.

Shortly after noon, the doorbell rang. The camera mounted outside the front door captured the images of three men in police uniform. Her brothers. Carlo, Bruno and Antonio.

"Here come the Keystone Cops," Steve murmured, making Martha laugh.

Kate stared reprovingly at the two of them. "They are my brothers, you know."

"You have to admit," Martha said, her eyes twinkling with merriment, "they do tend to trip over one another in their zeal to protect you. It can be quite comical to observe. Remember the time all six of them dropped by while you were hanging a painting in the dining room?"

Without waiting for her to reply, Martha turned to Steve. "As usual, they insisted on helping, then got into an argument about who was the best man for the job. There was a lot of shouting and posturing, and then they all went for the hammer at the same time. Carlo had finally wrestled control of it, when it flew out of his hands and hit the wall. Made a nice round hole, too. Kate had to hire someone to repair the plaster. While they were arguing over whose fault the hole was, she picked up the hammer and hung the painting herself."

Steve chuckled. "Sounds like them, all right. Once, right after we were married, Kate was frying bacon while talking to Franco on the phone. The bacon got a little too crisp, which set off the smoke alarm. Kate told Franco she had to hang up, that something was burning. Five minutes later, sirens blaring, a fire engine screeched to a halt outside our apartment building. All six brothers arrived minutes later. We were the talk of the complex for the next week."

The sound of their hearty laughter filled the room. Feeling invisible, Kate stared from Martha to Steve. They were entirely too chummy to her way of thinking. Not only did they seem to have forgotten her presence, but also the presence of the men on her doorstep. She didn't see what was so funny. After all, this was her family they were laughing about.

"My all-time favorite story," Martha went on, "is the one where they sat her down to tell her the facts of life. Can you picture the six of them surrounding one poor twelve-year-old? Carlo starts off by explaining that a woman's reproductive system is like a flower, and that it has to be carefully nurtured for it to bloom properly. Roberto interrupts him and says no, no, no, that's wrong. It's like a defenseless animal that needs to be protected from nasty predators. Five minutes later, all six of them are rolling around on the floor, trading punches. When they finally composed themselves, Kate calmly told them they were all wrong. She then proceeded to explain, in painstaking detail, the exact path the sperm swims to meet the egg. When she finished, all six of them were red faced. They couldn't get away from her fast enough.''

Grinning widely, Steve turned to Kate. ''You never told me that one. It's priceless.''

''I—'' She opened her mouth to say that he wasn't the only one who could keep secrets, and immediately lost her train of thought at the laughter in his eyes. Spellbound, she swallowed hard. How could anyone stare into the vivid blue of those smiling eyes and not fall under his spell? Much as she wanted to, she couldn't look away.

This was the side of him she found the hardest to resist. This was the man she'd first met and fallen in love with. A man full of laughter and mischief. A man like no other.

As she continued to stare at him wordlessly, the laughter faded from his eyes, and another, deeper emotion took its place. Hunger. Hunger for her. She knew an answering yearning was reflected back at him in her own eyes.

The doorbell pealed again. With an effort of will, Kate tore her gaze from Steve's. A glance at the monitors told her that her brothers were fast losing patience. With any luck, they would bring with them the news that the identity of her biggest fan was now known, that he was securely behind bars, and that she and Steve could get on with their lives. Separately.

''Is someone going to answer that,'' she asked, ''or do you want me to get it?''

As she'd known it would, her comment got an immediate response. Steve rose and headed out of the room.

''Merciful heavens,'' Martha murmured.

When Kate looked over, Martha had one hand across her

heart, while the other fanned wildly back and forth in front of her face. "What?"

"The two of you."

"What about us?"

Smiling ruefully, Martha said, "Herb was a wonderful man, Kate, and I loved him to bits. But the air never crackled like that when we looked at each other. Talk about electricity! My poor old heart goes into palpitations just thinking about it. Is it always like that between you?"

Kate turned unseeing eyes to her column. "Always."

"And you don't want to try to work things out?"

"As...stimulating as being with him always is, the pain and loneliness are far worse. So no, Martha, I'm not going to try to work things out. Unless I see some visible signs that he's really changed, that he's ready to open up to me, that's one road I'm not going to travel."

"No signs so far, huh?"

"There are no billboards along that highway."

"Pity." Martha spoke with what sounded like true regret.

A minute later Steve returned with Carlo, Bruno and Antonio in tow.

"Any leads?" Kate asked when they'd seated themselves stiffly on her leather sofa.

"Nothing." Carlo shook his head. "Like you already said, no one saw anything at the post office yesterday."

"What about fingerprints?" Steve asked.

"They lifted a few good lateral prints from both the basement and the living room," Antonio offered. "But so far we've had no luck matching them up with anything on file. We're still working on it."

Steve nodded as if he'd expected as much. "And the letters? Do any of the prints on them match the prints you found in the living room?"

"We couldn't get anything useful from them," Bruno said. "If there were any prints to be found, they were smudged by other people handling them. The only clear prints we got were from Martha and Kate. And you."

"Maybe you'll have better luck with this one." Steve handed him the envelope containing the latest letter. "None of us have touched it."

"So we're not any further ahead than we were yesterday?" Kate asked with a sinking heart.

"I wish I had better news for you, Katie," Carlo said sympathetically.

"Keep your chin up, kiddo," Bruno added. "We're bound to turn up something soon."

"Bruno's right," Antonio said. "Just lay low for a little while longer. We'll have this guy before you know it."

Kate prayed they were right. Because, scared as she was by the threat her biggest fan posed, the threat Steve posed was far larger. If she wasn't careful, if she so much as let her guard down, she was afraid the worst would happen.

She was terrified she would fall in love with him all over again.

*Chapter 8*

The roses wouldn't die.

Each morning, when Steve walked into Kate's office, their fragrance assaulted him like a fist to the nose. Every time he looked at them, sitting squarely in the middle of the coffee table, he found himself grinding his teeth.

Four days had passed since the flowers had been delivered. Four long days during which Kate's gaze had never once lingered on his for longer than the second or two it took to establish contact. Four endless days during which their conversation had remained carefully neutral. Four interminable days during which he'd worked by her side, slept in her guest bedroom, jogged with her on her morning runs, followed her on scheduled errands and wished, whenever he looked at them, for the blasted roses to shrivel up and die.

He'd never sent her flowers. Nor had he surprised her with unexpected gifts. Was that what she wanted? Tokens of affection? Pretty words?

She was a woman who dealt in words, who made her living by arranging them on the page in such a manner that they aroused the emotions of the people who read them. And he was a man who mistrusted words. Intensely.

Oil and vinegar. When you shook them up, they mixed temporarily. Eventually, however, they separated once more. The way he and Kate had. The way they would again, once her biggest fan was found. For his peace of mind, he prayed it would be soon.

Unfortunately, a review of the pictures Martha had taken had revealed no obvious suspects. Nor had any of the pictures taken since by Kent. No more letters had arrived. No fingerprint matches had been made by the police. No disturbances had interrupted them. It seemed that Kate's biggest fan was taking a break. For now.

Perhaps he was trying to lull them into a false sense of security before striking again. Perhaps, now that he was aware that Kate had hired protection, he'd given up and gone on his merry way. It was a tempting thought, but Steve didn't believe it for a minute. His gut told him that this guy meant business. Deadly business. Without a doubt, he would strike again. The only questions were, when and where?

And would Steve still have a shred of sanity left when that time arrived?

Willing his mind to focus on the job at hand, he concentrated on the day's schedule. That was when it dawned on him that today was Friday, and that the whole weekend yawned before him. Martha wouldn't be coming in tomorrow. He'd be alone with Kate. Other than a few errands, the schedule was bare.

Though they'd been alone every night for the past four nights, somehow this felt different. More…intimate. Weekends were for lovers, time to shed the cares of the work world, kick back your feet and relax. Together. When he and Kate had been married, he'd lived for those rare weekends when he'd had some free time to spend with her. Nine times out of ten, they'd whiled away those hours in bed. But that was then, and this was now. What was he going to do with himself for the next forty-eight hours?

Glancing across the room, he saw Kate, brow furrowed in concentration as she composed the first draft of that day's column. She wore a vividly striped pink-and-white cotton shirt over a pair of white shorts. The shirttail was untucked, and the sleeves had been rolled up to her elbows. She'd left the top three buttons undone, exposing a creamy length of throat that invited further inspection. As usual, her long hair was secured at the nape of her neck by a wide barrette, and her feet were bare. To Steve, she looked utterly delectable. And totally unreachable.

It wasn't right that all he had to do was look at her to feel anew the silky softness of her skin beneath his fingertips. It wasn't fair that he could still taste the mouth that had kissed his with a fervor that had made his mind spin. It went beyond all human endurance that the soft moans she'd made whenever he'd touched her just so, and the way she'd called out his name when she'd reached the pinnacle of her desire, continued to echo in his ears. No man should be tortured the way he was being tortured by the mere sight of the woman he used to love.

Surely, by now, and after everything that had happened, he should have reached the point where he could look at her and not want her. Yet, despite everything, he did. Desperately. Heaven help him.

Thoughts like these were what drove him to his flute every night. He played until he was exhausted and his fingers ached, and then he played some more. Still, it didn't stop him from wanting her. He was beginning to think nothing would.

It was just his wounded pride driving his fantasies, he told himself. Wounded pride was what made him want to test the waters, to see if he could make her want him the way she had when they were married. Wounded pride, and nothing more. She'd killed any feelings he had for her the day she asked him for a divorce.

When he looked away, his gaze collided with Martha's. There was a knowing, almost sympathetic look in the older woman's eyes that told him she'd seen him staring at Kate. Had she also seen the depth of his yearning?

Martha cleared her throat. "Think I'll head into the kitchen for a glass of lemonade. Anyone else thirsty?"

"I'll stick with my water," Kate said, sounding distracted.

"Lemonade sounds good to me," Steve said.

"Two lemonades coming up."

After Martha left the room, Steve returned his attention to the schedule. Though his photographic memory had already implanted it in his brain, he needed something other than Kate to occupy him. A seeming oversight caught his attention. It amazed him he hadn't seen it earlier.

"No date with David tonight?" He was proud of himself when his voice sounded casual.

"No." Kate's fingers flew over the keyboard.

He was either a masochist or a fool, he told himself, because he couldn't let it go. Even though she'd told him it was too soon to tell what her feelings were for David, and that she wasn't in a hurry to fall in love with anyone, he couldn't leave well enough alone. "Trouble in paradise?"

She glanced up, a faraway look in her eyes, and he knew her thoughts were centered on the column she was writing. "What?"

"I just assumed you'd have a date with David tonight."

Her eyes cleared, and she seemed to focus on him. "Why?"

Steve shrugged. "It's Friday."

"And?"

"You're single. It only makes sense you'd have a date. Besides, a guy spends all that money on flowers, he wants to see you more than once. I just assumed tonight would be one of those times."

"Well, you assumed wrong." She returned her attention to the computer screen.

"I thought he called you a couple of days ago."

With a weary sigh, Kate looked up again. "He did."

"And he didn't ask you out?"

"He asked. I said no."

He had no business feeling so ridiculously happy. Her next words confirmed it.

"Until this guy is caught, I don't see any reason dragging anyone else into this mess."

What was he hoping? That being with him again had made her see how empty any other relationship was? Idiot. "Very sensible of you."

She nodded. "I thought so. Anything else you want to know?"

*Nothing much. Just two simple things. How could you walk out on me the way you did? And why do you keep on insisting that I left you?* "No."

"Then I have a question. Do you have a date tonight?"

The words took him by surprise. "No."

"Why not? You're single. It's Friday night...." She gazed at him expectantly.

Steve grinned and shook his head. "Touché."

Her answering grin made his heart thump. Thank goodness Martha chose that minute to walk back into the room, before he did something stupid. Like kiss Kate.

He drained the icy glass of lemonade in one long gulp. It didn't come close to quenching his real thirst.


At eleven o'clock, Jock Oldham phoned.

"Hey, buddy," he said when Steve answered. "Sorry it took so long to get back to you, but I think I have the information you need."

"I'm listening."

"All the birds, except one, are still snug in their nests."

Steve's pulse rate accelerated, and he gripped the receiver tightly. "Which little birdie's learned to fly?"

"Lyle Benedict."

Lyle Benedict. The low-life drug dealer who had threatened to kill Kate to keep Steve from testifying against him.

"When did he get his wings?"

"A month ago. Good behavior."

The same time Kate had started receiving those letters. Steve felt a stirring of triumph. This was too much of a coincidence to be ignored.

"Where can I find him?"

"Rumor has it he's found religion." Jock's voice dripped sarcasm. "These days, according to his parole officer, Lyle's hangout is the Light of Hope Ministries on the North Side. They run a soup kitchen. Supposedly Lyle spends his time there, witnessing to the homeless."

Like Jock, Steve didn't believe for a minute that Lyle Benedict had reformed his ways. If the man was hanging around a soup kitchen, it was because he had an ulterior motive. And Steve knew exactly what that motive was: revenge.

When he ended his conversation with Jock, he crossed the room and stood beside Kate's desk.

"Yes?" she asked, without looking up.

"Can you take a break?"

Slowly she raised her gaze to his. "Why?"

"We have an errand to run."

"You mind telling me where we're going?" Kate asked when he stopped at a red light a few blocks from her house.

"We're going to pay a visit on a man named Lyle Benedict." Steve kept his gaze on their surroundings. So far, he'd seen nothing out of the ordinary.

"Why?"

"Because he was released from prison at the time you started receiving those letters."

He felt her gaze settle on him. "You think he's my biggest fan?"

"I think there's a good chance he is."

"Why?"

"Because I'm the one who put him in prison. And because he swore to get revenge."

She digested his words in silence for several seconds before asking, "What do you want me to do?"

"Look him over very carefully. See if you recognize him

as someone who's been hanging around the post office. Listen to him speak. Try to determine if it's the voice of the man who...shoved...you...."

His words trailed off when he saw the woman walking along the opposite sidewalk. She was pushing a stroller. Inside, sat a little girl who appeared to be just over two.

Steve's heart twisted. If she had lived, Molly would be that age. Would she have looked like that now? Would he have had that same look of contentment on his face while rolling her stroller down the street?

A glance at Kate told him that she, too, was observing the stroller's progress. He couldn't see her eyes, couldn't tell if the sight of that beautiful child stabbed at her heart the way it did his. Probably not, he decided, because she didn't carry around the burden of guilt that he did.

Behind him, a horn blared, and he realized the light had changed.

Damn! He'd never had such difficulty keeping his mind on the job before. Then again, he'd never shared any emotional ties with a client, either. It was a good thing Kent was bringing up the rear, Steve decided, because he definitely was not at peak performance level.

With trembling hands, Steve steered the car forward.

Neither one of them said a word about the child.


When Steve and Kate climbed out of his car in front of the Light of Hope Ministries, they were confronted by a forlorn-looking church whose grimy, buckled, stained-glass windows were protected by steel bars. A heavy red wood door creaked loudly when he opened it.

Inside, all was hushed and reverent and stiflingly hot. Squinting through the dimness, it took Steve only seconds to determine that Lyle Benedict was not among the gathered worshipers in the sanctuary.

A staircase to their left led them down one flight and through a pair of open doors. The aroma of tomato sauce drew them to a large room where fans whirred, doing little more than stirring up the heavy air. Approximately fifty men, women and children sat eating at tables that had been scattered across a worn hardwood floor. Another twenty people stood in the line that formed to their right and filed past two serving tables.

"I'm looking for Lyle Benedict," Steve addressed the man dishing out potatoes.

"Over there." The man inclined his head toward the other end of the room.

Turning to Kate, Steve said, "I can't stress how vitally important it is that you let me handle this. Just listen and observe."

She gave him a reassuring smile. "Don't worry. I won't interfere. Just pretend I'm invisible."

Fat chance of that ever happening. Reaching out, he gave her hand a quick squeeze. "Thanks."

Her fingers curled around his, and she squeezed back. The warmth of her hand, and her smile, traveled straight up his arm and into his heart.

"I'm the one who should be thanking you," she said.

*You have a job to do, Gallagher,* he reminded himself sternly. *Get a grip.* Squaring his shoulders, and ignoring the pounding of his heart, he turned his gaze to Lyle. "Let's go."

His quarry sat at a table reading the Bible to a grizzled man who, despite the heat, wore a hat, scarf, gloves and winter coat. This really was taking the act too far, Steve thought distastefully. Obviously Lyle had seen him coming and was putting on a show for his benefit.

When he reached the table where Lyle was sitting, he placed his body protectively in front of Kate's. "Hello, Lyle."

Lyle's head whipped around. After gazing up at Steve for several seconds in seemingly stunned surprise, a wide grin split a face that still managed to look amazingly youthful and innocent despite his years on the street and behind bars.

"Stevarino, my man! What brings you here, brother?"

As if he didn't know. Steve wondered how many hours Lyle had spent in front of a mirror, perfecting his reaction. He had to have known that Steve would eventually track him down, especially after he shoved Kate in front of that bus. Because Steve knew Lyle, knew the way the man's mind worked, he was certain Lyle had prepared well for this confrontation.

"You're what brings me here, Lyle. I came to see you. Is there somewhere private we can talk?"

Bible in hand, Lyle stood and squeezed the homeless man's shoulder. "Excuse me, brother. Enjoy your meal. Remember, you are not alone."

The same cocky swagger that Steve remembered so well brought Lyle to his side. Only now, for some reason, it seemed less cocky and defiant, more confident, purposeful.

Lyle pointed to an empty table that was set well apart from the rest. "We can talk there. No one will bother us. People tend to mind their own business around here."

For six months, after he'd infiltrated the nefarious street gang called the Crows, Steve had been Lyle's best friend and confidant. Though he'd despised what the gang had stood for and the drug trade they'd trafficked in, he'd grudgingly found himself liking Lyle, even respecting him in a way. Like his reawakened desire for Kate, he was amazed to discover that a remnant of that emotion still remained.

Lyle settled his gaze on Kate once they'd taken a seat across from him at the empty table. Steve tried to read something in the other man's eyes: recognition, surprise, evil intent. All he saw was polite interest.

"My wife," Steve said by way of introduction.

"Pleased to meetcha," Lyle said.

True to her word, Kate just nodded.

Lyle certainly looked the part he'd chosen to play, Steve reflected. Gone were the torn T-shirts, the gold chains and earrings, the black bandanna tied around his head, and the ever-present cigarette protruding from the corner of his mouth. In their place Steve saw a clean-shaven man who was neatly dressed in jeans and a white, short-sleeved shirt. If he didn't know any better, he could almost believe Lyle was the convert he professed to be.

Folding his hands in front of him, Steve centered his gaze unblinkingly on Lyle. "So, you've finally made your mama proud. I bet she's thrilled to have a preacher in the family."

Lyle nodded gravely, as if he didn't hear the sarcasm in Steve's voice. "She is at that." Then, grinning at Steve for all the world as if he were happy to see him, he added, "So, Stevie boy, it's been a long time."

"We haven't exactly been keeping the same company."

Lyle gave a soft bark of laughter and ruefully shook his head. "Ain't that the truth? Man, you can say that again."

Steve nodded at their surroundings. "Kinda quiet around here. Must get boring, just hanging around."

"Boring? Are you kiddin', man? This is where the action's at!" Lyle's voice grew impassioned. "Lives are at stake here. No, Stevie boy, I'm anything but bored."

According to the law of the hood, by all rights Lyle should be plotting his revenge, not hanging out here. He'd been betrayed by the man he'd thought of as a brother. It was his sworn duty to seek vengeance. So why was Steve suddenly feeling as if things didn't add up, as if something was going on here that he didn't understand?

"Rumor is, you've found religion."

Lyle raised the Bible in his hand. "It's no rumor, bro. It took the good Lord a good number of years to knock some sense into this thick skull of mine, but I've finally seen the light. I've mended my ways. From now on, I walk the straight and narrow. I've made it my life's goal to bring the good word to others."

"Witnessing here won't put food on your table, clothes on your body, or a roof over your head," Steve pointed out.

"Yes, but it does nurture my soul. That's what's important, brother. My soul."

"So is money for food, shelter and clothing. How are you paying for those?"

Lyle's fingers caressed the worn leather cover of the Bible. "I work nights busin' tables at a restaurant a few blocks from here."

Steve wasn't going to take Lyle's word for it; he intended to check this claim out. "How are your brothers in the hood dealing with your...shall we say, change of heart?"

Sadness flickered in Lyle's eyes. "There is no hood, Stevie boy. Not for me, anyway. Like I told you, I'm a changed man."

"Lay off the bull, Lyle," he said harshly. "I'm not buying."

Instead of blustering about being unjustly accused, Lyle stared at him calmly. "You gonna tell me why you're here?"

"I'm here to warn you."

"About what?"

Steve leaned forward until he was almost nose-to-nose with the other man. In a voice that was no less menacing for its softness, he narrowed his eyes and said, "If I find out you're the one threatening my wife, not even the God you profess to love so much is going to be able to save you."

Steve had expected one of two reactions: exaggerated innocence or heated denial. But Lyle didn't act at all the way Steve had anticipated. Nor did he look the least bit intimidated by the threat Steve had made. What he looked was concerned. And that took Steve aback.

"Someone's threatenin' this pretty lady here? And you think it's me?"

Steve clenched the hands he'd folded on the table and resisted the urge to wrap them around the other man's throat and squeeze until the truth spilled out. He wished he had the evidence that would toss Lyle back behind bars, but so far the man had been crafty enough not to implicate himself. All Steve could do was poke, prod and provoke, in the hope that Lyle grew angry and careless enough to trip himself up.

"I don't just think it's you, Lyle. I know it is. You're the one sending her those threatening letters. You're the one who pushed her into the street Monday morning. You've got a score to settle. I understand that. But you settle it with me. You stop threatening my wife. She has nothing to do with us.''

Lyle spread his arms, as if inviting Steve to search him. "I haven't threatened anyone, Stevie boy. Like I told you already, I got no score to settle. The slate is wiped clean. You're lookin' in the wrong place."

Steve felt his lip curl. "Is that so? Then why do I have this vivid recollection of you shouting at the top of your lungs, while they were dragging you away to your cell, how you were going to get me and everyone I ever cared about, if it was the last thing you ever did?''

"I'm not the person I was then," Lyle said. "Like I told you before, man, I've seen the error of my ways. I'm not interested in revenge."

"Then explain this. Why did my wife start receiving those letters the minute you were released from prison?''

Lyle shrugged. "Coincidence? How should I know, man? All I know is, I didn't send them. And I didn't do no pushin', either.''

No heated protest. Just calm denial. This wasn't going at all the way Steve had expected. Could he be wrong? Could Lyle really have changed? Was Kate's biggest fan someone else entirely?

He sent a questioning glance Kate's way. *Is he the man?* She shook her head, and mouthed the word "no."

"You could have paid someone to do your dirty work for you," he said to Lyle, not yet willing to give it up.

Lyle looked amused. "With what? Busin' tables ain't exactly put me on Easy Street."

Steve didn't want to believe that the Lyle he saw sitting before him was a different man from the one he'd helped lock away. People just didn't shed their skin overnight, like a molting snake. Lord knows how much he'd wanted to change what he really was, deep inside. For a time, he'd even believed he'd succeeded, until one regrettable event had proven how wrong that belief had been. He was no longer fool enough to hope it could really happen.

"Isn't this the part where you quote me passage and verse to convince me of your innocence?" Still hoping to provoke some sort of reaction, Steve made his voice deliberately insolent.

Lyle's smile was both sad and understanding. "No, man. One thing I've learned is that you can't convince a brother who's determined to disbelieve."

"You've got that right, at least. Want to tell me where you were Monday morning around eleven?"

Lyle thought a minute. "With my parole officer. I can give you his number, if you like."

"I like." Steve committed the name and telephone number to memory. "What about one o'clock that same day? Where were you then?"

"Here, like always. Ask anyone. The man who runs this place has an office in back. Reverend Hopkins. He'll tell you how much time I spend here."

Frustrated that things hadn't turned out at all the way he'd planned, Steve pushed his chair back. Out of the corner of one eye, he saw Kate follow suit.

"I'll be watching you, Lyle," he warned. "Make one wrong move, and you're going back to the slammer for a long, long time."

Lyle stood, too. "Watch away, Stevie boy. Watch away. I got nothin' to hide."

Taking Kate by the elbow, Steve ushered her away from the table.

"Stevie," the other man called softly.

Pausing, Steve glanced over his shoulder.

"It does my heart good to see you and your old lady still together. There's too much divorce these days. Seems like no one takes their marriage vows seriously anymore. What God has joined together, let no man divide. Right, bro? Be happy, man. Keep the faith. You'll catch this guy."

Until Lyle brought it to his attention, Steve hadn't realized he'd referred to Kate as his wife. Not once, but several times. It would have been easy to chalk the mistake up to a slip of the tongue, and he was half tempted to do so. But this was an afternoon for facing truths, unpalatable though they might be. Steve had learned two very important things during this visit. Number one: In all probability, Lyle wasn't the man they were looking for. And number two: In his heart, he still thought of Kate as his wife.

He waited until Kent had signaled the all clear and they were back in the car to speak. "You really didn't recognize him?"

"I've never seen him before," she confirmed.

"What about his voice? Did it sound familiar?"

"No. The voice of the man who pushed me was deep, almost bass. Lyle's definitely a tenor. I don't think he's the man we're looking for, Steve."

"Unfortunately, neither do I." He hesitated. "About me introducing you as my wife..."

Kate held up a hand. "You don't have to explain. I know it was just for effect. You were hoping Lyle would trip himself up by admitting that he knew we were divorced."

If only that were true, he thought.

"What are you going to do now?" she asked.

"Check out Lyle's alibi. Just to be sure."

"And after that?"

With all his heart, Steve wished that Lyle was the man they sought. He was a known entity, someone they could track and eventually outwit. Instead, the person stalking Kate was still an unknown, shadowy figure who was all the more dangerous because of that anonymity. Her biggest fan could be anyone, from an old school chum she'd unwittingly slighted to the Pope himself. The only thing they were certain of at this point was that the person who'd shoved her in front of that bus was male. With every passing moment, their suspect pool only grew, instead of diminishing. Damn.

Oh, they'd keep an eye on Lyle. Steve wasn't a fool. But in his gut he knew nothing would come of it.

"Look elsewhere," he said.

"I'm sorry," Kate replied. "It's obvious this has really gotten you down."

He should be the one comforting her, he thought guiltily. "I'm sorry, too." Shaking off his bad mood, he adopted a businesslike attitude. "But I'm not down. I prefer to look at this positively. After all, we've just eliminated one player from the field. We have one less suspect to concern ourselves with."

He was thankful when she let the matter drop. Instead, she surprised him by asking, "Do you play Scrabble?"

"Why?"

"I'd like to invite my next-door neighbor, Mrs. Edmund, and her friend, Clara Mae Edgington, over to play this evening."

So, she'd been thinking about the weekend, too. Was she just trying to fill the empty hours, or did the thought of their being alone together disturb her as much as it did him?

He also wondered why, despite her assertion that she didn't want to put him in danger, she hadn't invited David. After all, she was willing to entertain her next-door neighbor. Could it be that she wasn't as enamored of him as Steve had supposed?

"I guess I could manage a game or two," he said.

Kate's smile was wry. "Your enthusiasm is overwhelming."

He grinned. "I don't suppose you could talk Mrs. Edmund and her friend into a game of Trivial Pursuit?"

She looked scandalized. "With your photographic memory? That would hardly be fair, would it? A word of advice, though. Don't let their sweet-old-lady act fool you. When it comes to Scrabble, Clara Mae and Mrs. E. are ruthless."

"I'll keep that in mind."

"One more thing," she added, as if the idea had just occurred to her. "When you're making up next week's schedule tomorrow, I want to slot a visit to the cemetery on Sunday."

The image of the toddler in the stroller flashed in his mind. Had the sight of that little girl prompted Kate's request?

"The cemetery?" he asked, his chest tight.

"Yes. I want to take flowers to my mother's and Molly's graves."

Other than the funeral, he'd never been able to visit his daughter's final resting place. "Do you do this often?"

"Every Sunday."

Relief coursed through him. "It's not safe, Kate. We need to vary your routine."

"Then we'll go in the morning, instead of the afternoon." The look in her eyes told him she'd brook no resistance on this one. "I need to do this, Steve. I'll understand, though, if you don't want to come. Kent can go with me, instead. I won't mind."

He'd never said goodbye, he realized. Not in his heart, anyway. Maybe it was time.

"That won't be necessary. I'll go with you."

# Chapter 9

Mrs. Edmund looked as if she had just stepped out of a nineteenth-century painting. The elderly woman was slight and stooped, with snow-white hair, paper-thin skin and piercing blue eyes. Despite the warmth of the night air, she wore an ankle-length print dress. A matching kerchief covered her hair.

In contrast, Clara Mae Edgington had broad, upright shoulders and a solid body that hinted at a robust constitution. Her outfit consisted of a no-nonsense black, knee-length dress and a pair of sturdy black shoes. Ace bandages encircled her ankles, and her stockings had been rolled down to form a ridge just below her knees. Though she didn't need it, like Mrs. Edmund, she relied on a cane to help her maintain her balance.

After ushering the two women into the living room, Steve had murmured something about refreshments and disappeared into the kitchen, leaving Kate to handle the greetings.

"Thank you for inviting us over, dear," Mrs. Edmund said as she made her slow way to the card table Kate had set up in the middle of the floor. "I've been looking forward to our game ever since you called. Haven't I, Clara Mae?"

"It's all she could talk about," Clara Mae confirmed. "Thank you for the invitation, Kate. Although why a pretty young woman such as yourself would want to waste the evening with a couple of old biddies is beyond me."

"Old biddy, indeed," Mrs. Edmund harrumphed. "Speak for yourself, Clara Mae. You're only as old as you feel, and right now I feel about twenty-seven."

"You may feel twenty-seven, but you look seventy-seven," Clara Mae retorted.

Smiling, Kate pulled out Mrs. Edmund's chair and waited while the older woman gingerly settled herself. She only hoped that she had half her neighbor's energy, and her youthful outlook on life, when she was the same age. One thing was for certain: there never was a dull moment when Mrs. Edmund and Clara Mae were around. Which was exactly what Kate was counting on.

"I'm glad you both could come. I've been looking forward to tonight, too." More than they would ever know.

Truth was, she had invited the women over because she'd panicked at the thought of spending the weekend alone with Steve. And to cut down on his flute playing. Beautiful and haunting as the music was, like his presence, it aroused emotions in her that she didn't want to deal with. Plus, it was driving her crazy. Why couldn't he just while away his free time watching ESPN, like any other normal adult male?

Instead, night after night, he sat in her den, or in his room, and played songs about life and love. "Danny Boy." "Clair de Lune." "I'll Take You Home Again, Kathleen." "When A Man Loves A Woman."

And night after night, Kate lay awake, listening and wanting him. Last night, he'd played "Unchained Melody," and it had been all she could do to force herself to remain rigid in her bed, teeth clenched and arms held stiffly at her sides, while she fought the urge to go to him. Like the words to the song, she'd hungered for his touch and his love with a ferocity that had shaken her to her very being.

That was when she'd told herself it had to stop. She was to the point now that she even wished her biggest fan would do something—anything—to take her mind off Steve. If something didn't happen soon, she might even be driven to calling her brothers and asking them to take turns coming over. Not that they didn't do that already. But weekends were traditionally the time they devoted to their own private lives. And a weekend without any warm bodies to run interference between her and Steve was definitely *not* what the doctor had ordered.

She was spending too much time with him. That was the problem. His proximity was making her forget what had torn them apart in the first place. Or maybe she was remembering all the wrong things, like how incredible they'd been together physically. That he'd been her only lover probably fed into the hunger that seemed to grow exponentially with every passing minute.

He was the sum of all the fantasies she'd ever had. The only way she could see of changing that was to become involved with someone else. *Call David,* the voice inside her head kept urging. But David wasn't the man who was going to make her forget Steve. She knew that now. She would only be using him for her own selfish purposes if she continued to lead him on, and that she would not allow herself to do.

If she didn't get a break soon, though, she was afraid she'd start hoping for the impossible. She was afraid she'd start believing that she and Steve could make things work, an event as probable as her column winning the Pulitzer prize.

The theory behind the Scrabble invitation had been twofold. First, Mrs. Edmund and Clara Mae would serve as a much-needed buffer between her and Steve. In addition, both women were avid players. Kate would have her hands full getting them to quit after three or four games. Mrs. Edmund might appear frail and shrunken with age, but when it came to her games, she had incredible stamina. Kate would be lucky to shoo the duo out the door by midnight.

And that was the whole point of the exercise. If she exhausted Steve enough, both physically and mentally, it was her dearest wish that he'd be too drained to pick up that blasted flute. He'd go straight to bed, and for once Kate could get a good night's sleep. That was what she really needed to put things into perspective. A good night's sleep, and she'd be able to meet his gaze again and not ache for the feel of his mouth on hers. A good night's sleep, and she'd be able to look at him and not yearn to have their bodies, naked and straining, entwined.

A good night's sleep. That was the ticket. She was determined to purchase it, no matter the cost.

Steve emerged from the kitchen balancing a tray that held a pitcher of freshly squeezed lemonade and four frosty glasses. He had a smile on his face, the same smile that had stolen her heart the first time she'd laid eyes on him. The smile that still made her heart thud madly no matter how many shields she threw up to try to deflect it.

Yes, Kate thought darkly as her mouth went dry and her stomach dipped with desire, her plan had better work. Because if it didn't, she was in trouble. Big trouble.

"I'd like you to meet our fourth for the evening," Kate said.

Because she hadn't wanted to alarm Mrs. Edmund and Clara Mae unnecessarily, she and Steve had agreed beforehand that she would introduce him as a friend and fellow Scrabble enthusiast. An incident that had occurred shortly after Kate had moved into the house was the catalyst for this decision. On that bright, sunny summer morning a year earlier, her brothers had shown up en masse in police cars, sirens wailing and guns drawn, because a Peeping Tom had been reported in the area.

Kate had been chatting on her front porch with Mrs. Edmund, who had just finished relating the tale of her new pacemaker. The sight of all those drawn guns had so shaken the woman that Kate had been terrified the pacemaker wouldn't be able to handle the stress. One thing she wanted to avoid at all costs was a repeat performance of that day's events. Since, as far as they knew, her biggest fan was no danger to anyone but her, she felt it best that Mrs. Edmund remain ignorant of his existence.

For that reason, she'd also insisted that Carlo question the elderly woman after the break-in on Monday, instead of Steve. Mrs. Edmund was used to her brother's histrionics and would take no undue notice of his interrogation.

As Kate had anticipated, Mrs. Edmund had attached little importance to Carlo's questions, and her brother had discovered that she'd seen nothing suspicious at the time of the break-in. Fortunately, since Kate lived across the street from a park, there were only four houses on her block. Other than Kate and Mrs. Edmund, no one else was home during the day. Which meant no pesky rumors were floating around to disturb the older woman and set her pacemaker off-kilter.

Unfortunately, by glossing over the real reason for Steve's presence, she'd created a situation she hadn't anticipated. It quickly became apparent that both women had taken an immediate shine to Steve. Equally apparent was that they'd decided he was the man for Kate.

"You should have told me your young man was such a handsome devil," Mrs. Edmund said, primping her hair and smiling at Steve. "If you had, I might have gussied myself up more."

"You look radiant just the way you are," Steve told her.

And she did, Kate realized, as she watched the way her neighbor beamed at Steve's words. It was amazing how the attentions of an attractive man erased the years from her face, giving Kate a glimpse of the youthful beauty Mrs. Edmund must have been. Kate felt a pang in the region of her heart. Surely she couldn't be jealous of Steve's attentions to Mrs. Edmund? Surely things hadn't deteriorated that far? No. The idea was preposterous.

"I like him," Mrs. Edmund pronounced, as if they'd all been waiting breathlessly for her assessment. She turned to Clara Mae, who had taken the seat opposite. "What about you, Clara Mae? What do you think?"

"What's not to like?" Clara Mae said, making no effort to hide the fact that she was examining Steve from head to toe. "If I were a few years younger, I might try to steal him away from you, Kate."

"And I would have the devil of a time resisting such charm," Steve said, handing each woman a cold glass of lemonade.

"Now that's what I call gallantry." Clara Mae was clearly pleased. "It's obvious your mother brought you up well."

Kate's gaze flew to his to see how he would react to the mention of his mother. When they'd been married and she'd tried to bring the subject up, he'd always withdrawn inside himself, declaring that no good could come of discussing what was past.

"Thank you," he said softly. To Kate's surprise, he added, "She was a special lady. It would have made her proud to hear you say that."

"Ah." Clara Mae heaved a regretful sigh, and patted his arm consolingly. "She's passed. When?"

"Twenty years ago."

"Too young, too young." Clara Mae's eyes filled with sorrow. "I'm sorry. You still miss her, don't you?"

"Yes," he said. "I do."

Over the heads of the elderly women, Steve's gaze searched and sought out Kate's. The message in his eyes was easy for her to read. *Help me out of this,* they begged. While she was half tempted to ignore the plea and see what other revelations the two women could wring from him, Kate couldn't help but take pity at his obvious discomfort.

"Shall we get started?" she said quickly, taking a seat.

"Ready when you are," Mrs. Edmund replied, flexing her fingers while Clara Mae pulled a tattered and worn paperback dictionary from her purse.

Steve handed Kate a glass of lemonade before sitting down in the empty chair across from her. Almost immediately, their knees knocked together.

"Excuse me," she murmured, trying to ignore the surge of heat that shot through her at the contact.

"Sorry," he muttered, his gaze averted from hers.

They both shifted in their seats. Once again, their knees knocked together, and once again they exchanged apologies. Kate bit her lip in consternation. When she'd set up the card table, she hadn't noticed how small it was. Mrs. Edmund and Clara Mae could sit at it with ease. But Steve, with his long legs, did not have the same luxury. And she was the lucky woman sitting across from him.

It didn't help matters that he'd changed out of his suit into a pair of navy-blue shorts and a bright red-, blue-, and yellow-striped polo shirt that made his eyes seem bluer than a summer sky. He looked so sexy her breathing went haywire every time she glanced at him. Though she tried to keep those glances to a minimum, her knees continued their run of bad luck. While she and Steve set up the Scrabble board and chitchatted with the women about current events, their knees kept rubbing together. Since Kate was wearing shorts, too, the feel of his bare limbs against hers had her body humming like an electrical power station. She moved uncomfortably in her seat, trying to find a position that would keep her knees in the safety zone.

Mrs. Edmund leaned toward Kate, engulfing her in a cloud of White Shoulders cologne. "You okay, dear?"

"What?" Still distracted by Steve's knees, Kate turned her attention to her neighbor.

"You look distressed. Anything wrong?"

Kate forced herself to stop fidgeting and plastered a smile on her face. When Steve's knees brushed against hers again, she didn't so much as move a muscle, although she felt the heat all the way down to her toes.

"I'm fine," she croaked in a high voice. She cleared her throat and added in a more normal tone, "Are we ready?"

As hostess, Kate went first. The combination of letters she'd drawn only allowed her to form the word "act" across the center of the board.

"Ten points," she announced to Clara Mae, who was keeping score.

Mrs. Edmund went next, turning "act" into "lactic." The play moved to Steve, who formed the word "course" using the second *c* in lactic.

Kate was just beginning to relax and enjoy herself, when Clara Mae turned "lactic" into "prophylactic." It was Kate's second hint—Steve's knees rubbing against hers being the first—that the evening wasn't going to go as smoothly as she'd hoped.

Clara Mae must have picked up on her agitation, because she said, "I assure you, it's spelled correctly, Kate. Feel free to challenge, though, if you wish."

Kate was well aware that the word was spelled correctly. It was the meaning of the word that gave her pause.

"I believe you," she said. "I'm not challenging."

"You still don't look happy," Clara Mae said. "Tell you what. I know it's pushing the rules a bit without a challenge and all, but I'll look the word up. It'll set your mind at ease."

"Really, Mrs. Edgington, there's no need—"

"Oh, yes there is," Clara Mae demurred, nodding her white head firmly. "A triple word score is involved here. We're talking eighty-seven points. I want everyone satisfied that it's spelled correctly. When I win, I want there to be no taint on my victory."

She opened her dictionary, found the entry she sought, then leaned toward Kate. "Here it is. See? 'Prophylactic. A device, usually a rubber sheath, used to prevent conception or venereal infection. Condom.'"

Kate couldn't help herself. She glanced across the table at Steve. His eyes twinkled as their gazes met, and he looked as though he were struggling mightily not to laugh. She felt a glow of warmth at their shared humor.

"Thank you," she said to Clara Mae, swallowing back her

own laughter as she formed the word "quiet" using the *e* in "course."

"Speaking of prophylactics," Mrs. Edmund said, "that gives me the perfect word." She then proceeded to lay down the tiles that transformed "course" into "intercourse."

Kate felt the heat rise in her cheeks. This time she didn't dare look at Steve, although she thought she heard him make a choking sound.

"Don't look so shocked, dear." Mrs. Edmund's arthritis-twisted fingers patted Kate's hand. "It's a perfectly legitimate word."

"I know," Kate managed to say.

"The standard definition is an exchange of thoughts and feelings." Mrs. Edmund replaced her used tiles. "Like what we're doing here. Of course, I prefer the more intimate connotation, that being sexual relations. Making love is the most wonderful expression of intimacy. It's the giving and sharing of not just bodies but souls that makes it so special. Don't you agree, young man?"

"Absolutely," Steve said.

As if drawn by a magnet, Kate looked across the table and found his gaze trained squarely on her. His eyes were clouded with the same memories that chased relentlessly through her brain, memories of the many times they had indulged in sexual intercourse together.

Kate's mouth went dry, and her hands shook. Quickly, before he could read in her eyes how much she still wanted him, she looked down at the table and hid her hands on her lap.

Why had she ever been foolish enough to think that the presence of these two women would be enough to save her from his hold over her? And why now, after untold hours during which she'd played canasta, mah-jongg, poker and Scrabble with Mrs. Edmund without the conversation growing any more personal than was she seeing a young man, had the woman chosen to take their social intercourse to new, unexplored heights?

"I'm not embarrassed to admit," Mrs. Edmund continued, "that over the years my Herman—God rest his soul—bought his share of prophylactics. I've no doubt Clara Mae's Waldo did the same."

Clara Mae nodded her head vigorously. "He did indeed. Yes sirree. You see, we weren't as lucky as you young people. We didn't have the wide variety of contraceptive devices that are available today. But that didn't mean we weren't any less passionate. Not at all. I daresay we were as lusty as any young lovers."

Kate sat there, dumbfounded. She couldn't believe she was having this conversation. It felt surreal, almost like a dream. If someone had told her earlier that, this evening, she would be sitting with her ex-husband and two elderly women discussing the definition of sexual intercourse and its relationship to prophylactics, she would have told said person that she had a few screws loose. Maybe it was because she'd never had a mother to discuss such things with—and her brothers had zealously avoided the subject, if at all possible—but it made her distinctly uncomfortable. Of course, Steve's presence didn't help any.

And she'd been worried about Mrs. Edmund's pacemaker. The way her heart was pounding, if the subject wasn't changed soon, *she'd* need a pacemaker of her own.

"Why is it," Mrs. Edmund asked, eyeing Kate's red cheeks, "that you young people always assume we've forgotten what it's like to be young and in love?"

"Maybe," Steve offered, sounding reflective, "it's because there are times when we forget ourselves."

Mrs. Edmund gave him a coy look. "A good-looking man like you? With all those hormones running amok? I don't think there are many times you forget."

Steve's smile was broad. "Mrs. Edmund, are you flirting with me?"

"No, dear." She aimed a sly look at Kate. "You may be a handsome devil, but I wouldn't want to take unfair advantage of my hostess. She doesn't get out much, you know."

"No," Steve said, his gaze speculative as it moved to Kate, "I didn't know. Tell me more."

Mrs. Edmund didn't need further invitation. After barely pausing to draw breath, she launched into speech.

"She's never said as much, but I think someone hurt her very deeply. I don't think it was too long ago, either. I get the sense that the pain is still raw, still very close to the surface. She must have loved him very much."

What was it about her that made people talk as if she weren't even in the room? Kate wondered in desperation. And just how could she put a stop to it?

"Did someone hurt you?" Steve asked softly.

Kate felt her temper rise at his concerned suitor act. He knew darn well someone had hurt her, and that *he* was the someone in question. "Yes," she said curtly.

"I thought so." Mrs. Edmund's voice was smug with satisfaction. "It's taken you until now to risk dating again, hasn't it?"

"Yes," she admitted, a little more gently, because she didn't want to hurt the older woman's feelings.

"Didn't I tell you, Clara Mae? And here you thought she was just picky."

Clara Mae gave a woeful shake of her head. "Guess you were right, Janet. Appears I owe you five dollars."

"I'll put it on your account."

"How did he hurt you?" Steve asked.

Instead of answering, Kate nodded toward the playing board. "It's your turn."

He laid down his tiles, and Clara Mae recorded his score.

"How'd he hurt you, Kate?" he repeated.

Much as she wanted to ignore the question, she couldn't. Steve looked like he really wanted to hear what she had to say. And a part of her wanted to answer, while he was sitting there, unable to walk away. This was an opportunity he hadn't afforded her while they were married. Maybe this was the only way they *could* talk about it, as if it had happened to two different people.

Clenching the hands she held in her lap, she said, "He wouldn't open up to me. Everything was a big secret with him. He made me feel…insignificant. Finally, I couldn't take it anymore."

Mrs. Edmund's eyes were bright with sympathy. "I'm so sorry, dear."

Kate tore her gaze away from Steve to ponder the older woman. "Did you and your husband communicate well?"

"Herman and I talked about everything." A nostalgic smile curved the woman's lips and her eyes grew soft and dreamy. "He was my best friend. We had no secrets."

"What about arguing?" Kate pressed. "Did you do that, too?"

"Heavens, yes!" Mrs. Edmund laughed with delight. "Sometimes I just wanted to kill that man. But then our tempers would cool, and we'd make up. And the making up more than compensated for the fighting."

Kate shot a pointed glance to Steve before turning her attention to Clara Mae. The look on his face told her he was sorry he'd pursued this line of questioning. Good.

"What about you, Mrs. Edgington? Did you and your husband fight?"

"Like cats and dogs. Those were the days." Clara Mae sighed. "I wouldn't have missed them for the world."

"Well, my…the man who hurt me wouldn't fight. He always walked away. What do you think about that?"

Mrs. Edmund made a soft tsking sound. "No matter how fast you run, you can't escape your problems. No, that wouldn't do me at all."

"It didn't do me, either," Kate said flatly. "I felt more alone when I was with him than when he was gone. So I ended the relationship. When I told him I wanted a di…out, he didn't protest."

"Oh, you poor thing," Clara Mae said. "That must have hurt."

Only pride kept her from admitting exactly how much it

had hurt. How much, despite the passage of eighteen months, it still hurt.

There was an odd look on Steve's face as he turned his gaze on her. "You left him because he wouldn't fight with you?"

He sounded incredulous, as if he couldn't believe his ears. Exactly why had he thought she'd left? Kate wondered. At the time, she'd thought she'd made her feelings and her reasonings abundantly clear. Of course, she hadn't been thinking all that clearly in the weeks before coming to her decision. Maybe she hadn't clarified things well. Still she couldn't stem the vindictive voice inside her that whispered if he hadn't understood why she was leaving, all he'd had to do was stick around long enough to ask. Instead, he'd calmly accepted her declaration and then walked out the door.

"Yes," she said, thrusting her chin forward. "I left him because he wouldn't fight with me." It was a simplistic explanation for what had happened, but it would do. "Can you think of a better reason?"

"Hell yes," he retorted. "Hundreds."

"Name a few."

"Gladly." He ticked off on his fingers. "For starters, we have mental, verbal and physical abuse. Infidelity. Desertion. Incompatibility. Care to hear more?"

Kate could see Mrs. Edmund and Clara Mae listening closely while they watched the verbal interplay. The game was totally forgotten as their heads shifted back and forth between her and Steve like spectators at a tennis match. It was obvious they'd picked up on the undercurrents in the conversation. They might not understand where the flow was going to take them, but they were clearly fascinated by the interchange and planned on sticking around for the ride. Kate was too wound up to care.

"There's no need. I think my reason for ending the relationship was as valid as any of those you listed."

"What if he had a reason for always walking away?" Steve asked.

"Like what?" she challenged. "What could possibly make him walk away, other than that he just didn't care?"

Adrenaline raced through her veins. This was it. After what seemed like forever, the moment she'd been waiting for had finally arrived. She could feel it in her bones, taste it on the air. She'd finally goaded him past the point of no return, and he was going to give her the explanation she'd longed for. The explanation she deserved.

Steve opened his mouth, then closed it again. A minute later, he shrugged. Seeming to remember that they weren't alone, he smiled at the older women. "How should I know? I was just making a point."

It was all Kate could do to keep her shoulders from slumping. She should have known better. If the past had taught her anything, it was that Steve was a man who kept his own counsel at all costs. Especially when they had an audience. Well, she wasn't quite ready to end the conversation just yet.

"For the sake of argument," she said, "let's say you're right. Let's say he had a reason for walking away. Why didn't he ever tell me what that reason was? Maybe if he had, I wouldn't have felt so frustrated. I wouldn't have felt so alone."

His voice lowered and he looked away. "Maybe he wanted to, but couldn't."

"Why not?" she pressed.

His head came up. "Some people just aren't... approachable."

"What's that supposed to mean?"

"You have to admit, Kate, that you take your independence seriously. You don't like letting people do for you. You don't like needing anyone. Maybe he didn't confide in you because he didn't want to feel weak next to you."

Of all the explanations he could have offered, this was one she'd never expected. Kate felt stunned. Was he telling her the truth? Had she made him feel weak? Gazing at him now, so big, strong and remote, it was impossible to believe.

"Steve has a point," Mrs. Edmund said. "This isn't meant

as a criticism, dear, but you are the most self-sufficient woman I've ever met. It would take a special man not to be intimidated by your strength.''

Kate barely heard the woman. She was too busy staring at Steve.

''What are you saying? That if I had been soft and weak and clingy all the time, he would have been able to confide in me?''

Steve rubbed a hand around the back of his neck, and she could see the frustration in his eyes. ''No, Kate. I'm sure your independence was part of what drew him to you. I was just offering a hypothetical explanation for his silence.''

He glanced at Mrs. Edmund and Clara Mae, and Kate knew he was searching for the words that would defuse the situation. ''You know how we men stick together. Anyway, it doesn't matter anymore. It's over.''

''Nothing's really over unless you want it to be,'' Mrs. Edmund offered.

''Fiddlesticks,'' Clara Mae said. ''Sometimes things are broken beyond the point of repair. Remember, all the king's horses and all the king's men couldn't put Humpty-Dumpty together again.''

Good point, Kate thought. And her relationship with Steve was far more scrambled than poor Humpty had been. It would take a miracle to put it back together again.

''You are such a pessimist, Clara Mae,'' Mrs. Edmund groused. ''Well, I'm an optimist. And I'm of the opinion that joy is always there for the taking. Kate's an optimist, too. Aren't you, dear?''

''To tell you the truth, Mrs. Edmund, I haven't been feeling very optimistic lately.''

''That's just temporary.'' Mrs. Edmund waved her hand. ''Hormones. Trust me, you're an optimist. If you and your young man really wanted to, you could fix that relationship. The question is, do you want to fix it? Personally, if I had someone like Steve waiting in the wings, I wouldn't even consider it.''

Clara Mae shook her head vehemently. "You couldn't be more wrong, Janet. Not about Steve here—I agree with you on that—but about Kate and her relationship. And about me. I'm not a pessimist. Never have been, never will be. What I am is a realist. As Mark Twain once said, 'We are all like the moon in that we all have our dark side that we never show to anybody.' The difference between an optimist and a realist is that a realist knows all about that dark side, while an optimist foolishly doesn't believe it exists."

Mrs. Edmund sat quietly for a moment before saying, "That's the biggest load of poppycock I've ever heard."

"Which just proves my point," Clara Mae retorted. She looked at Steve. "What about you, young man?"

"What about me?"

"Which camp do you fall in? Optimist, pessimist or realist?"

"I'm a realist from way back."

"So you've seen the dark side, too."

His jaw tightened and his expression turned inward. Kate knew he was thinking about his father and everything he and his mother had suffered at the man's brutal hands. "Too many times to count."

"I thought so." Clara Mae's tone was reflective. "Beneath all that charm, you have that look about you. The one that says you've been to hell and back, and lived to tell the tale. I daresay you've got a dark side yourself."

Steve turned his gaze on Kate. His eyes were cloudy and tempestuous as he welded her to her seat with a look that seared into her very soul. She got the distinct feeling he was trying to issue her some kind of warning.

"I daresay I do," he said.

For a moment or two she wondered what he meant, then pushed the thought aside. She had other, more pressing matters to occupy her mind. Of utmost importance was the way this conversation had gotten entirely out of hand. The evening that was supposed to be relaxing and diverting had turned out to be anything but.

"We were discussing Kate's relationship here," Mrs. Edmund reminded. "Not people's dark sides."

Kate drew a deep, shuddering breath. It was time to regain control over the situation. "Steve's right. The relationship's over. It won't accomplish anything to discuss it further."

"Then let's not," Clara Mae said.

"Fine with me," Mrs. Edmund agreed.

Though what Kate really felt like doing was throwing herself on her bed, pulling her pillow over her head and crying her eyes out—for what she wasn't exactly sure—she pushed her hair back off her face and smiled shakily at the three people assembled around the table. "Popcorn, anyone?"

# Chapter 10

They were in the middle of the second game, Clara Mae having handily won the first, when Mrs. Edmund leaned toward Steve and asked, "So, young man, what is it that you do for a living?"

Kate tensed. Her fingers clenched around the tile she'd just drawn, and her gaze flew across the table. She relaxed slightly when the reproving look in his eyes told her he remembered their pact and that he'd be careful in the way he answered Mrs. Edmund's question. He wouldn't reveal anything that could possibly alarm the older woman. At least, not deliberately.

"I'm the owner of a company that specializes in protection services for both corporations and individuals," he said.

The way in which he worded his reply had Kate suppressing a smile. She knew he was trying to make his work sound so boring that Mrs. Edmund would eagerly drop the subject. Unfortunately, he didn't know the woman like Kate did. Mrs. Edmund approached new things with the openness of an infant discovering its world. When she had learned that Kate was a newspaper columnist, she'd spent the better part of an hour quizzing Kate on all aspects of that work. Steve's description of his job would only serve to whet Mrs. Edmund's appetite for knowledge. There would, Kate knew, be more questions. Lots of them.

As Kate had predicted, the minute the woman finished her turn, she aimed eyes bright with interest toward Steve. "Protection services? Do you mean security guards?"

Steve nodded. "Training and supplying security guards accounts for approximately seventy-five percent of our work."

"I have a nephew who once worked as a security guard at a toy factory," Clara Mae offered as she laid down her tiles. "Said it was the most boring job he'd ever had, and that it was all he could do to stay awake. He quit after two weeks to take a job as a presser at a dry cleaner's. Been there ten years now. Never happier."

"Clara Mae, that's not very polite," Mrs. Edmund admonished. "You'll offend our guest."

Steve smiled. "I'm not at all offended. I'm well aware that the job can seem rather...tedious at times. It's not for everyone. Which is why we look for employees who understand the importance of the service they're providing, and who aren't easily bored."

"You said seventy-five percent of your work was supplying security guards," Mrs. Edmund commented. "What's the other twenty-five percent?"

Kate shot him a warning look. In return, he gave her a benign smile that set her teeth on edge. It was a smile she'd seen on her brothers' faces countless times. Loosely translated, it meant that Steve was feeling supremely confident in his ability to control the situation, and she shouldn't bother her pretty little head worrying about it. Inevitably, after one of her brothers flashed her that same superior smile, all hell would break loose. Kate prayed it wasn't about to break loose here and now.

"We provide personal protection services for those individuals who require it," Steve said.

Clara Mae perked up. "You're a bodyguard?"

"I've acted in that capacity once or twice." The smile was still on his face, but his tone had grown cautious.

"Now that sounds a lot more interesting than being a security guard," Clara Mae said.

"It has its moments," Steve allowed.

When his gaze met Kate's, she saw the irony in his eyes, and the repressed laughter. Despite her best intentions, she found herself drawn to him like a mouse to the cheese in a baited trap. That very same look was what had so disarmed her the day she'd met him. Because of that look, she'd surrendered her virginity to him not long after. And, because of that look, she'd fallen head over heels in love with him and married him.

How many times had she wished that the first thing he'd aimed her way would have been that smug, superior, I-can-handle-things smile that never failed to nudge her temper up a notch. If he had, she never would have fallen for him. At least she thought not, since the theory had never been put to the test. It really didn't matter at this point. Back then, she hadn't been able to resist his appeal. If she didn't find a way to resist it now, the trap would once again slam closed. She would be lost. And it would be her undoing.

Though she tried with all her might, she couldn't look away. Her heart steadfastly ignored the frantic messages her brain repeatedly telegraphed, demanding that she get control of herself. Time seemed to stand still as the laughter in his eyes was replaced by a new, far different, far more elemental emotion.

Kate's heart thudded frantically, and her mouth went dry. Desire swept through her with the force of a flash fire, devastating her emotions and leaving her weak and trembling. The tile that she'd been clutching since Mrs. Edmund's unexpected question slipped from her fingers and tumbled to the floor.

"You dropped your tile," he murmured in a husky voice. Cheeks reddening, Kate managed to tear her gaze away.

Bending over in her seat, she combed unsteady fingers through the carpet, searching for the fallen tile.

"How fascinating," Mrs. Edmund commented, and for a heart-stopping moment Kate thought the woman was referring to her silent exchange with Steve. Mrs. Edmund's next question put her mind at rest, at least in that regard. "Have you ever guarded someone famous?"

To Kate's relief, when she righted herself in her chair, Steve was concentrating on his tiles. Self-reproach left a bitter taste in her mouth. She was too old and experienced in the ways of men—one man, anyway—to ever again allow herself to be seduced by a mere look. How could she have been so weak? The solution was simple. She needed to end this enforced nunhood of hers, to get out more. Once her biggest fan was safely out of the way, she was determined to do exactly that. And she was going to forget that there ever existed a man who could obliterate any resistance on her part with a mere look.

"Normally," Steve said, "I work the administrative end of the business. My firm, however, has handled security for a number of well-known entertainers when they've performed in Pittsburgh."

He smiled when Mrs. Edmund and Clara Mae oohed and aahed their delight at such a close brush with celebrity. Kate let her guard down for the first time in what seemed hours. This was the way she'd wanted the evening to go: a lot of chatter to pass the time, without that chatter becoming too personal. No suggestive words on the playing board. No meaningful glances across the table. She'd even grown, if not exactly used to the feel of Steve's knees against hers, resigned to their constant pressure. She could go for minutes at a time without noticing their warmth.

"Kate had some alterations done on her house earlier this week," Mrs. Edmund said. "New locks, outside lights and such. Did your company do the work?"

So much for letting her guard down, Kate thought, as alarm bells went off in her head. She didn't want the discussion to go anywhere near the work she'd had done on the house, because it could potentially lead to the reason for it.

Steve shook his head. "The bulk of the work was contracted out. My company just oversaw the job."

"I was thinking of having some similar work done on my house. As soon as possible, really. Could you oversee it for me?"

The bells in Kate's head started clanging. Before she could think of something to say to steer the conversation onto a safer topic, Steve said, "Certainly. Is there a reason you feel it needs to be done so soon?"

Mrs. Edmund looked embarrassed. "I just haven't felt as safe lately."

"You haven't?"

"No. A couple of rather odd things have occurred over the past few weeks. They've got me thinking it might be time to take a few extra precautions."

Steve's eyes narrowed. "What odd happenings?" he asked sharply.

The look on his face told Kate that he thought whatever it was that Mrs. Edmund had seen, it had something to do with her biggest fan. For a brief moment, she squeezed her eyes shut. She could feel it coming. Disaster. Like a runaway freight train, it was barreling their way.

She shot him a warning glance, shoved her knee against his and mouthed, "No!" He paid her no heed, his attention centered squarely on the elderly woman.

"Nothing in particular, just several things that all added up in my mind," Mrs. Edmund said. "Now that I think about it, I feel rather silly."

"Please," Steve urged. "I'd like to hear. What was it you saw that bothered you? After all, this is my business. I can tell you if you have anything to be worried about."

Mrs. Edmund shrugged. "Very well, if you insist. Three weeks ago, a man started jogging by my house. I noticed him because he always had on the same black spandex shorts and muscle shirt. He also wore a headset, like he was listening to the radio.''

"How often did this happen?" Steve asked.

"Every day for almost two weeks. He'd go by the house four or five times. I haven't seen him at all this week."

"Was it always the same time of day?"

Mrs. Edmund nodded. "Early evening, right after dinner."

"Sounds like a jogger to me," Clara Mae commented. "Nothing unusual in that. This time of year, most sensible runners are out in the early morning or evening hours to avoid the heat of the day. From what I've heard, they also tend to follow the same route for a while, especially if they find it a challenging one."

Mrs. Edmund tossed her friend a patient look. "Then why haven't I seen him at all this week?"

"Simple," Clara Mae responded. "He got tired of running past your house, and went in search of a change of scenery. Give him a couple of weeks. He'll be back."

"Was there something about him that made you suspicious of him?" Steve asked.

"It was the way he looked around him when he passed by," Mrs. Edmund replied. "If he was seriously into his exercise, he wouldn't have had the time to take in the little details. But this man seemed to be constantly looking around him, like he was trying to memorize everything he saw. And he stared really hard at the houses on this block. It made me uneasy. I'm probably being paranoid, but I think he was casing the neighborhood."

"Take it from me," Clara Mae said, "you're being paranoid.

"Maybe I am. Still, there's one thing I don't understand, one thing that doesn't fit."

"What's that?" Steve asked.

"He wasn't sweating. Not a drop." Mrs. Edmund shot Clara Mae a look of triumph. "How many joggers do you know who can run for an hour straight in eighty-degree weather without breaking a sweat?"

"Maybe he's one of those people who don't sweat very much," Clara Mae defended. "They do exist, you know."

Mrs. Edmund turned to Steve. "My theory is that he was only jogging on our block when he could be seen by one of us. The rest of the time, he was walking, probably plotting how he was going to break in."

"Was there anything else?" Steve asked.

"Yes. The last time he passed by, I happened to be out taking my daily constitutional. Two blocks down, he got into a car. There was another man in the driver's seat. The jogger said a couple of words, and they drove off. It just didn't settle well with me."

"Bah," Clara Mae said. "You've been watching too many detective shows, Janet. I told you before, the guy is probably in training, and he chose this neighborhood because of its hills. And the man in the car was most likely his personal trainer."

"And I told you that any self-respecting personal trainer monitors and directs his client's exercise. He doesn't sit in a car and wait. I think the man in the car worked for the jogger. Sort of like a chauffeur."

Clara Mae snorted her derision. "Janet, I love you dearly, but you couldn't be more wrong. If this guy was wealthy enough to have a chauffeur, he'd be jogging in an affluent neighborhood, not mingling with the riffraff."

"We aren't riffraff," Mrs. Edmund said heatedly. "We're solidly middle class. This is a wonderful place to live and raise a family. Most people in this town own oodles of things that any self-respecting burglar would be thrilled to get his hands on. Take, for instance, all the gizmos Kate has in her den. Computers, television, CD player. Perfect items for fencing, especially if someone wanted some quick drug money."

"So now he's a drug addict?" Clara Mae's eyes widened incredulously.

"You wouldn't happen to have recorded the license plate number, would you?" Steve asked.

The two women stopped their bickering to give him their full attention.

"You really think this is important?" Clara Mae asked.

"Yes," Steve replied. "I do. So, Mrs. Edmund, did you happen to write down the license number?"

"All I know is, the car had a Pennsylvania plate."

"What kind of car was it?"

"Buick. LeSabre. Black. Late model, I believe. Not more than two or three years old, anyway. Oh, and it had a decal from Portman Motors on it."

Steve's smile grew broad. "Mrs. Edmund, I could kiss you."

The elderly woman tilted her head and peered up at Steve with eyes that were frankly assessing. "As tempting as I find your offer, it also makes me think you weren't asking all those questions out of idle curiosity. There's something more here, isn't there? You weren't just humoring an old woman and her silly fears, were you?"

This was it, Kate thought. The runaway freight train had hit, and the debris was falling all around them. Steve was going to tell Mrs. Edmund everything, even though he'd promised not to. And when he did, Kate would be dialing 911.

"Steve," she said sweetly through gritted teeth. "You promised. Remember?"

He looked at her then, and her heart plummeted. "I'm sorry, Kate," he said, not sounding the least apologetic. "But where your safety is concerned, all bets are off."

He turned his gaze back to Mrs. Edmund. "I'm afraid we haven't been quite straight with you. I'm not here tonight to play Scrabble. Nor am I Kate's date, as we've led you to believe. I'm her bodyguard."

Kate groaned. She wished there was room under the table for her to draw back her foot and kick him in the shins. Hard.

"Bodyguard?" Mrs. Edmund asked, a puzzled look on her face. "Why does Kate need a bodyguard?"

Kate strained to hear a tremor in the woman's voice, a

faltering that would indicate her neighbor was in distress. But she saw and heard nothing. Yet. So far, Mrs. Edmund seemed to be taking things in stride. She wasn't clutching at her chest and straining to breathe. Of course, when Steve explained about Kate's biggest fan, which he was drawing breath to do this very second, things would probably change dramatically.

"She's received some threatening letters," he said.

As if to emphasize the gravity of his announcement, the grandfather clock chimed the hour. Kate flinched.

"What kind of threats?" Clara Mae asked.

"Death threats. The writer signs himself as her biggest fan."

Kate closed her eyes in despair. If there was a guardian angel who watched over pacemakers, it was her fervent wish that he was here, this very minute, in the room with them.

"Has he done anything besides write letters?" Clara Mae asked. "After all, words—and paper—are cheap. He could send threats until the cows came home, but they wouldn't mean a lick unless he acted on them."

Kate opened her eyes to see Mrs. Edmund and Clara Mae leaning as far forward as their chairs—and the table—would allow. The intent expressions on their faces reminded her of moviegoers who were so into the action on the screen that they literally sat on the edge of their seats.

"On Monday, someone pushed Kate in front of a bus." Steve paused to acknowledge both women's indrawn breaths of shock. "Shortly after that, someone broke into her house. Nothing was stolen. The intruder just wanted to let her know he was here."

"Her biggest fan," Clara Mae breathed.

Steve nodded. "He was telling her that he could get at her whenever he wished."

"So that's why Carlo was asking me all those questions," Mrs. Edmund said.

"Yes," Steve replied.

"What I saw really was important, wasn't it?"

"It could be the key to breaking this thing wide open."

"How exciting!" There was an eager look on Mrs. Edmund's face.

Kate felt her mouth drop open. "Exciting?"

"I'm sorry, dear." Mrs. Edmund looked apologetic. "I don't mean to make light of your plight. But I do have to admit that things were rather dull around here before you moved in. Your brothers have provided me with a vast amount of entertainment. I've grown rather used to their lively comings and goings. This new development just adds more spice to the pot."

"You're all right, then?" Kate asked. "Your pacemaker's not skipping a beat?"

The older woman's brow furrowed. "It's ticking just fine, dear. Why wouldn't it be?"

"Remember that afternoon a year ago? The Peeping Tom in the neighborhood? When my brothers scared you? It went haywire. I was afraid it would do the same thing when you heard about my...situation."

"Oh, that." The elderly woman waved her hand in a dismissive gesture. "Your brothers didn't scare me. That was just a little malfunction. The doctor fixed it right up. It's been working perfectly since then."

"You mean the sight of all those loaded guns didn't set it off?"

"Of course not, dear. I was in the Army Nurse Corps during World War II. Served in North Africa. That's where I met my Herman, you know. But I digress. When you operate through sniper fire, precious little frazzles you after that. It would take more than a crazed fan, and the sight of a couple of drawn guns, to startle this old heart of mine. I'm just sorry I didn't pay closer attention to the license plate of that car. If I had, you might be able to find out who its owner is, and whether or not he has something to do with the letters you've been receiving."

"Don't be sorry, Mrs. Edmund," Steve replied. "You've been more help than you realize."

"Really?"

"Really," he insisted. "You have a wonderful eye for detail. Based on your description, even without the license plate number, if we search the records of individuals who have bought black Buick LeSabres at Portman Motors for the past three years, we have a good chance of locating that car and its owner. Did anyone ever tell you you'd make a great detective?"

Mrs. Edmund looked pleased. "Thank you, young man. I try to make it a point to be observant."

"And you don't know how grateful I am that you do. What I need you to do now is describe, in as much detail as you can, both the jogger and the driver."

Clara Mae extended the pad and the pen she was using to keep score. "Would you like to use these?"

Kate knew it wasn't necessary for Steve to write down anything, that his photographic memory would unerringly record whatever Mrs. Edmund related to him. Instead of explaining, however, he took the pad and pen and offered Clara Mae his thanks. Several minutes later, after he'd diligently recorded every word, he pushed back his chair and stood.

"If you ladies will excuse me for a minute, I need to make a couple of phone calls." He smiled at them and headed for the den.

"It really is a shame," Mrs. Edmund commented as she watched his retreating figure.

"Don't worry," Kate said distractedly, her gaze also following Steve from the room. He had always been impressive to watch, both coming and going. Tonight, wearing those navy-blue shorts that showed off his trim waist and powerful thighs to advantage, was no exception. "Everything will work out. Steve will see to it. He'll keep me safe."

"I'm sure he will, dear. I'm sure he will. He looks capable of doing just about anything he sets his mind to. But when I said it was a shame, I wasn't referring to your letter writer. Although that, too, is a shame. A sorry shame. I was referring to the fact that you and that young man aren't dating."

Kate came back to earth with a jolt. Dismayed, she forgot all about Steve's lean body and muscled thighs.

"You'd make a perfect couple," Mrs. Edmund went on. "Maybe when this is all over, you should give it some thought. Don't you agree, Clara Mae?"

"Absolutely." Clara Mae gave a wistful sigh. "Just looking at him brings back such memories. You don't see a man like him very often."

"No," Mrs. Edmund said softly, reflectively. "You don't."

Kate turned her eyes toward the ceiling and prayed for forbearance. Forbearance to survive the rest of the evening with her sanity still intact. Forbearance to survive what lay ahead until her biggest fan could be caught. Forbearance to ignore the traitorous tug at her heart that wished she and Steve could be a couple once more. But most of all, she prayed for the forbearance to withstand the emptiness that would again consume her when he was gone.

# Chapter 11

The gathering broke up shortly after midnight. Steve escorted Mrs. Edmund home and settled Clara Mae into her taxi. Then he went into the den and dismissed George from his duty at the television monitors, a duty necessitated because the ruse he and Kate had agreed to play had required that he not wear his headset. For the past four hours—except for the phone calls he'd made after Mrs. Edmund's revelation—he'd been out of contact with his men outside, and George had been responsible for Kate's safety. Steve had hated every minute.

Still he couldn't help being elated that they'd gotten an unexpected lead. Mrs. Edmund, bless her observant eyes, might have actually found Kate's biggest fan for them. Hopefully, if all went well, in as little as two or three days they could know the identity of this man who wanted to do Kate harm.

Of course, the police would arrest him immediately. The question was, could they hold him for very long? Without an eyewitness account to place him as the man who had shoved

Kate in front of that bus, it was doubtful that attempted murder charges would be filed. The most they could hope for was that his fingerprints matched those the police had taken from Kate's house. Still, breaking and entering—especially when nothing was stolen—was no guarantee of a long prison sentence. If the man had no criminal record, he could be put on probation and set free.

If that happened, Kate would still be in danger. Grave danger. She would have to apply for a protection from abuse order. What worried Steve was that his years as a cop had taught him the reality of just how ineffective those orders were. In most cases they weren't worth the paper they were written on.

The sad truth was that an astounding number of women were murdered by the men against whom protection from abuse orders had been issued. A protection from abuse order, had his mother ever obtained one, most certainly wouldn't have stopped his father's murderous rage. A person might as well try to halt a charging bull with a feather as try to stop a deranged man intent on inflicting bodily harm. If Kate's biggest fan was determined to get to her, he wouldn't let a piece of paper stand in his way.

That small detail was one Steve had yet to share with Kate. He just hadn't been able to find the words to explain that, even after her biggest fan was unmasked, this whole sorry episode might not be over. And if he had been able to find the words, he knew he'd put off telling her until the last minute, in the hope that something would happen to change what seemed to be an inevitable outcome.

While the last thing Steve wanted was for Kate to have to suffer another attempt on her life, he couldn't help wishing that he could somehow manipulate the cagey SOB into doing something foolish. Something that would serve to put him behind bars for life.

Now that Steve thought about it, maybe he could make it happen. There were ways. He knew several policewomen who were more than adequately trained to serve as decoys.

One, in particular, owed him a favor. It would be an easy thing to hire her to impersonate Kate and to have her try to lure this guy out of hiding. All he had to do was come up with the proper plan. And get Kate out of the way while he executed it.

Kate wouldn't go for it. In fact, he knew she'd vocally prohibit it. Especially if someone else, no matter how skilled and well trained, would be exposed to danger on her account. But then, who said he had to tell her about it? After all, he'd managed to keep her in the dark the last time her life was in danger. If he'd managed to elude her discovery for several weeks, he could easily manage one little sting operation without her finding out about it. Surely, once it was all over and she was finally and truly safe, she'd thank him for it.

After rinsing the lemonade glasses in the kitchen sink and placing them in the dishwasher, Steve wandered into the living room. Kate stood in the middle of the floor, struggling with one of the card table's legs and muttering beneath her breath.

"Mind if I take a shot at it?" he asked.

For a minute she looked as though she were going to refuse—that stubborn independence of hers again, he thought with a trace of bitterness. To his surprise, though, she stood back. While he dealt with the recalcitrant table leg, she busied herself straightening knickknacks that didn't need straightening and plumping pillows that didn't need plumping.

"Thanks," he said after he'd stowed the card table in the closet.

"For what?"

"Letting me help."

"It was just a card table leg."

"Maybe to you," he allowed. "But there was a time when you wouldn't have let me do even that one small thing for you. As a matter of fact, you would have acted like my offer was the worst of insults."

She looked rueful. "I was that bad?"

If he were at all chivalrous, he would lie through his teeth, tell her no, she hadn't been bad at all. But then, he'd never been accused of being the least bit chivalrous. When it came down to it, he preferred his truth served sunny-side up, not down, and that was the way he served it to others.

"Yes, Kate, you were."

She surprised him by agreeing with him. "I suppose I was. I guess I spent so many years fighting my brothers for the right to make just one tiny decision on my own, it was only natural the tendency would spill over into other areas of my life. It was always difficult for me to accept help from someone else."

"Was? Are you saying you don't find it difficult anymore?" He allowed the skepticism he was feeling to color his voice.

"Oh, it's still difficult," she acknowledged with a wry grin. "Just not as much as it used to be." A teasing light entered her eyes. "And you thought I couldn't be taught any new tricks."

For countless seconds, desire blinded him to all else but the light in her eyes and the curve of her lips. Lord, but he wanted her. Even though he knew better. Even though she'd made it more than plain that she didn't want him. At least, not in a till-death-do-us-part way.

"What brought about this miraculous change?" he asked to keep himself from reaching out for her.

She extended one arm, indicating the room in which they stood. "This old house, for one. It didn't take me more than thirty seconds to discover I was no Bob Vila, and that if I needed something fixed right, I was going to have to hire someone with the ability to fix it."

"What else?"

"My column. After it was syndicated nationwide, and the mail started pouring in, I realized I couldn't handle it, the writing and the research all by myself."

"So you hired Martha."

"Yes." She paused before adding, "And then a crazy man

started stalking me, and I didn't know how to protect myself. So I went to you.''

"Do you regret it?" The words burst from his throat before he could bite them back.

"No, Steve," she said softly. "I don't."

They stared at each other for a long moment. Somehow, she managed to looked proud, defiant and vulnerable all at the same time. And utterly beautiful. Just looking at her made his blood beat wildly in his veins and his heart hammer in his chest. Heaven only knew what would happen if he touched her.

That was a lie. Past experience, along with eighteen months of self-imposed celibacy, told him exactly what would happen if he so much as laid a finger on her. He'd go up in flames like kindling that had been dried in the Sahara.

The room was entirely too warm, he thought, as perspiration broke out on his forehead. He swallowed hard and reached up to loosen a tie that was nonexistent since he no longer wore his suit. He must have telegraphed some of what he was feeling to Kate, because an expression of uncertainty crossed her face. She licked her lips nervously before looking away.

"I think I'll go to bed," she said.

Bed. The word hit him like a sucker punch. The last thing he wanted to think about was her lying in bed. Unless, that is, she was waiting for him to join her.

"I think I'll do the same." He heard the strain in his voice. After giving the alarm system a final check, he turned out the living room lights and followed her up the stairs.

"No flute playing tonight?" she asked, stopping before her bedroom door.

He shook his head. "I'm too tired." When what he interpreted to be a flicker of relief crossed her face, he added, "Does my playing bother you?"

"No," she denied quickly. Too quickly. "Of course not."

A three-year-old could see through that feeble lie, he thought on a sudden surge of irritation. She was the one who had always complained that he wouldn't talk to her, yet she couldn't be bothered to share with him the one small fact that his flute playing annoyed her?

"If it bothered you so much, you should have said something."

Her chin went up in the defensive gesture he knew so well. "I already told you, it doesn't bother me. In fact, your playing is quite beautiful. It's just...sometimes it keeps me awake."

She really did look exhausted. Her face was pale, and she had dark smudges under her eyes. For a man who was supposed to be so observant, it had taken him an embarrassing amount of time to realize that she hadn't been sleeping any better than he had.

Paradoxically, her weariness only made her seem more beautiful to him. And, paradoxically, for as much as she'd hurt him in the past, he wanted her more than ever.

Maybe it was because she needed him, really needed him, for the first time. Maybe it was just lust, because it had been so long since he'd been with a woman. Or maybe he needed to be near her because once her biggest fan was found and somehow neutralized she'd be gone from his life for good.

Was it just his flute playing, or was there something else keeping her awake? Was it thoughts of her biggest fan, or was, perhaps, her sleeplessness due to his presence in her home? Steve couldn't stem the ridiculous hope that it would be the latter.

His irritation drained out of him, leaving a burning sensation in his chest and a longing for the bottle of antacid that was a mile away in the den. "I'm sorry, Kate. I didn't realize the music carried so far."

She gave him a tired smile. "You don't have to apologize. I know you didn't do it on purpose."

That was certainly the truth. If he'd wanted to keep her awake purposely, he would have found a more inventive—and much more intimate—way to do so. And, afterward, they both would have slept like babies.

*Stop it!* he ordered himself sternly. *You've got to keep your wits about you. You've got to stop thinking about her like this. She's a client, nothing more.*

If he was smart, he'd say good-night and shut his bedroom door, putting some much-needed space between them. These were the dangerous hours, the time between dusk and dawn when defenses were down and the impossible seemed possible. Even though he knew he should, he was loath to leave her.

"They really are something, aren't they?" he asked, just to keep the conversation going.

Her brow furrowed. "Who?"

"Mrs. Edmund and Clara Mae."

"They're something, all right," she agreed with a chuckle. "When Clara Mae spelled out 'prophylactic,' I thought I was going to lose it."

His answering laughter echoed off the walls in the small hallway. "Now you know how I felt when Mrs. Edmund turned the conversation from social to sexual intercourse."

"Boy, do I ever," she said with a wide grin.

Steve felt a pang squeeze his heart. This was too much like old times. How he missed this kind of sharing with her, the laughter that, in the beginning anyway, had never seemed far away. He hadn't expected to share a moment like this with her again.

"This evening didn't turn out at all the way I thought it would," he found himself saying.

Her answer sounded heartfelt. "You can say that again." Yawning behind one hand, she reached the other toward her bedroom door. "If you want to play your flute tonight, you don't have to worry about keeping me awake. I'm so tired, I think I'd sleep through an air-raid siren."

"You do look exhausted."

Kate turned to face her bedroom door, but not before Steve saw the self-mocking gleam in her eyes. "Just what a woman wants to hear from a man."

Though the words were offered in a teasing manner, they

cut straight through him. His hands clenched at his sides, and he felt a nerve pulse in his cheek. A man could only take so much, and no more. She'd left *him,* after all. What right had she to complain, even in jest, that he wasn't speaking to her in the manner *she* wanted?

"What do you want to hear from me, Kate?" he asked in a low voice. "How beautiful I think you are? How I haven't been able to touch another woman since you left me? How I still want you so badly I ache? Just what exactly do you want to hear from me?"

Slowly, her movements wary, she turned to face him. "I didn't mean—"

"To goad me?" he cut in roughly, before automatically biting back his sudden surge of temper. When he was in control again, all that remained was a residue of frustration, a feeling that was becoming too familiar since he'd agreed to be her bodyguard. At least that feeling he could handle.

Why this woman? he wondered. Why did Kate have the power no other woman possessed to rob him of his reason and steal his soul?

Her continued silence told him that she didn't want to take the discussion further, but he wasn't quite ready to let it go. "You invited Clara Mae and Mrs. Edmund over here tonight to put a buffer between us, didn't you?"

"Yes," she admitted.

"Why?"

She rubbed the back of her hands across her eyes before lifting her chin and meeting his gaze head-on. "Because I still have feelings for you. There, I've said it. I don't want to, but I do. Nothing's been the same since you've been gone, Steve. And now that you're here with me again, I'm feeling things I don't want to feel. The simple truth is, I invited those two women here tonight because I was afraid."

Her honesty caught him unprepared and obliterated any defenses he might have built. "Of what?"

"That I'll do something stupid, like throwing myself at you."

His high school chemistry teacher had assured him that, under temperatures of 3,000 degrees or so, it was virtually impossible for bones to turn to liquid. But that was precisely what Steve's bones did when he looked at Kate and saw the naked yearning in her eyes. She still wanted him, as much as he wanted her. That was heady stuff to a man whose ego had taken such a severe beating. Only one question remained. Was he ready to start things up between them again? Could he bring himself to take the risk?

He wasn't sure of much of anything, except that she was the most beautiful thing he'd ever seen, and that he wanted her. Desperately. Anything else held no meaning for him at that moment.

"I don't think it would be stupid at all for you to throw yourself at me," he told her.

"Trust me," she said with a brittle laugh, "it would be a disaster."

"You're so beautiful," he murmured.

"Don't," she protested, putting her hands out protectively in front of her.

"Don't what?"

"Don't talk that way."

"Why?"

"Because I have no power to resist you when you do."

He took a deliberate step toward her. "Good. Because I certainly have no power to resist you."

A look of desperation crossed her face, but she stood her ground. "Isn't it against the rules for you to become romantically involved with a client?"

"Absolutely." He took another step. This time, she took a step back.

"What would you do if an employee behaved this way toward a client?" There was an edge of panic in her voice.

"Fire him." He continued moving purposefully toward her.

One more backward step trapped her against her closed bedroom door. She swayed a little on her feet, and it was the most natural thing in the world for him to reach out and pull her close.

She didn't resist.

The sensation was incredible. Beneath his questing fingers, the skin of her arms felt like silk, and the scent of her went straight to his head. Like a piece of modeling clay, her body contoured itself to his. They fit together perfectly, as if some benevolent god had molded her just for him. And oh, the sensation of her softness to his hardness!

Her eyes were dark orbs of sensuality that bothered, bewitched and beguiled him almost to the point of insanity. As he gazed down at her, her lips parted invitingly. He slowly lowered his head, intent on only one goal: possessing their lush fullness.

"Can you guarantee that things will be different this time?" she asked.

Her unexpected question made Steve pull back a fraction. He frowned at her. He didn't want to think of anything beyond the present moment: not the past, and certainly not the future. All he wanted was to indulge the desire racing through him. Judging by her earlier reaction, she'd wanted the same. So why was she spoiling it now?

"You know I can't make that kind of promise," he said, when his brain had cleared enough to process her question and frame a response.

"Then I'm begging you, Steve. Don't do this to me. Don't make me fall in love with you all over again. If it didn't work out, I don't know what I'd do."

Her plea served to bring the fever pitch of his desire down a notch or two. "It's just a kiss, Kate. That's all I'm asking. A kiss, and nothing more."

Her smile was sad. "But don't you see, it would be more than that to me. And I'm just not ready."

It was the smile that did him in and brought him back to his senses. Though his body ached with unsatisfied passion, he wasn't ready for this any more than Kate was. It cost him what little self-control he had left to settle his lips briefly against her forehead before releasing his hold on her.

"Thank you." Her voice was unsteady.

He didn't want to do any more talking. His control was shaky enough as it was.

"Go to bed, Kate," he said roughly. "Before I change my mind."

Steve waited until her bedroom door had closed before making his way to the end of the hallway. His earlier exhaustion had disappeared, replaced by a desire that showed no signs of abating. There was no question that he was wide-awake and that flute playing was not an option, no matter what Kate said.

He chuckled grimly and shook his head in self-mockery. Had he really thought he'd finally be able to get a good night's sleep? He should have known better. With Kate under the same roof, but in a different bed, it just wasn't going to be possible. Not in this lifetime, anyway.

What he needed, he decided, was a cold shower, followed by a few pages of the most boring book he could lay his hands on. He wasn't certain, but he thought he'd seen a copy of this year's federal budget on the bookshelf in Kate's den. She'd probably used it for a column or two. A few pages of that, and he'd be guaranteed some shut-eye for sure. He'd go get it the minute he was out of the shower.

A second later, all thoughts of his cold shower were driven from his head by the sound of shattering glass.

## *Chapter 12*

The sound, which Steve judged to be coming from the living room, was followed by a soft thud and then silence. A silence that was broken a heartbeat later by the wail of the security alarm.

Kate's bedroom door flew open and she stepped into the hallway. "What was that?" she cried.

"I don't know," he said grimly, striding past her to the top of the stairs. "But I intend to find out."

Hands on the railing, he leaned forward and mentally cursed the darkness that greeted his searching gaze. The only illumination came from a low-wattage light fixture located a good ten feet behind him, and what little light spilled through Kate's open bedroom door. It wasn't enough to enable him to see into the living room, let alone discover what had caused the commotion.

His imagination ran wild with all the possible items that could have caused a window to shatter. A bomb that was ticking away precious seconds while he just stood there, trying to figure out what to do. A tear gas canister. A brick with a threatening note wrapped around it.

Of course, it was entirely possible that the culprit was something as innocent as a rock kicked up by a passing car, or a breaking tree branch. Although how a tree branch could come crashing through a window when there wasn't so much as a breeze outside was anyone's guess. And when he'd helped Clara Mae into her taxi earlier, there hadn't been a rock in sight.

No, whatever the object was, it had been hurled through the window. Even more ominous, the hurler had breached his security. That was unacceptable.

"Stay there," he ordered Kate as he raised the two-way radio mouthpiece to his lips. "Talk to me, George," he barked. "What the hell just happened?"

Still scanning the darkness below him, he listened in growing dismay to the bad news George delivered.

"Damn!"

"What did he say?" Kate asked.

Whirling, he came up smack against her, the action knocking them both off balance. His hands shot out to span her waist at the same time that she clutched at his shoulders. Once they'd regained their footing and were no longer in danger of falling, he found himself staring into her wide, frightened eyes. The warmth of her soft breasts against his chest sent tremors through him and made his breathing grow erratic. Unbidden, he felt consumed by an urge to kiss her, to run his hands over every inch of her body. Self-disgust filled him as he roughly pushed her away. How could he be thinking of *that* at a time like this?

"I thought I told you to stay where you were." His voice came out harsher than he'd intended.

Her reply was shaky but determined. "If you think I'm going to stay up here while you wander into who knows what down there, you've got another think coming."

Steve heaved a resigned sigh. "I don't have time to argue with you, Kate."

"I thought you never argued."

His hands fisting at his sides, he quickly counted to ten. "You know what I mean."

"Yes, unfortunately, I do. That doesn't change the fact that I'm coming with you."

He knew it was pointless to protest further. She wasn't going to back down, at least not without a lot of persuading on his part. And, based on what George had just told him, he didn't have the time to be persuasive.

"Stay behind me," he ordered. "Stick close, and do exactly what I tell you." After she nodded her assent, he turned to face the bottom of the stairs.

"What did George say?" she asked again as they took a careful step downward.

"Someone created a diversion in the park." He took another step, and Kate followed. "When my men went to check it out, a kid ran out of the shadows and threw an object through the window. George saw it all on the monitors in the van."

"So you don't know what the object was?"

"No." Steve felt his jaw tighten.

They were more than halfway down the stairs when he smelled the smoke. He listened for the answering crackle of flames but heard nothing except the steady clanging of the security alarm. Both he and Kate jumped when the smoke alarm suddenly emitted its high-pitched shriek.

"Damn!" he cried.

"Is the house on fire?" She had to yell to be heard over the noise of both alarms.

"No, it's a smoke bomb."

"What's that mean?"

"It means that in a few seconds the air around us is going to be unbreathable. We've got to get out of here, Kate. Now."

He dashed up the stairs and grabbed a couple of towels from the bathroom, pausing only long enough to run water over them. Without stopping to wring out the excess moisture, he rushed back to Kate's side and handed her a dripping towel.

"Put this over your nose and mouth," he ordered. "Try not to inhale too deeply." Into his mouthpiece he yelled, "It's a smoke bomb. We're coming out the front."

Taking her by the forearm, Steve led her quickly down the remaining stairs. Smoke had already filled the front hallway, and was rolling steadily toward them like some ghostly fog. Steve felt his eyes start to water almost immediately. Beside him, he heard Kate cough.

A rush of urgency had him fumbling for the light switch. Unfortunately, the smoke was already so thick, the added illumination did little to help.

When they reached the front door, his fingers skidded across the smooth wood surface of the walnut writing table that stood to the right of the door frame. "Where's the card?" he yelled, and started coughing himself.

"In the drawer," she yelled back.

Heedless of any damage he might do to a piece of furniture that was obviously a treasured antique, he yanked the drawer open and felt around inside. He almost went weak with relief when his fingers closed upon the thin plastic card that would release the front door lock. His movements clumsy, he tried twice to slip the card into the slot, and twice missed his mark.

When he missed his mark a third time, Kate reached around him to grab hold of his hand. With her guidance, the card hit home. A second later he heard the welcome sound of tumblers falling into place, and the door swung open.

Lungs bursting, he and Kate hurtled out into the fresh air. They collapsed into a heap on the front lawn, where they lay gasping like two fish out of water.

"Are you okay?" he asked when he'd drawn enough oxygen to speak. His throat felt raw.

She nodded, still gulping in air. "I don't...mean to be critical...at a time like this, but...we wouldn't have had...so much trouble getting out...if you hadn't put in that...blasted keyless lock system."

Leave it to Kate to try to start a fight at a time like this, he thought with grim amusement. "I disagree. With the old lock…you still would have…had to insert a key. It would have taken just as long, if not longer, to open it."

"Are you okay?" George asked, rushing up to them.

"We're fine," Steve told him. "The area secure?"

"Yes."

"Good." Off in the distance, he heard the sound of sirens. If Kate's biggest fan was hanging around anywhere close by, knowing that the police were on their way would be enough for him to make himself scarce.

The problem was, he didn't think the guy had ventured anywhere near Kate's house that night, which raised a whole host of questions he wasn't sure he could answer.

"Where's the kid?" he asked George.

George looked shamefaced. "I'm sorry, Steve. He got away."

Steve swore. The curse was vulgar, highly descriptive and nothing he should have uttered in front of a woman. But that was how he felt at the moment, and he didn't have the strength, or the lung power, to apologize.

"How could he get away? You were supposed to have been positioned to cut off all escape routes."

"He ran like the wind," George explained. "And he seemed to know the neighborhood even better than we do."

"Did you get a good look at him? Would you recognize him if you saw him in a line-up?"

Again he saw regret on George's face. "It was too dark, and he was careful to stay away from the streetlights. All I know is he was about six-two, skinny and wore jeans and a T-shirt."

"Well, that certainly limits our list of suspects." Steve didn't bother to hide his sarcasm.

"I'm sorry," George repeated. He looked so disheartened, for a minute Steve thought the man might actually cry. "It's all my fault. I allowed my attention to be diverted. I should have known the disturbance in the park was just a decoy."

Steve held up a hand. "There'll be plenty of time for recriminations later. We don't have much time to speak, since the police will be here in a minute. Did the kid leave anything behind?"

"A backpack full of books. There was also another note."

"What did it say?" When George aimed a tentative look at Kate, Steve added, "She's going to find out sooner or later. It might as well be sooner."

"The note said that her—" George inclined his head at Kate "—I mean your…time is running out."

Steve had expected as much. Whoever had done this had planned it out thoroughly. "What about the books?"

"You're not going to like it," George said.

So what was new? "Just tell me."

"All black market. The subjects cover kidnapping, bomb building, assault rifles and ways to obtain them, how to commit murder without being caught. You get the drift."

Yes, he got the drift. The sadistic SOB who called himself Kate's biggest fan was toying with them, and enjoying himself thoroughly in the process. To him, they were marionettes on a stage, and he was pulling the strings and making them dance to his tune. It was only a matter of time, though, before he tired of his games and tried to make good on his promises. The note he'd left in the backpack said as much. If the look on Kate's face was any indication, she was thinking the same thing.

The sudden force with which the fury that was the bane of his existence surged through him took Steve's breath away. Struggling for control, he dug his fingers into the grass. A hard, hot hatred coursed through him, bathing everything he saw—Kate, George, the house, the yard—in a glow of red blood-lust. At this very moment he longed only to resort to one thing: violence. Specifically, violence against this unknown fan. The bloodier the better. How he longed to use his fists against the man, to pummel him to a bloody, unrecognizable pulp. How he ached to wrap his fingers around this psychopath's throat and squeeze until the man's eyes bulged out. Given time, Steve knew he could come up with a thousand different ways to torture and torment his adversary past the limit of all human endurance.

The pleasure he felt at his thoughts sent a wave of disgust through him. He was little more than an animal. Was this keen yearning that felt almost sexual in nature how his father had felt in the moments before he'd unleashed his temper on Steve and his mother?

*The violence stops here,* he repeated to himself, over and over again. Though it seemed that hours had passed, he knew it was only seconds until his fingers finally relaxed their death grip on the grass and his emotions were once again under control. Now, of all times, it was important that he not give in to the darker side of his nature.

He glanced at Kate and despaired, as he'd done a thousand times before, that anything short of an exorcism would ever be able to make him the kind of man she needed. The kind of man who wasn't tortured by murderous thoughts and rages every time his anger was aroused. The kind of man who would never hurt her. How appalled Kate would be, and how repelled, if she ever knew of the dark forces that swirled through him. How terrified she would be if she realized the tenuousness of the hold he had on them.

"The evening hasn't been a total loss," she said, surprising him.

"What do you mean?"

"First, answer me this. That boy who threw the smoke bomb. He wasn't my biggest fan, was he?"

"No," Steve said. "The boy doesn't fit the profile. Whoever your biggest fan is, he's not some pimply faced teenager."

She nodded as if she'd expected as much. "Then we've learned something tonight. Something important. Whoever my biggest fan is, he isn't working alone."

That was the problem, Steve thought, as a chill raced up his spine. This fan of hers, whoever he was, was no ordinary stalker. Ordinary stalkers normally didn't have the wherewithal to get others to do their dirty work for them. Nor did they want others to do that work. For ordinary stalkers, the thrill was the fear or love or whatever emotion they wanted to engender in the object of their fixation.

The good news was, the man had finally done something that would guarantee him a lengthy jail sentence. Still something was definitely wrong. What happened tonight made no sense at all. Stalkers just didn't behave this way. At least, none of the stalkers Steve had encountered in the past had. Obviously he was missing a piece of the puzzle. A vital piece. And he'd better locate it pronto, if he wanted to keep Kate safe.

"What I've been thinking," Kate said, "is that maybe he never was working alone. Maybe he wasn't the one who pushed me in front of that bus. Maybe he wasn't the one who broke into my house. You know what that makes him?"

"What?" Steve asked, still wrestling with the problem.

"A phantom. A man without substance. A man who can appear and disappear at will. A man who is impossible to catch."

The torment in her eyes and the hopelessness in her voice caught at his heart. He felt the anger within him begin to stir again and ruthlessly suppressed it.

"We're going to find him," he promised. "And when we do, he will be punished."

She bit her lip and looked away. "I wish I could feel as confident about that as you seem to."

"I won't let you down, Kate," he said, and prayed that it would be so.

The sirens were much closer now. The police would be arriving any second, and there would be no time for him to think, much less plan what their next step should be. The new variable that had been added to the equation that was her biggest fan would have to be analyzed later.

"Oh, no!" Kate cried. Scrambling to her feet, she lunged past him and headed for the front door.

Because her action caught him off guard, it took him a

second to react. When he caught up to her, heart racing, she'd nearly reached the house. Barring her way, he demanded, "What the hell do you think you're doing?"

She tried to dodge around him, but he anticipated her move and successfully blocked it.

"Fred and Wilma," she cried. "They're still in there. They'll suffocate!"

Steve bit off an epithet. Those damn birds again. "You're not going back in, Kate. Not until the smoke has cleared and it's safe."

She appeared not to have heard him, because once again she tried to get around him. "I can't leave them in there. They'll die!"

He reached out and steadied her with his arms, his grip firm without being brutal. "You're not going back in," he repeated when she stopped struggling. "It's too dangerous."

She gazed up at him imploringly. The tears that gathered in her eyes shimmered in the glow of the outside lighting. *Please, God,* he prayed. *Tell me she isn't going to cry. I won't be able to bear it if she cries.*

One lone tear made its way down her cheek, and she inhaled on a sobbing breath. "You don't understand. I'm all they have, Steve. They're depending on me. I can't just let them die. I can't."

Why were those blasted birds so important to her that she was willing to risk her life for them? he wondered in desperation. Out of the blue, the answer came to him. Molly. Though she probably didn't realize it, to Kate, the birds symbolized the child they had lost. Though she'd done everything in her power to give her unborn child a healthy start in life, Molly had died. It didn't matter that what had happened wasn't Kate's fault. She still blamed herself.

The way he still blamed himself.

Dangerous or not, Steve knew he was going to go in after the birds. He hadn't been there when Molly and Kate had needed him most. At least he could be here for Kate now.

"All right," he said. "I'll go get them. But only if you

give me your solemn promise that you won't budge from this spot.''

"I promise," she said immediately.

Over his shoulder he nodded at George. "Guard her with your life. If she moves so much as a muscle, tie her up." Putting the towel to his face, he sprinted toward the open door.

"Steve!" Kate called after him.

He turned. "What now?"

"Be careful."

For one last minute as several police cars screeched to a halt at the curb, lights flashing and sirens wailing, Steve's gaze held hers. Then, taking a deep breath, he plunged inside.

The minute Steve disappeared from view, Kate wanted to call him back. What had she been thinking? That was the problem: she hadn't been thinking. She'd merely been reacting. And, in so doing, she'd put Steve in danger. If she'd been thinking, she never would have let him risk his life for a couple of birds. Much as she loved them, Fred and Wilma were replaceable. Steve was not.

*So, if anyone's going to get hurt, you'd rather it be me. Is that it?* The words he'd spoken on the day she hired him echoed in her ears. When she recalled her reply—*Isn't that your job?*—shame filled her.

How arrogant she'd been! Add to that thoughtless, self-righteous and self-serving, and the picture that developed wasn't pretty. Yes, she'd hired him to protect her. Yes, there was an element of risk assigned to that protection. But the last thing she'd ever wanted was for Steve to get hurt. The mere thought made her heart ache. She'd never forgive herself if something happened to him.

Some of what was going through her mind must have shown on her face, because George said, "Don't even think of it, Kate."

"Think of what?" she asked, playing innocent.

He nodded toward her front door. "Going inside after him.

You heard what Steve said. If you make a move toward the house, I *will* restrain you.''

Kate believed him. Given his size and apparent strength, George could probably accomplish the task without breaking a sweat, even if she put up the mother of all battles. Before she could figure out a way to get past him, her brother Carlo thundered across the lawn.

''What happened?'' he demanded.

Kate returned her gaze to the front door. As long as she didn't look away, she told herself, as long as she maintained her vigil until Steve reappeared, he'd be fine. ''Someone threw a smoke bomb through my living room window.''

Carlo immediately began barking orders. Kate only half listened to the activity going on around her as her brother scattered men across her yard and throughout the neighborhood. When he sent another man back to the station in search of a gas mask, Kate knew that meant he was preparing to go inside to assess the damage and see what evidence could be recovered.

A gas mask. She wished Steve was wearing one now. How long had he been inside? Seconds? Minutes? Was he okay? Or was he lying on the floor, unconscious?

*Come out, Steve. Please come out. I don't care about Fred and Wilma, just you. Please be okay.* No matter how hard she prayed for him to appear, however, the doorway remained stubbornly empty.

''Are you okay?'' Carlo asked.

No, she wasn't okay. She wouldn't be okay until Steve was safely at her side. ''I'm fine,'' she said, her gaze fixed firmly on her front door.

''We need to talk, Kate. The sooner you tell me everything that happened, the sooner we can start tracking whoever did this. I don't want to waste any time. I want to strike while the trail is still hot.''

Kate couldn't talk. Couldn't Carlo see that? There was room in her mind only for Steve. Until he was safe, she had no energy to focus on anything else.

"If you'd like, I'll fill the officer in on the evening's events," George volunteered.

"Thank you, George."

"Who's this?" Carlo said, his tone suspicious.

"This is George. He works for Steve. He's one of the men guarding me."

"Doesn't look like he did that great of a job tonight."

Kate's chin went up, and she stole precious seconds from her vigil to glare at her brother. She wasn't about to let Carlo criticize Steve and the job he was doing. Not now. Not ever.

"I'm here in one piece, aren't I? If Steve and George hadn't been with me, who knows what might have happened?"

Carlo looked around him. "Speaking of Gallagher, where is he?"

Once again, her fear for Steve's safety overwhelmed her, and her gaze flew to her front door. "Inside."

"He didn't come out?" Carlo asked sharply.

"Yes, he came out. He went back in."

"Why?"

"To get my birds."

There was a brief silence as Carlo digested her words. She didn't have to look at him to know that he was shaking his head in amazed disbelief. When he spoke, she knew her hunch had been right.

"I knew the guy was a fool when he let you divorce him, but even I didn't think he was this stupid. I can't believe he went back in there for a couple of dumb birds."

Once again, Kate felt compelled to defend Steve. "He's not stupid. He only went in after them because he knows how much Fred and Wilma mean to me."

"So what you're saying is that even though he knew better he went in after those birds because you love them."

"Isn't that what I just told you?"

She sensed Carlo's gaze narrowing on her. "What's going on between you two? You're not falling for him again, are you?"

"No, Carlo," she said calmly. "I'm not falling for him again."

Her words carried the ring of truth, because that was what they were. The truth. After all, how could she fall for him again, when she'd never fallen out of love in the first place? She knew that now. Her bitterness and anger over his uncommunicativeness while they were married, and his seeming indifference when she'd asked for a divorce, had simply masked those feelings until tonight.

She still loved Steve. With a ferocity that was soul-shaking. Heaven help her.

"Good," Carlo said, his satisfaction evident. "See that you keep it that way. The man's all wrong for you."

Long ago, she'd come to the conclusion that the man whom all her brothers would approve of had never been born. Even in the remote likelihood that he had, if she actually met him, she knew he'd be so saintly and dull he'd bore her to tears within seconds. Still, she didn't need Carlo telling her that she and Steve were all wrong for each other. Her short-lived marriage had more than taught her that lesson. If there was one thing she knew, it was that her love for Steve was hopeless.

"Talk to George," she said wearily, waving a hand at the other man. "He saw everything that happened. I didn't."

A minute later, the two men were deep in conversation. Kate tuned them out and returned to her vigil. As the seconds continued to tick away and still Steve didn't appear, her anxiety grew.

*Come out, Steve. Please, please come out. I'll do anything you say without putting up a fuss. I won't goad you anymore and try to pick a fight. Just come out.*

"Are you okay, dear?" a voice asked.

With a start, Kate realized that Mrs. Edmund was standing by her side. She'd been focused so hard on her empty doorway, she hadn't heard the elderly woman approach. Now that she thought about it, she was surprised that both Carlo and George had let the woman onto her property. But then, both men knew who she was, and that she was no danger to Kate. Plus, if she wasn't safe with all these policemen milling about, she'd never be safe.

"I'm fine, Mrs. Edmund."

"What happened?"

"Someone threw a smoke bomb through my front window."

"How terrible! Is this related to the problem Steve told us about tonight?"

"Yes."

"You really are in danger, aren't you?"

The only danger Kate could think of was the danger Steve was facing. At the moment, everything else seemed immaterial. "It would appear so."

"Where is he?"

"Inside."

"Is it safe?"

"No, Mrs. Edmund, it's not." Kate bit her lip. "He went back in to get my birds."

"My hero!" Mrs. Edmund exclaimed, clasping her hands to her heart.

Kate looked at her neighbor in surprise. "Excuse me?"

When she spoke, there was a faraway look in Mrs. Edmund's eyes. "A hero is always easy to spot, Kate. He's not necessarily handsome—although Steve is certainly that—or rich, but he is always larger than life. He also has integrity and honor, and he's always kind to the weaker and less fortunate. In a word, he has character. Show me a man who will put his life on the line for a pair of parakeets, and I'll show you a genuine hero."

As she silently willed Steve to come out her front door, Kate thought about what Mrs. Edmund had said. She didn't know of any other man who would have done what Steve had tonight. Whether that made him a fool or a hero, she wasn't entirely sure.

She felt a touch on her arm and turned to the woman at

her side. "There's something I want you to see," Mrs. Edmund said.

"Yes?"

The elderly woman extended a gleaming wood cane. Kate took it and examined the beautifully crafted object.

"It was carved from oak by my husband's grandfather in 1850. His brother was a silversmith and fashioned the ram's head for it. Do you like it?"

"It's beautiful," Kate said reverently.

"I was going through some things in the attic the other day and stumbled across it. It polished up quite nicely, don't you think?"

"Yes, it did."

"I want you to have it."

Kate looked at her blankly.

"For a weapon. It could do some serious damage if you brought it down on a person's skull. I was going to give it to you tomorrow. But when I saw all the commotion out here tonight, I thought you might need it sooner."

Kate didn't want to think that she might have to defend herself that way. "It looks pretty valuable to me. Aren't you afraid of something happening to it?"

Mrs. Edmund shrugged. "I'd rather use a thing and have it lost or broken than hide it away and never see it. Besides, it's a little too long for me, but it looks just the right height for you. Carry it with you when you're out and about. Make your own fashion statement. And keep it by your bed at night."

"But—"

"Please, Kate. I'll sleep better knowing that you have it."

"All right, Mrs. Edmund. If you insist. Thank you."

The silver ram's head felt cool to the touch, the wood of the shaft smooth and remarkably substantial. It was probably an illusion, but she did feel safer just holding it.

"I know I have a sword somewhere up in my attic," Mrs. Edmund said. "If you'd like that, too, I'll try to find it. I can't guarantee its sharpness, however."

In a pinch, Kate thought she could use the cane to hobble someone. But to actually pierce someone's flesh with a sword... Her mind balked at the repellent thought.

"That's okay," she said quickly, amazed that her neighbor could nurture romantic fantasies about heroes one minute, and bloodthirsty thoughts about villains the next. "I'll make do with the cane."

Like a vision out of a dream, Steve appeared in the doorway with the birdcage, coughing but otherwise seemingly unharmed. Kate forgot all about canes and swords. Profound relief mixed with joy filled her. He was okay!

"Excuse me," she said to Mrs. Edmund. Heart hammering, she raced to the door. When she came to a stop in front of him, it took every ounce of her willpower not to fling herself into his arms.

"It took you so long to come out, I was afraid something had happened to you," she said.

Her words seemed to please him. "As you can see, I'm fine. The smoke's starting to clear a bit, so it wasn't too bad. The only problem was, I had a bit of trouble getting the blasted cage off the hook."

When she saw the towel draped across the cage, some of her happiness faded. She wondered if Steve had placed it there to protect the birds, or to protect her from a sight she didn't want to see.

"How...how are they?"

"It was too dark in there to tell."

"Have they made any sound at all?"

"No."

There was a pause as both of them stared at the silent cage. "Kate," Steve finally said.

"Yes?"

"If they're not all right, I want you to know that it's not your fault."

She looked up at him in confusion. "Why would I think that?"

"I just want you to know that."

She reached a hand toward the cage, then pulled it back. "I can't look."

"I'll look, if you want."

All Kate could manage was a nod of her head.

She couldn't watch while he peered under the towel. When she finally steeled herself enough to meet his gaze, she saw that his eyes were smiling.

"I think they'll live."

Kate pulled the towel away and was rewarded with an angry chirp from Wilma. Fred added his complaint a second later. Both birds began flying in frantic circles around the cage.

"Hi, my beauties," she crooned. "You had quite an adventure, didn't you? Lucky for you—for us—Steve was here to save the day."

When she glanced at Steve, she was surprised at the odd look on his face. "I can't thank you enough. What you did...well, it went beyond the call of duty. Mrs. Edmund was right. You are a hero."

His eyes went blank. "I'm nobody's hero, Kate," he said roughly, handing her the cage. "Now, if you'll excuse me, I have to speak to your brother."

After beckoning George to come stay with her, Steve stalked across her yard to where Carlo stood. Kate wondered why he was so angry. True to form, he'd run away instead of hashing out with her whatever it was that was bothering him. Though she knew that should anger her, she couldn't seem to summon up any answering indignation.

Shrugging, she devoted her attention to Fred and Wilma, cooing at them until they'd both calmed down. It really didn't matter one way or the other if Steve was angry with her. All that mattered was that he was safe.

# *Chapter 13*

Feathers fluttering furiously and chirping at the top of their lungs, Fred and Wilma sent a shower of seeds cascading onto the pristine surface of his grandfather's gleaming mahogany desk. While he spoke into his headset to George, Steve's gaze roved the library of the mansion his maternal grandparents had called home. His home, now.

The furniture might be vintage Edwardian, and the books lining the mahogany-paneled walls leather-bound first editions, but he still hated it. With a passion. To him, every room was as cold and unfeeling as the couple who had lived there for the forty years prior to their deaths.

He kept telling himself he was going to get rid of it, sell the whole place, lock, stock and barrel. But for some reason, he never quite managed to pick up the phone to call a Realtor. Although officially his residence, he tried to spend as little time there as possible. That it was his only link to his mother probably had something to do with his ambivalence about selling.

Tonight, though, his hatred for the place wasn't important.

The only thing that mattered was that it was the perfect place for Kate to hide. Not only was the stone monstrosity a fortress, it was guarded by a security system that far surpassed the one he'd set up at Kate's house. It was also protected on all sides by an electrified fence. Kate's biggest fan wouldn't look for her here. At least, not initially.

It had taken over two hours for the smoke to clear and for the police to complete their investigation. When he and Kate had finally been able to reenter her house, the smell of smoke had been overwhelming. Once Kate realized it would take more than a good airing to rid the place of the odor, it hadn't been too difficult for Steve to convince her to come here. It also hadn't hurt that all six of her brothers had arrived by that point, and had added their voices to his. It was probably the only time they'd ever agreed unanimously on anything. But then, the Garibaldi brothers were overprotective, not stupid. They had grasped immediately the truth it had taken Steve much longer to convey to Kate: that she would be safer here than anywhere else.

With the resources Steve now knew the man who called himself Kate's biggest fan possessed, he would find them here sooner or later. In all likelihood, the way things were going, it would be sooner. They'd be foolish to believe otherwise. Which was why Steve had doubled the guard outside. For a little while, though, Kate would be safe. They would have some breathing room in which to plan their next move.

There was much to do. Topping the list was securing the home they'd just left. First thing in the morning, he would make the necessary arrangements for the living room window to be fixed, and for a cleaning crew to see to Kate's furniture, carpeting, draperies and wardrobe. Liza would be assigned the responsibility of purchasing whatever necessary clothing items Kate needed in the interim.

His gaze roved to where Kate sat on an overstuffed sofa. Her face was pale, her arms wrapped protectively around her shoulders. Reaction must have finally set in, because she was shivering. From where he stood, he could hear her teeth chattering.

Biting back a curse, Steve ended his conversation with George and strode to the bar. After pouring whiskey into a cut crystal glass, he sat down next to her.

"Drink this," he ordered. She gazed at him, an uncomprehending look in her eyes, and he added, "It'll help."

Obediently she tipped the glass back. She grimaced and shuddered as the liquid slid down her throat.

"Feel better?" He took the glass from her and placed it on a side table.

"A little."

Not enough, obviously, since she still continued to shiver. At least her teeth had stopped chattering. A quick perusal of the room failed to offer up a blanket or a throw he could wrap around her. Without taking time to ponder the wisdom of his actions, Steve gathered her close.

She went into his arms without protest, her body molding to his, seeking out his heat. Nestling his chin atop her head, he held her tightly, running his hands up her arms and over her back until the shivering finally stopped and she lay quiet against him. For a moment, he wondered if she'd fallen asleep. If she had, he knew he would sit there the rest of the night, holding her. Hell, he'd sit there throughout eternity, if only she'd let him.

Lord, but she felt good. Even though it was highly inappropriate, given the circumstances and their past, he felt desire stir. At the moment, he would have given all he owned to have one more night with her, to know the heaven that was the joining of their two bodies.

He really was the lowest of the low, to be having these thoughts, these feelings, these needs, when all he should be concentrating on was providing Kate with the comfort she so obviously needed. His only excuse was that he'd discovered he was still in love with her, and the knowledge had bowled him over.

He'd known it the minute he walked out of her house

carrying that blasted birdcage, and she'd looked so happy to see him his heart had practically exploded from his chest. Then, when she'd told him she'd been worried about him, it was all he'd been able to do to keep from dragging her into his arms and kissing her senseless.

All this time, he'd thought he was over her. All this time, when he'd told himself that her actions had killed any feelings he had for her, it had only been hurt pride. He loved her, always had, always would. That was why there hadn't been any other women. Because there was only one Kate.

She still had feelings for him, too. She'd told him so earlier that evening when he'd tried to kiss her. While that should encourage him and give him hope that she might come to love him again the way she had before, he knew better. And the reason he knew better was because she'd also asked him if he could guarantee that things would be different between them this time around. The sad truth was, he couldn't.

So far as he could tell, things weren't any different now than they'd been eighteen months ago. He certainly wasn't any different. While his love for her had always been enough for him, her love for him had not. Because of that, he hadn't been able to give her what she needed. And what he could give her had left her unsatisfied and wanting more. It would be foolhardy in the extreme to think they had a future.

His heart grew heavy with the knowledge that, one day all too soon, she would walk out of his life forever. The first time had been bad enough. This time would be far worse. This time he wouldn't have his wounded pride to fall back on. All he'd have were his pain and his longing.

Better that, though, than for her to get a glimpse of the monster that lurked within him. He'd take the pain of her leaving him any day over the disgust and loathing that would surely fill her eyes if she found out what he was really like, deep inside. The disgust and loathing Steve felt for his own father.

"What a fool I was," she said into his chest. Her fingers

clenched around the fabric of his shirt as she pounded her fist against him. "What a blind, stupid, careless fool."

The misery in her voice jolted him out of his self-pity. There would be plenty of time later for him to indulge in feeling sorry for himself. When she was gone, there would be all the time in the world. Right now, though, Kate was here, and she needed his comfort. That was what he would give.

"What are you talking about?"

"Tonight," she said. "It was all my fault."

"If you mean the smoke bomb, then I was the one at fault, Kate."

She leaned back in his arms and shook her head vehemently. "I'm talking about me. I thought I was the only one at risk. But I'm not. He's made it perfectly clear that he doesn't care who he hurts to get to me. I put Martha at risk by allowing her to continue to come to work every day. And I put poor Mrs. Edmund and Clara Mae at risk by having them at my home tonight. How could I have been so selfish?"

The anguish in her eyes was almost more than he could bear. "Shh," he crooned, gathering her close once more. "Don't waste your time thinking about it. What's done is done. The past can't be changed."

*Remember that,* he told himself. *Remember that when you start wishing for the impossible.*

"I have to think about it," Kate said. "You saw them tonight. Neither one of them can move faster than a snail. They never would have gotten out in time if that smoke bomb had been thrown when they were there. I'd never forgive myself if something happened to them."

"But nothing happened," Steve pointed out. "They're both fine."

"No thanks to me," Kate said bitterly. "No matter what Martha says, she's not coming back to work until this madman is caught. From this moment on, she's on paid leave."

"You'll get no argument from me on that." Not to mention that he never would have allowed Martha to lead Kate's biggest fan here.

"Want to hear something funny?" She gave a shaky laugh as she pulled away from him. Reluctantly he let her go.

"Right about now something funny would be really welcome," he said.

There was no laughter in the eyes that gazed straight into his. Her expression was deadly serious. "I'm so glad I can lean on you in this. I'm glad I'm not alone. Isn't that hilarious?"

Damn. To have her openly admit her need for him, even though it wasn't the emotional need he yearned for, was the answer to a dream. How was he going to be able to continue resisting her, if she went and did things like that?

"I'm not laughing, Kate."

"Neither am I. Thanks for going in after Fred and Wilma. It's the most unselfish thing I think I've ever seen anyone do."

"You must not get out much," he joked, trying to lighten the mood, to make her feel better.

"I'm serious, Steve." Reaching out, she traced a finger from his right cheek to his jaw, causing an electric shock to reverberate throughout his body. Her eyes darkened and her voice lowered sensuously. "I don't know anyone else who would have done what you did tonight. Do you know how special you are?"

"Kate," he said hoarsely.

"What?"

How could one little word be so provocative? The sound of it, husky and beguiling, wrapped itself around him like a beckoning arm, drawing him closer and pulling him even further under her spell. Another moment, and he'd be lost.

Steve swallowed. "If you keep touching me like that, looking at me like that, and talking to me like that, I'm going to kiss you."

Instead of pulling away as he'd expected, she leaned closer. Her breasts brushed against his arm. Her finger moved from his jaw to his lips. Deliberately, tantalizingly she traced their outline. It was all he could do not to pull that questing finger into his mouth and suck. Hard.

"Good," she said. "I want you to kiss me."

His heart thundered. She was slowly, methodically driving him insane. With what little control he still possessed, he repeated, "I haven't changed, Kate. I'm the same person I was eighteen months ago, when you left me."

Her finger stilled against his lips; her chin set defiantly. "I don't care."

"You will later."

"Maybe," she conceded. "Maybe not. Right now, all I know is I need this. I need you."

Her beautiful brown eyes gazed at him with warmth and desire. It was the way she'd looked at him when they first met, the way she'd looked at him during the early days of their marriage. He hadn't been able to resist that look then, and he couldn't now.

"Kiss me, Steve."

A wild hunger—to touch and be touched by her—inflamed him. While his reason pulled him one way, his desire, a thousand times stronger, pulled him another. With a groan, his mouth claimed hers, his mind whirling drunkenly with the taste and feel and smell of her.

Her mouth was voracious as her lips parted and her tongue sought and tangled with his. Hot with urgency, her hands undid the buttons on his shirt, then slid restlessly across his chest. Her touch nearly drove him crazy. Sinking his hands into the hair at the nape of her neck, he pulled her so close he could barely breathe. He wanted to inhale her, to make her essence his. In that moment, he knew he could kiss her a thousand times, make love to her a thousand more, and still it wouldn't be enough.

It was the danger that had made her toss her normal caution to the wind. Danger always intensified every sensation. That was one of the first things he'd learned as a cop. After meeting death head-on and surviving, things tasted different, sounded different, smelled different, felt different. Needs, especially that most basic human need to connect and feel close to another person, were exaggerated.

That was all it was, he told himself. The danger. That was why she was kissing him this way. Nothing more.

The knowledge didn't stop his erection from hardening painfully. It didn't stop his questing hands from searching out the softness of her breasts and thumbing her nipples into taut buds that just begged for suckling. And it most certainly didn't stop his heart from yearning for the impossible: that they could start over, with a fresh slate, and live happily ever after.

Taking one of her hands, he pressed it against his hardness. "Feel how I want you, Kate."

She didn't shy away from the contact. Instead, her hand caressed his length, inflaming him even more. Her eyes, when he looked into them, gleamed with a naked hunger that left him reeling.

"I want you, too, Steve," she breathed. "I'm wet for you. If you want to take me now, here, I'm ready."

He nearly exploded when she said that, and his mouth ravaged hers with a savage fierceness. There was nothing more in the world he would rather do than lay her against the cushions of the sofa, remove the clothing from both their bodies, and slide his aching length inside her.

Something, some small pocket of sanity, held him back from doing just that. Yes, she would make love with him now, if that was what he wanted to do. And the wonder of it would shatter them both. Despite that, in the morning she would despise both him and herself for her weakness. And for him, it would make the leaving, when the time came, that much more difficult.

Somehow he managed to summon the strength to pull his mouth from hers. He unclasped the hands that had locked around his neck and gently but firmly placed them in her lap.

"No," she moaned. "Don't."

Gritting his teeth against the wave of desire that once more swept over him, he prayed for strength. "This isn't the time or the place, Kate."

She looked as though she wanted to protest. To his relief, however, she nodded curtly and clamped her mouth shut. "You're right."

For a long moment, they simply sat there, staring at each other, their breathing ragged.

"I didn't want this to happen." He was speaking of more than the kiss.

She seemed to understand, because she nodded and said, "I know. I didn't, either."

His heart was still racing. "Now that it has, what are we going to do about it?"

"I wish I had an answer."

He wished he did, too. "We can't pretend it never happened."

"No," she agreed. "We can't."

"And we can't pretend that the problems that broke up our marriage have miraculously disappeared."

"That would be beyond foolish." She peered at him closely. "This has really shaken you up, hasn't it? Even more than it's shaken me."

He spoke without thinking. "I guess it has. It's just… What happened tonight was too much like that other time, when we were first married and—" Too late, he realized she'd been talking about them, not the smoke bomb, and that he'd said too much. Way too much.

"What other time?" He could see the curiosity in her eyes, and the confusion. "What are you talking about?"

"Nothing. It's not important."

As he'd known she would, she refused to let it go. "I think it is important. What did you mean, tonight was like that other time, when we were first married?"

This was it, he thought. This was where it all hit the fan. Maybe it was for the best. Because when she found out about his deception, he wouldn't have to worry about fighting his love for her. She'd never let him close enough for there to be anything to fight.

"Remember Lyle Benedict?"

Her brow furrowed. "Of course. What's he have to do with this?"

"Right after we got married, when I testified against him and he was convicted, he threatened to kill you."

Shock widened her eyes. "I didn't know that."

He steeled himself mentally for what was to come. "That's because I made a conscious decision not to tell you."

Fury quickly replaced the shock in her eyes. "Are you saying that my life was in danger, and you didn't tell me about it? How could you!"

He sat there, head erect, ready to take the punishment he knew would rain down on him. "I didn't want to worry you."

"You didn't want to worry me," she mocked. "But we're talking about my life here. Sounds like I had every right to be worried."

"In hindsight, no. Lyle never tried to carry out his threat."

"But at the time, you thought he might."

"Yes."

"And you decided, all on your own, that you weren't going to tell me about it."

He'd wrestled long and hard with his conscience over his decision. When he'd spoken to her brothers about it, they'd assured him he was doing the right thing. Kate was pregnant and highly emotional. She was also so very young and unspoiled, too sweet to be touched by such ugliness.

"I made certain you were safe," he told her. "You had nothing to worry about."

"Obviously. How could I worry when I didn't know there was something to worry about?" She crossed her arms beneath her breasts. "So, how did you make certain I was safe?"

Her voice was quiet and controlled. Too quiet. And far too controlled. He knew then that he'd lost her. Ignoring the pain that felt like a fist squeezing his heart, he gave her the answer she sought.

"It was relatively easy. If you weren't busy writing, you were sewing something for the nursery. About the only time you went out was to buy groceries or to go to the post office. All I really needed to do was keep a guard outside the apartment. Your brothers helped."

Her laughter held no humor. "So my brothers were in on it, too. I should have known."

Was it only minutes ago that her eyes had blazed with desire for him? Looking at her now, he found it hard to believe. Equally hard to imagine was the thought that she would ever again look at him with need.

"I did what I thought was right," he maintained.

"Well, it was all wrong," she said heatedly. "The right thing to do was to tell me about it, not treat me like some delicate piece of porcelain that would shatter at the slightest touch. I wouldn't have fallen apart, you know. I think I've more than proven that this past week."

Okay, he conceded, so maybe he'd been wrong. But he'd made his decision with the best of intentions. Did she have to sit there looking at him as though she were Little Red Riding Hood and he the Big Bad Wolf who'd just swallowed up grandma?

"Maybe," he said, fighting an answering anger, "I didn't tell you because I wanted to shield you from all the ugliness that was my life before you came into it. And maybe I didn't tell you because it was the only way I knew you'd ever let me take care of you. It's awfully hard, Kate, being with somebody who doesn't need you for anything."

That seemed to shake her up a bit, he noted in satisfaction. Her confusion didn't last long, however. She catapulted from the sofa and crossed the room, seemingly trying to put as much space between them as possible.

Back to him, she said in a voice raw with emotion, "I thought you cherished my independence as much as I did. I thought you didn't want a clinging vine."

"I didn't...don't." He thrust his fingers through his hair. "Hell, no matter how I try to explain it, I'm going to say it wrong. I didn't keep it from you to hurt you, Kate. Or to be overly macho and protective. Can't you see that?"

She whirled to face him. "You know what's really ironic? I was beginning to hope that maybe things had changed, that you had changed, even though you said you hadn't. But you're not going to change, are you? You have no interest in changing. I'll always need something from you that you can't give me. And I can't change who and what I am for you."

"Have I ever asked you to?" he said softly.

"No, Steve." Her eyes filled with sorrow. "That's the problem, don't you see? You've never asked me for anything, except to be a warm body in bed next to you at night. All you've done is walk away when the going got tough."

"Meaning," he said, "when you were spoiling for a fight."

"Exactly. You'll never open up to me. If you can't even confide in me when my life is in danger, how can I expect you to share what you're feeling in your heart?"

"I don't know what you want me to say."

She sighed. "Nothing, I suppose. It's impossible, isn't it? You and me, I mean."

"It always was impossible." He paused, then asked the question that had lain heavy on his mind since the Scrabble game. "Did you really leave me because I wouldn't fight with you?"

"It's a little more complicated than that. But yes, that was part of the reason. Why did you think I left?"

"Because you fell out of love with me."

She gazed at him for a long minute before replying, "It would have made things a whole lot easier if I had."

Was she saying that she'd still been in love with him when she asked for the divorce? If that was the case, did she love him now? Just a little bit? He opened his mouth to ask, then decided the question would have to wait. She'd been through a lot that evening, and she looked dead on her feet.

Besides, he wasn't sure he could take it if her answer wasn't the one he wanted to hear. And it really was a moot point, since she wasn't about to forgive him for not telling her about Lyle Benedict's threat.

"It's nearly three o'clock," he said softly. "You should go to bed. We'll talk more in the morning."

A bitter light gleamed in her eyes, and her smile was sad. "I knew you wouldn't ask."

"Kate—" he began, then stopped. Now really wasn't the time.

"What?"

He heard the note of hope in her voice and steadfastly ignored it. "Nothing," he said. "Get some sleep."

# Chapter 14

Kate had never been so furious with anyone in her life. How dare he! How dare Steve not tell her about Lyle Benedict and his threat.

All her life, in one way or another, men had conspired to protect her. Her brothers after her mother died, and then Steve after they married. At least now she knew why he'd followed her every move during the first weeks of their marriage. She should have known better than to fall for a man who was just like her brothers. Trouble was, she hadn't known he was just like them, until after she'd said, "I do."

And whose fault was that? Hers and hers alone. She'd been so feverishly in love that she'd taken the ultimate step—lovemaking, which had led to an unplanned pregnancy, which had led to marriage—before she'd gotten to know him. So even though she was furious with Steve, she was even more furious with herself. Not only had she married a man she really didn't know, but, after it had proven a disaster, she'd allowed herself to hope they could start all over again, even though she knew nothing had changed. The old adage was definitely true: there really was no fool like an old fool.

For the better part of the next day, Kate studiously avoided Steve's company. Since the house was so huge, it wasn't hard. If he walked into the library, she went into the kitchen. If he came in there, she stalked to the bedroom he'd assigned her and slammed the door. She knew she was behaving childishly, but she was still so angry she could spit. By ten o'clock that evening, though, she knew they had to talk.

Predictably she found him hard at work in the library. "I still want to go to the cemetery tomorrow," she announced without preamble.

Steve didn't bother looking up from the paperwork spread across the huge mahogany desk. "No."

Her voice rose disbelievingly. "No?"

He looked up then. "After last night, it's too dangerous. Surely you can see that."

After last night, all she could see was the impossibility of them ever working things out. "I told you before that I wasn't going to let this nut control my life. I want to go to the cemetery, Steve. And I want to go tomorrow. I *need* to go."

"No."

She wasn't about to be deterred. "I don't believe this is your choice to make," she said, hands clenched at her sides. "I hired you, remember? And I can fire you. Now, I'm going to the cemetery tomorrow. The only question remaining is, who will be going with me—you, or my new bodyguard?"

For just a minute, as their gazes warred and she saw a fury equal to her own in his eyes, Kate thought she'd gone too far, and that he was about to tell her in no uncertain terms exactly what she could do with this job. Angry as she was at him, it was the last thing she wanted. Steve was the only person she trusted to keep her safe, particularly after last night's events.

"Me," he finally said through gritted teeth.

Relief coursed through her. "Thank you," she replied with as much dignity as she could muster.

Turning on her heel, she marched out of the room. She'd won the battle, and the victory should taste sweet. So why did it taste like ashes in her mouth?

The sudden brightness jolted Kate out of a deep sleep. Disoriented, and not yet ready to wake up, she pulled the covers over her head and tried to recapture a rapidly fading dream.

"Rise and shine," she heard Steve say.

"Huh?" Blinking, she lowered the covers and rose up on her elbows. When her pupils adjusted to the light, she peered blearily at the bedside clock. "It's only five-thirty. What are you doing here?"

"You wanted to go to the cemetery. I agreed to take you. I'm ready to go."

Hands in his pockets, he leaned indolently against the door frame. He was fully dressed in a navy blue suit and white cotton shirt. A mocking gleam lit his eyes. Even though she was still furious with him, and his behavior this morning only served to make her madder still, Kate's heart skipped a beat just looking at him.

And she'd thought her behavior the day before was childish. This little stunt of his gave new meaning to the word.

"It's five-thirty in the morning, Steve," she said wearily. Turning on her side, she pulled the covers up to her chin and closed her eyes. "Only grave robbers go to the cemetery at this ungodly hour."

"Which is exactly why we're going. So your biggest fan won't be lurking about."

Drat the man, but what he said made sense. She was a creature of habit. If her biggest fan knew that—which he undoubtedly did, since he seemed to know everything else about her—it would be an easy thing for him to lie in wait. She cracked an eyelid and saw Steve glancing at his watch.

"You've got exactly ten minutes to get dressed and meet

me downstairs," he said. "Better get moving. Time's a wastin'. Of course, if you'd rather go back to sleep..."

Kate tossed her covers aside and glared at him. "I'll be ready."

"I'll see you downstairs, then."

A lock of hair fell over one eye, and she impatiently brushed it away. "You're enjoying this, aren't you?"

With a smug smile, he pulled away from the door frame and stood erect. "Very much, thank you."

When the door closed behind him, she picked up her pillow and threw it. Since it was stuffed with feathers, it was heavy enough to make a satisfactory thud against the wood. Kate wasn't certain, but she thought she heard Steve chuckle.

Exactly ten minutes later, wearing sweatpants, a T-shirt and tennis shoes, she met him at the front door.

Steve nodded his approval. "I like a woman who's punctual."

It took a great effort of will, and much gritting of teeth, but she refrained from slugging him.

Neither one of them spoke during the ten-minute drive. When they passed through the cemetery gates, the sun was just beginning its climb over the horizon.

They went to her mother's grave first. Steve accompanied Kate, while three bodyguards stationed themselves at strategic points throughout the cemetery.

After paying her respects to her mother, Kate climbed a small hill. The headstone that marked her daughter's final resting spot lay adjacent to the spreading branches of an old oak tree. Steve lagged several steps behind. When she glanced back at him, she couldn't help noticing how reluctant he seemed. He looked for all the world like a man walking to his execution.

A familiar tightness filled Kate's chest when she reached the grave. Kneeling before the marble marker that was inscribed with their daughter's name, she traced the letters with loving fingers. Molly Marie Gallagher.

Would the sharp ache of her loss ever leave her? Kate wondered. Would she ever be able to come here, to think of Molly, without her heart contracting with an unbearable pain?

Blinking back tears, she looked over her shoulder at Steve, who still stood a good five feet away. Understanding dawned. "You've never been here, have you?"

"Not since the funeral," he said in a choked voice.

His face was pinched, his body rigid, his hands clenching and unclenching by his sides. It was obvious to Kate that the last place on earth he wanted to be was here.

"Why not?"

"I can't bear it."

"And I can't stay away," she murmured softly.

There was a long silence while they both stared at the grave.

"It's all my fault," Steve said, the words erupting from him like lava from a volcano.

Kate blinked. "What is?"

"That Molly died."

She stared at him in shock. "Why would you think that?"

"Because it's true." He thrust his fingers through his hair, then turned away.

After rising to her feet, Kate crossed to stand behind him. For the first time, she realized that his pain was as fresh, as cutting as hers, and her heart went out to him.

"Why would you think that, Steve?" she repeated, raising a hand to his shoulder.

His sigh came from the depths of his soul. "You begged me not to go out that night. But I wouldn't listen. The investigation into Quincy's activities had reached a critical point, and I was gung ho to get everything wrapped up before the baby was born. And then I came home, and you were gone. All that was left was a note, and the blood. So much blood. Maybe if I'd stayed with you, the way you wanted, this wouldn't have happened." His voice broke. "Maybe our little girl would be alive today."

Heart aching for him, Kate forgot all about her anger. She

also forgot that three other people were watching them. Had Steve been carrying this terrible burden around with him all this time? How had he been able to bear it?

"Oh, Steve." She moved to stand in front of him. "It's not your fault."

A nerve pulsed in his jaw. "How can you be so sure? You were all alone. If I'd stayed, maybe I could have gotten you to the hospital quicker. Maybe Molly would have had a chance."

To see tears shimmering in his eyes, and to witness his proud shoulders bowed beneath the weight of his pain, was almost more than Kate could bear. Swallowing back her own tears, she shook her head.

"No, Steve. You couldn't have saved her. If you had stayed home with me that night, Molly still would have died. It was just one of those things that sometimes happen, and it happened to us."

His throat worked. "I thought you must hate me."

She laid a gentle hand against his cheek. Then, closing the gap between them, she folded her arms around him. With a shudder, his arms tightened around her like a vise.

"I could never hate you," she said.

"Oh, God," he cried brokenly. "It still hurts so bad."

"I know, I know," she soothed, her tears joining his. Children weren't supposed to die before their parents. It was not the natural order of things.

Arms wrapped around each other, their tears mingled together. When they quieted, Kate felt a healing calm spread through her veins. It soothed her heartache, made her feel whole once more. She looked again at the small marble headstone, and the overwhelming grief was gone.

They'd needed this, she realized. They'd needed to open their hearts to each other, to share their pain in a way they hadn't been able to after Molly died. Now they could finally heal.

"I think I'll be able to come here now," Steve said.

"And I think I won't have to come so often."

He took a step back from her, and her arms fell to her sides. "It's time to move on, isn't it?"

"Yes," she agreed with a nod.

Moving on meant not forgetting their daughter, but accepting that she was gone, that their lives would and must continue without her. Although she'd never felt closer to Steve than she did at that moment, it also meant accepting the death of their relationship. He had opened his heart to her in a way he never had before. Would it be so foolish to hope that this could lead to a new beginning?

Something whistled past her cheek, and Kate heard what sounded like two hollow pops. The pops were followed by the splintering of bark on the old oak tree. Before her startled brain could process what was happening, she found herself facedown on the ground. Steve lay on top of her.

"What are you doing?" she complained, spitting out blades of grass.

"Someone's shooting at us." His voice was tense, and she saw that he'd drawn his gun. "We have to move, Kate. We're an open target right now. When I count to three, you're going to keep as low to the ground as you can while running for the other side of the tree. I'll cover you. Okay?"

Heart thudding with fear, she nodded.

He gave her shoulder a reassuring squeeze. "Don't worry. I won't let anything happen to you. Trust me?"

Above their heads, the bark of the tree splintered again. Kate flinched. What about Steve? she wondered. Who was going to make sure nothing happened to him?

"Yes," she said, her voice shaky. "I trust you."

"Good girl. Ready?"

She drew a deep breath. "Ready."

"One, two, three. Run!"

An adrenaline surge propelled her to her feet as shots continued to ring out around them. The two seconds it took them to reach the safety of the tree seemed an eternity to Kate. When they finally crouched behind it, her heart raced like a jackhammer.

"Are you okay?" she asked, eyeing him for signs of blood. "You weren't hit, were you?"

"I'm fine," he reassured her. "What about you?"

"I'm okay."

One minute passed, then two. There were no more hollow pops, no further splintering of wood. An eerie hush settled around them. The birds had stopped chirping in the trees. The grasshoppers had stopped rubbing their wings in the grass. Kate heard nothing but a nerve-racking quiet.

The sudden silence was almost worse than being shot at. Was her biggest fan on the move? she wondered. Was he creeping up from behind them while they surveyed the ground in front of them? The thought made the hackles rise on her neck.

"Where is he?" she whispered.

"I don't know." Steve spoke into his mouthpiece. "Kent thinks he's closing in on him."

Kate bit her lip. "He was lying in wait for me, wasn't he? Since he didn't know where I was, he just decided to wait here for me to show up. And I, like a fool, walked right into his trap."

"I told you we shouldn't have come."

So much for their new beginning. "I don't think now is exactly the time for I-told-you-so's," she said.

"You're right," he agreed. "I'll save them for when I get you out of here."

And, if she was smart, she'd gladly listen to every one of them a dozen times over, if it meant they were safe.

"For what it's worth," Steve said, "I don't think he meant to kill you just yet. Standing out in the open like we were, he would have had plenty of time to take aim. Either he's a lousy shot, or he deliberately missed. Given the number of shots he fired into the tree, I'd vote for the latter. The bastard's still toying with you."

With a shiver, Kate remembered the whistle of sound past her cheek. It had been a bullet. If her biggest fan was indeed still toying with her and had intended to miss, he'd cut it awfully close.

Far off to the right, she heard a shout. When she turned to look, she saw a figure dressed in black fleeing into the distance. About a hundred yards behind, Kent raced after him.

"Damn!" Steve swore into his mouthpiece a minute later.

Kate sagged. "He got away, didn't he?"

Steve nodded grimly.

As Kate looked around at the open expanse of the cemetery, for the first time she understood the enormity of the task Steve had undertaken in trying to protect her. She certainly hadn't made it easy on him. If anything, she'd made a tough job even tougher.

Two attacks in less than thirty hours. Things were picking up. Her biggest fan had moved from bare hands to smoke bombs to guns. What weapon would he choose next? And how long, she wondered, until he wearied of his games and decided to put an end to things?

"If this guy really wants to kill me, he has a good chance of succeeding, no matter what we do," she said. "Doesn't he?"

Steve's mouth was a tight, grim line. "That's what I've been trying to tell you since you hired me."

Off in the distance, Kate heard the first wail of a police siren.

"Who called the police?" she asked.

"Kent."

She should have known. Unfortunately, if the police were on the way, her brothers wouldn't be far behind. The last thing she wanted at the moment was another long interrogation—with the police, or her brothers.

"I don't suppose we could duck out of here before they arrive?"

Steve stood up and extended his hand toward her. "No, Kate, we can't."

She took his hand and allowed him to pull her to her feet. "That's what I thought."

Despite her exhaustion, Kate couldn't sleep. She had too much on her mind: Steve, her biggest fan, the tangled mess that her life had become. After tossing and turning for over two hours, she put on the robe Liza had purchased for her and headed barefoot for the library. Since she couldn't stomach warm milk, she hoped that if she read for a while, she might be able to numb her brain to the point where she could nod off.

At the foot of the spiral staircase, she stepped onto the cold marble floor of the foyer. To her right, she saw that the sliding wood doors leading into the living room had been closed. From behind them came the strains of a flute. So Steve couldn't sleep, either. At least here, in this huge house, the sound didn't travel the way it did in her much smaller home. Here, he could do his playing in peace. And she wouldn't be tormented and tantalized beyond all measure by its beauty and emotion.

She tiptoed past the closed doors. The one thing she didn't want to do was alert him that she was still awake. She'd had enough I-told-you-so's for one day. Plus, seeing Steve, and feeling the jumble of emotions that the sight of him always aroused, was guaranteed to keep her awake, not put her to sleep.

Fred and Wilma chirped joyously when she entered the library.

"Shh!" she whispered, finger to her mouth. "Not so loud. We don't want to disturb you-know-who."

After lavishing attention on the birds, she perused the floor-to-ceiling shelves that lined an entire wall of the room. Steering away from the leather-bound first editions, which she deemed far too expensive and in too pristine a condition to be touched by mortal hands, Kate concentrated her search on the bottom shelf, far right corner. Nearly hidden from view until one was almost upon it, it was stuffed with paperbacks. Smiling, she crouched down and pulled out a medical thriller. This was definitely more her speed.

She was about to turn away when she saw the scrapbook. Intrigued, she pulled it out and opened it, then caught her breath when she saw that it was filled with newspaper columns. Her newspaper columns.

Had Steve cut these out, collected them? Since he was the only one living here, the logical conclusion was that he had. From the looks of things, except for the week he'd spent as her bodyguard, he'd saved every column she'd written from the day they met. Why? Why would he bother to keep tabs on a woman he no longer loved? Assuming, that is, he'd ever loved her to begin with.

With a snap, Kate closed the book. There was only one way to find out. Leaving the medical thriller behind, she marched out of the room.

# Chapter 15

**K**ate hesitated before the closed living room doors. Why was she even bothering? She was just setting herself up for more frustration. Because she knew what would happen when she confronted Steve with the scrapbook. He'd put her off with some excuse or other, the way he always did. She wouldn't learn anything.

The strains of "Too-ra-loo-ra-loo-ral" floated into the foyer. The song, about a mother singing a lullaby to her child, was beautiful. The notes were rich and soaring, the emotion that fueled them raw and heartfelt.

Was Steve thinking of his mother as he played? Were memories of his tragic past still haunting him and driving him from his bed each night? Was he allowing the notes of the song to speak of his pain and suffering, the way he wouldn't allow his voice?

Her hands clenched at her sides. If so, it was wrong. All wrong. He should be disclosing his pain, his anger and his confusion to another human being, not the cold, unfeeling instrument in his hands.

Barring the scene in the graveyard, though, he'd never willingly confided in her. He'd shared his laughter, but not his anger and his pain. Other than a brief mention when they'd begun dating, he'd never spoken of his mother, or of the beatings they'd endured at the hands of his father and the awful way she had died. He'd always kept his deepest feelings to himself. She'd loved him, loved him still, yet she hadn't been important enough to him for him to unburden himself to her.

Kate's anger grew with every moment that passed as she stood there, listening to him play. When the melody reached a fever pitch, she could contain herself no longer. Shoving both doors wide, she stormed into the room.

He stopped playing immediately. "Is something wrong?"

"Yes, Steve, there is." Her voice vibrated with her fury, and she could feel her body shaking from the force of it. "Night after night, you pour your heart out to that flute. You tell it things you've never told another living soul—things you haven't told me, anyway. And it's driving me crazy. Will you, for Pete's sake, put that thing down and talk to me? Tell me what you're telling it. For once in your life, stop running and hiding. Tell *me* what's bothering you."

Slowly, his gaze on the flute, he lowered the instrument to his lap. "If you want to know the truth," he said, still looking down, "I'm getting tired of running myself. I don't want to do it anymore. It's not getting me anywhere."

A surge of hope obliterated her anger. "Then don't," she said softly. "Talk to me, Steve."

For one of the few times she could remember, the eyes he raised to hers were totally unguarded. "What do you want to know?"

"Why don't we start with this?" She held up her hand. "What does it mean?"

His lips curved wryly at the sight of the scrapbook. "So you found it."

"I was looking for something to read. It was stuffed in

with the paperbacks. And you haven't answered my question.''

"What does it mean?" He drew a deep breath. "It means, Kate, that you're the first thing I think of when I wake up in the morning, and the last before I go to sleep each night. When I can sleep. It means, dammit, that I love you. I always have.''

Her heart lurched with joy. *She* was the reason he couldn't sleep at night. He loved her. They did have a chance, after all.

Instead of leaping into his arms and smothering him with kisses, the way she longed to, Kate forced herself to remain where she stood. Now that he'd started talking, she wasn't about to let him stop until he'd told her everything she wanted to know.

"That's the first time you've ever spoken those words to me," she said.

"I know."

"Say them again."

"I love you, Kate," he said seriously.

"You could sound a little happier about it," she joked, smiling.

He didn't smile back. "I'm not happy about it."

Some of the joy leaked out of her heart. Could it be, even after she'd all but spelled it out to him, even after the way she'd thrown herself at him the other night, that he didn't know how she felt?

"Would it help," she said, "if I told you that I still love you? That I've never, for one minute, stopped loving you, either?"

For a brief moment, sheer joy blazed in his eyes. Then the emotion was snuffed out, like the flame of a candle.

"No, Kate, it wouldn't."

She felt the first stirring of unease. "Why not?"

"Because, in the end, it doesn't matter. What matters is that nothing has changed, as you so rightly pointed out when I told you about Lyle Benedict. We, as a couple, won't work.

The problem that broke us up in the first place still exists. It's not going to go away."

She didn't understand. "But you said you were tired of running. You're not going to walk away from me anymore. When the going gets tough, you're going to stick around and fight it out. That's all I've ever asked, Steve."

The expression in his eyes was bleak. "I said I'm tired of running, Kate. I didn't say I was willing to fight. I'll never be willing to do that."

And until he was willing, they had no future. They both knew it, although she didn't want to believe it.

"Will you at least tell me why?" Her voice was thick with unshed tears as she watched her hopes for a future with him shatter and fall away. "I think you owe me that much."

"Yes, I'll tell you, Kate. For what it's worth. There seems little point in trying to hide it any longer."

He stood and crossed to the fireplace. Back to her, he placed his hands atop the mantle and stared up at the oil painting hanging there.

"I won't fight with you, Kate, because I'm just like my father. I've got this terrible rage lying deep in my soul, and if I ever let it loose, I'm terrified I'll hurt you. Or worse."

Even though she should have seen it coming, given what she knew of his past, his words took her completely by surprise. Why had she never glimpsed this fear before, never guessed at it? Because it went beyond her powers of belief to think that Steve would undeservingly raise his hand to anyone.

"You're nothing like your father," she protested hotly. "You chase into smoke-filled buildings so that two birds don't suffocate, for goodness' sake. How could you ever think you're like him?"

He raised a hand, and she fell silent.

"Once, when I was eight or nine, after one of his rages, I balled my fists at him and threatened to kill him when I got bigger. Know what he did? He laughed. I'll never forget what he said next. He said, 'You're just like me, boy. You're just like me.' And his voice was filled with pride.''

Steve turned to face her then, and she saw the agony in his eyes. "I screamed at him that I wasn't, that I never would be. Then I ran into the bathroom and slammed the door shut. That's when I saw my reflection in the mirror. And the face staring back at me was his. I had the same murderous glint shining in my eyes that I always saw in his. And I knew at that moment that he was right. I *was* just like him.''

He was breathing hard. "God, the hatred that filled my heart! I knew then that I had to harness it, to keep it deep inside me, so I wouldn't hurt the people I loved the way he hurt my mother and me. That's why I won't fight with you, Kate. Now or ever. I couldn't bear it if I ever harmed you.''

Kate's heart ached for him. "Why didn't you tell me this before?''

"Because I was ashamed. Because I was afraid you'd look at me with fear and loathing.''

"You were just a boy," she said, tears spilling onto her cheeks. "A boy being manipulated by a master manipulator. Can't you see that?''

"No, Kate, you're wrong. Until the day my father set me straight, I was also a boy who used his fists whenever he felt he'd been crossed. Kids were terrified of me. It took me years to harness my temper. Since then, I've only lost it once. And the lesson I learned only reinforced that, at all costs, I have to keep it in check.''

"What happened?''

He sighed. "It was after I first joined the police force. Quincy and I were on a routine drug bust. Somehow, things went wrong, and Quincy ended up being held at gunpoint. I managed to get the gun from the perp, but in the struggle to do so, I nearly beat the man to death. Only Quincy's intervention stopped me from killing him.''

"You were under stress—''

"Don't make excuses for me,'' he said, his voice harsh.

"What I did was wrong. I knew it at the time, and still I couldn't stop myself."

"The violence stops here," she murmured. "The plaque in your office. Now I know what it means."

"Yes, now you know. Want to hear something crazy? Even though it hurt like hell, a part of me was glad when you asked for the divorce, because it meant you'd be safe. I'd never harm you."

She crossed the room to stand at his side. "You'll never harm me, Steve. No matter how angry you get. I know that the same way I know that the earth is round and the sky is blue. Why can't I make you see it?"

"Because I know the rage, Kate. I've felt it more times than I can count." Taking her hand, he raised it to his chest. "And it's still alive, right here, deep inside me, like a dormant volcano just waiting to blow. I can't take the risk."

He let her hand go, but she held it where it was, against the warmth of his heart. "What if I'm willing to take it?"

"I won't let you."

"But things would be different this time," she protested. Needing to convince him with her touch as well as her words, she raised her hand and lovingly brushed the hair back from his forehead, then trailed her fingers down his cheeks and across his lips. "Now that I know why—"

"The knowing won't change anything," he interrupted, his mouth moving against her fingers. After capturing her wandering hand between his, he gently but firmly lowered it to her side. "Whenever I feel in danger of losing my temper, I'll still walk away, Kate. I saw what that did to you the first time around, how desperately unhappy you were. I won't put you through it a second time. If you give it some thought, you won't put yourself through it, either."

That he was right didn't make it any easier to accept. Kate had never understood it when she'd read a book or watched a movie where two people who were obviously in love walked away from each other. Now, for the first time, she did. And the pain of it was beyond anything she'd ever felt before, including the loss of her daughter.

"So," she said, drawing a shaky breath, "what this means is that when we find my biggest fan and put him behind bars..." She couldn't go on.

"We each go our separate ways," he finished for her.

"There's nothing I can do to change your mind?"

"I wish you could. You don't know how I wish that, Kate."

She squeezed her eyes shut against the pain. When she opened them a minute later, she'd come to a decision. "Can I ask you a favor?"

"Of course."

"While we're together, for however long it is, I want us to share a bed. Will you do that, Steve? Will you hold me at night? Make love to me? Will you give me the memories that I can hold on to...later?" She felt her lower lip start to tremble and sank her teeth into it. "Please?"

A muscle jumped in his jaw as he gazed at her for untold seconds. Then, in a burst of motion, he reached out and hauled her into his arms. "God help me," he cried, burying his face in her hair. "I'm not strong enough to turn you away."

But he was strong enough to walk out of her life, Kate thought with a twinge of bitterness before shoving the thought from her mind. Tonight she would concentrate only on Steve. On the strength of his arms around her. On how good it felt to have her head cradled to his chest. On the way his heart beat beneath her ear and the heat from his body seeped into hers.

She lifted her head and raised her lips to his. "Kiss me, Steve. Make love to me."

With a groan, his mouth crushed hers. Kate melted against him, her fingers clutching at the fabric of his shirt. The kiss deepened, her mouth parting beneath his as his tongue stabbed into her in a motion that she felt all the way to the core of her femininity. Feverishly, restlessly, his hands slid over her arms and back, until finally his fingers sank into her hair and pulled her mouth so tightly against his it hurt. And still she strained to get closer.

When he raised his head, he caught her beneath the knees and lifted her into his arms. His eyes glittered with a desire that left her weak with wanting.

"You're sure you want this, Kate?"

She didn't hesitate. "I've never been more sure of anything in my life."

His long strides carried her up the stairs and into a bedroom where a huge, mahogany four-poster dominated the masculine room. After turning on a bedside lamp, he set her on her feet.

"Let me undress you," she said, reaching for his shirt buttons.

Gaze locked with his, Kate allowed her fingers to do their work. When the last button had been freed, she slid the fabric off his shoulders and let it fall softly to the floor. His chest rose and fell rapidly as she tangled her fingers through its soft mat of hair.

"Your heart's pounding," she teased as her hands roved from his chest to his hard stomach.

"That's because you're driving me crazy," he replied through clenched teeth.

She sent him a coquettish look. "Want me to stop?"

"Never."

She reached for his belt, and he inhaled sharply. Heady with her power over him, she knelt before him and removed his pants. Though his body was as familiar to her as her own, she felt as if she were seeing it for the first time. Wonder filled her at his perfection. She wanted to touch and kiss and stroke every inch of his skin. When his erection sprang free, she reached for him.

Steve's hands shot out, and he pulled her to her feet. "Not tonight, Kate," he said, shaking his head. "It's been too long. If you touch me like that, I might not be able to hold back."

His fingers slid her T-shirt from her sweatpants. "Besides, it's my turn to undress you."

Slowly, tantalizingly he relieved her of her clothing. When she was finally naked, she trembled with her need.

Steve's gaze roved hotly over her. "You're so beautiful, Kate. You're the most beautiful thing I've ever seen."

A wave of desire washed over her, leaving her weak and yearning. "Love me," she begged.

"Always." He spoke the word as if it were a vow.

This time, when he took her in his arms, she could feel that he trembled, too. After sweeping back the covers, he gently laid her on the cool sheets, then covered her body with his. While his mouth sought hers, his hand slid between her legs, stroking her, readying her.

"You don't know how many times I've dreamed of holding you like this," he said.

"Not any more than me," she replied, gasping with pleasure as his mouth moved from her lips to tease the nipple of one breast.

When he entered her a moment later, Kate shuddered with pleasure. How she'd missed this! How she'd missed him!

Steve moved slowly at first. Then, when she wrapped her legs around him, his movements grew faster, more frenzied.

"I'm sorry, Kate," he groaned, lifting up on his elbows to gaze down at her. "I thought I could be gentle, take my time. But I can't. Lord help me, I can't."

"I don't want you to be gentle," she said.

Her fingers clutched at shoulders that were slippery with sweat, and her eyes closed as he drove into her with hard, urgent strokes. As she arched beneath him, meeting every thrust with an answering one of her own, a familiar sensation started building deep inside her. It grew and swirled until she literally exploded from the force of it. Sobbing his name, Kate wrapped her arms around his neck as their bodies convulsed together.

"Thank you," he said a minute later, arms still around

her. The words were muffled because his face was buried in her hair.

"For what?" she asked, a playful smile curling her lips.

When he lifted his head and gazed down at her, the look in his eyes was anything but playful. "For the gift of your love," he said softly. "No matter what happens in the future, I will always have this night with me."

Kate's smile faltered as reality—the knowledge that their time together was limited—threatened to pierce the veil of sensual fulfillment that enclosed them like a caterpillar in a cocoon. Not tonight, she told herself. Tonight, there was just the two of them. Tonight, and for as long as it took them to find her biggest fan, she refused to think of anything but the satisfaction they could find in each other's arms.

Drawing a long, ragged breath, she banished all sad thoughts and forced the smile back to her lips. "Are you tired?" she asked, her voice heavy with promise as, reaching up, she idly twirled a finger through his hair.

His answering smile was knowing. "Why do you ask?"

Kate's heart pounded with love and need. "No special reason," she teased. "I just thought that if you weren't too tired or too worn out, maybe I could show you a thing or two."

He rolled onto his back, and pulled her on top of him. "Show away," he invited.

She complied willingly.

When Kate woke, late morning sunlight spilled across the massive bed. She was alone. Dressing quickly, she went looking for Steve. She found him in the kitchen, pouring coffee into a mug.

"Can I have some?"

"Of course."

He handed her the coffee he'd already poured. Before she could make eye contact, he turned and reached for another mug.

"Last night was wonderful," she said, after taking a sip.

"Yes," he replied. "It was."

"I can't wait until tonight." She dropped her voice seductively. "Of course, we don't have to wait until then."

He turned to face her. The light of awareness, of shared intimacy that she'd expected to see in his eyes was glaringly absent. He seemed distant, preoccupied. There was a frightening emptiness in his face.

"What is it?" she asked. "Is something wrong?"

"There won't be a tonight, Kate," he said.

"But...I thought you agreed—"

"Carlo just called. Your biggest fan's behind bars."

The words hit her like a blow. Pain squeezed her heart like a fist. *No,* she wanted to cry in protest. *Not yet. I'm not ready.*

"When?" she asked.

"Last night. Carlo's been keeping an eye on the post office. One of his men caught the guy red-handed while he was trying to mail another letter to you. Not only does he own a black Buick LeSabre that he purchased from Portman Motors three years ago, but his prints match those we found in your house. When confronted with the evidence against him, he confessed. The bond hearing was first thing this morning. He pleaded guilty and is being held in the county jail without bail, awaiting sentencing. With any luck, it'll be a long time before he's free to walk the streets."

Kate knew she should be deliriously happy that the threat to her life had been removed. Instead, all she felt was a rising desperation, because the way Steve was acting told her that he meant to follow through with what he'd said last night. Despite his avowals of love to her and hers to him. Despite the incredibly sweet hours they'd spent in each other's arms. Unless she could think of something fast, he was going to walk out of her life. Or, to be more precise, he expected her to walk out of his.

"Did he say why he did this to me?"

Steve shrugged. "Not that I'm aware. Do these kooks ever need a reason?"

"I suppose not." She let out a long breath. "So, it's finally over."

He nodded. "Yes, it is."

"It's safe for me to go home now."

"Yes."

She could still smell his scent on her body, still feel his touch, and he stood there looking at her as if he'd already said goodbye. The hopelessness of the situation made her want to break down and cry. Instead, she lifted her chin and stared at him defiantly.

"You want me to go? Is that what you're saying?"

The knuckles of the hands he'd wrapped around his mug showed white. "I think it would be best."

"You can still say that, after last night?"

Though her words sparked a flare of emotion in his eyes, his voice was empty when he spoke. "To prolong things would only make it harder on both of us. I've already called a cab. It will be here in a few minutes."

So this was it. The end of the road. She'd only had one night with him. It was far too little.

Kate carefully placed her mug on the kitchen table. "I'll go, Steve, if that's what you want. But I won't say goodbye. I'll never say goodbye."

"Then I'll say the words for you. Goodbye, Kate."

Dry-eyed, her pain too deep for tears, Kate stared at the blinking cursor on her computer monitor. As they had been for the past hour, her fingers were poised over the keyboard, waiting for the words to come. But they wouldn't come, no matter how hard she willed it. The screen remained blank. She had no room in her brain, or her heart, for anything but thoughts of Steve. Even the knowledge of a looming deadline wasn't enough to spur her into action.

Most of her columns were an effort to make sense of the world she lived in. They usually began with one simple question: why? Then, in nine hundred words or so, she'd figure out the answers for herself and others. If only it were that easy for her to figure out the solution to her problem with Steve.

Her gaze roved to the bank of computer monitors on Martha's desk, and a lump formed in her throat. Even though it would mean that her biggest fan was still on the loose, she wished with all her heart that Steve was sitting there right now. But he would never sit there again. The last thing he had said to her before the taxi drove off was that someone would be by later that week to collect the monitors.

Drawing a shaky breath, she returned her focus to the computer screen. She was a professional, she told herself. She had a column to write. People were depending on her to get the job done. For however long it took, she would put her misery behind her and do what she had to do. Slowly she began to type.

She wasn't sure how much time had passed when she suddenly realized that she was no longer alone in the room. At the same time, she realized one other thing: whoever the intruder was, he or she had gone to great pains not to be heard.

Kate's fingers froze on the keyboard. A frisson of fear raced up her spine. Too late, she remembered that she'd left her front door unlocked and the security system turned off. The gesture had been a rebellious one, a reaction to everything she'd been through the past week. Now it just seemed foolish. And incredibly stupid.

"Hello, Kate," she heard a familiar voice say, and her fear heightened a notch. "It's been a long time."

Heart pounding, she swiveled around in her chair. The first thing she saw was the gun pointing at her heart. Even before she saw the crazed light in his eyes, she knew that a terrible mistake had been made. Her biggest fan hadn't been caught. She was staring straight at him.

"Quincy," she said.

# *Chapter 16*

The woman wore a long-sleeved dress. Her lank hair had been combed forward to cover the bruises on her cheeks. Dark glasses failed to hide the black-and-blue marks around her eyes. When she looked up from the money he'd placed in her hands, Steve saw tears streaming down her cheeks.

"But this is your own money," she said. "I can't take it. I'll never be able to repay you."

"You don't owe me anything, Mrs. Johnson," he replied. "I'm the one who's repaying a debt. You don't want me to get behind in my payments, do you?"

"No, I...I suppose not."

Still seeming hesitant, she glanced across the reception area to where her two too-quiet children sat with Liza. Steve took advantage of her preoccupation to press his point home.

"If you can't take the money for yourself, take it for them. Later on, when you're in a position to do so, help someone else in need. That will be payment enough."

"All right," she said, much to his relief. "Thank you.

You're a good man, Mr. Gallagher. It's nice to know there are still some of you left.''

The compliment made him uncomfortable. If only she knew the thinness of the line separating him from her husband, she'd grab her children and run screaming from the building.

''You have a bus to catch,'' he reminded her. ''You don't want to miss it.''

''No, we don't. God be with you.''

''And with you, Mrs. Johnson.''

With a nod, she gathered up her children and ushered them into the waiting elevator. As usual, after the doors closed, Steve felt drained. Instead of returning to his office and the workload awaiting him, he remained rooted to the spot, unable to summon up the command that would force his body to move. Inevitably, as they had a thousand times already, his thoughts turned to Kate.

Letting her go that morning had been the hardest damn thing he'd ever done. Although he'd known it was the only answer for them, he'd almost begged her to stay a dozen times. When her taxi had finally driven off, he'd felt as if his heart had gone with it. As, in fact, it had.

He wished he could turn back time to the hours before Carlo's phone call, when she'd lain in his arms and he'd found heaven on earth. If he could turn back time, he'd freeze it there, so that he would never have to let her go.

The phone call. Something about it niggled at him. He couldn't help thinking that a couple of the puzzle pieces were still missing. Everything had been wrapped up too smoothly, too effortlessly for him to completely trust it, he supposed. It was probably just his disappointment that he hadn't been in on the capture. Kate's biggest fan was behind bars. That was all that mattered. She was safe.

Which meant that, once again, he was all alone. A fresh wave of pain washed over him. How was he going to live without her? How was he going to make it through the next minute without her by his side?

He had work to do, he reminded himself. A lot of it. Work had helped him in the past. It had gotten him through the deaths of both his daughter and his marriage. It would see him through this. It had to.

"You have a phone call," Liza announced, jolting him out of his reverie. "A Jock Oldham."

Since he'd phoned Jock earlier that day to let him know the case had been wrapped up, he found it odd that his friend would be calling back so soon. "I'll take it in my office."

Liza surprised him by extending the receiver. "He says he can't wait that long."

Steve's earlier reservations flooded back full force. Something was wrong. Very wrong. In his gut, he knew whatever it was, it involved Kate. Heart thumping and adrenaline surging, he crossed the room and snatched the receiver from Liza's fingers.

"Gallagher here."

"I'm afraid I've got bad news, buddy," Jock said without preamble. "Turns out the guy who was arrested for stalking your ex-wife is Quincy Ellis's brother-in-law. Not only that, but everything he did, he did under Quincy's explicit orders. Or so he now swears."

Steve sucked in a harsh breath. "Why?"

"He claims he had no choice, that Quincy was black-mailing him, and that he was terrified not to do what he'd been told. He also claims that killing your ex-wife was never part of the plan. She wasn't even the real target. I'll give you two guesses who Quincy was really after."

There was no guesswork involved in his answer. "Me," he said dully.

"You got it."

Like the tumblers of a lock under a master thief's fingers, the missing puzzle pieces fell into place. He finally understood. All those near misses. It had never been about Kate. All along, it had been about him. That was what had been niggling at him. He was the target. Kate was just the bait.

Quincy was the only one who truly knew the extent of

Steve's love for Kate, and he'd used that knowledge to his advantage. He'd forced Kate to hire a bodyguard, knowing she'd come to Steve. Then he'd played with them, with their emotions, like a cat with a cornered mouse. Quincy had wanted Steve to know that, even behind bars, he was a force to be reckoned with. And that when and if he was ever released, he'd be exacting his revenge. Personally.

For once, when the familiar rage filled him, Steve welcomed it. Visions of exactly how he'd make Quincy pay for every second of anguish the man had caused Kate swirled drunkenly through his brain. They were followed by the echo of a familiar voice. *You're just like me, boy. You're just like me.*

His rage died immediately. Self-disgust left a sour taste in his mouth and an ache in his gut, and he found himself yearning for the bottle of antacid that was out of reach on the desk in his office. How could he have let himself go like that? But then, hadn't he always known that this was the way he would react in times of great stress? Wasn't this the very thing he'd fought against for most of his life? The very thing he had to continue fighting with every ounce of his strength?

"Why didn't Quincy's brother-in-law say anything about this last night, when he was arrested?" Steve asked Jock. "Why plead guilty to all the charges? Why change his story now?"

"Because," Jock replied, "last night, this morning even, circumstances were different."

"How were they different?"

There was a brief pause, then Jock said, "Less than an hour ago, he was charged with aiding in the escape of a known felon. I hate to be the one to tell you this, buddy, but Quincy's broken out of jail."

Steve drove like a madman. Repeated phone calls to Kate's house continued to go unanswered. While the rational side of his brain told him that she was probably out running errands, that Quincy wasn't stupid and would go underground

until the heat cooled off, his gut told him that his former
friend would waste no time coming after him. And that meant
he was going to try to get Kate. He'd had an hour head start.
To Steve, it seemed a lifetime.

When his car screeched to a halt in front of Kate's house
and he saw the note that had been taped to her front door,
Steve knew he was too late. Quincy had Kate.

He didn't bother to close the car door when he jumped out
onto the sidewalk. It took him less than two seconds to reach
the porch and grab the note. Hands shaking, he read the
words that had been cut and pasted to the page.

As much fun as this game's been, I'm wearying of playing. Time for a trade, old pal. I give you Kate, and you
give me your life. Sound fair to you? If you want to
know where to find her, think two words: déjà vu. Come
alone and unarmed, buddy. Otherwise, I won't be able
to vouch for her safety.

*Déjà vu,* Steve thought, the sense that you've already ex-
perienced something you're encountering for the first time.
His brow furrowed and his panic rose. What the hell did
Quincy mean? How would thinking of déjà vu help him find
Kate?

It took him the better part of the next thirty minutes before
he finally figured it out. Quincy was holding Kate at the old
warehouse where he had conducted his illegal drug business.
He planned on taking Steve down in the same place that he
himself had fallen.

When her fear faded to the point where she could think
beyond her immediate survival, Kate called herself all kinds
of a fool. After all the precautions, she'd been caught woefully unprepared. Now here she lay, on the floor of a vehicle,
hands and feet bound, eyes blindfolded, mouth taped, body
covered by a blanket, and she didn't have a weapon any-

where near her. She'd left the whistle and pepper spray on the bedside table in Steve's bedroom. The cane Mrs. Edmund had given her reposed on the floor beside her computer. Quincy had her purse. She was totally unarmed.

*Except for your brain, Kate,* she told herself. *Use it. Think of a way out of this mess.*

For the first few minutes, she tried to keep her wits about her, tried to figure out where Quincy was taking her. But the vehicle made far too many turns, and she quickly became hopelessly disoriented. They could be in China for all she knew.

Finally, after what seemed hours, they rolled across gravel and came to a halt. After untying her legs, Quincy roughly pulled her to her feet. A hot breeze smelling of diesel fuel and the river lifted her hair from her face. Other than the roar of a jet in the distance and the soft lapping of water, there was no other sound. Kate kicked out blindly at her captor, missed, and sat down hard on her backside.

The next thing she knew, she was hauled to her feet and the barrel of the gun had been shoved into the middle of her back.

"I wouldn't try that again, if I were you," Quincy breathed hotly into her ear.

The tape over her mouth muffled her cries of outrage and frustration. She should run, she knew, but where would she go? She couldn't see, and repeated shaking of her head refused to dislodge the blindfold. With her luck, she'd only tumble into the river. Bound and gagged as she was, she would surely drown. That is, if Quincy didn't shoot her first.

Once again, her fear took over, nearly paralyzing her. Whatever was going to happen was going to happen here. Wherever "here" was. From the silence, and the general feel of decay and isolation, she knew she couldn't count on someone witnessing her plight and coming to her rescue.

Using the gun in her back as a prod, Quincy gave her a shove. "Move," he commanded.

Kate moved.

A minute later the pressure of the gun eased, and she heard a door screech open. Taking her by the arm, Quincy thrust her inside. Kate barely had time to register the blessed coolness before she was pushed forward.

She stumbled and lost her balance. Since her hands were bound behind her back, she had no way to break her fall. Unprotected, her chin slammed into a concrete floor. The impact was blinding. Pain drove through her, and she tasted blood.

Quincy left her no time to nurse her injuries. After dragging her to her feet, he propelled her relentlessly forward. Ignoring her pain, Kate concentrated on not falling again.

They climbed a pair of metal stairs that clanged hollowly in the silence. At the top of the stairs, Quincy shoved her through another doorway. A final shove, and she tumbled onto a bare mattress whose springs squeaked with age.

Winded, she lay quietly, trying to still the pounding of her heart and the ache in her jaw. She heard the flare of a match, and then silence. A minute later, she felt Quincy's fingers fumbling at her ankles as he rebound her legs. By the time she realized what was going on, it was too late to fight back. When she was once more immobilized, he undid the knot of her blindfold.

Candlelight bathed the room in a soft glow. Through the dimness, Kate saw that it was very small. Other than the narrow bed on which she lay, the only other furnishings were a scarred metal desk, some empty bookcases lining the wall and a filing cabinet. A thick layer of dust covered every surface. There were no windows.

The mattress beneath her back smelled mildewy. What she could see of it was stained. Kate decided she was better off not knowing the source of the stains.

Quincy removed the tape from her mouth, and she gingerly moved her jaw to see if it would function. When it did, she opened her mouth to scream.

"Go ahead," he said calmly, moving to perch on a corner

of the desk. "Scream yourself hoarse. There's no one to hear you."

She did scream once, out of sheer desperation and a faltering hope that someone might be nearby. The echo of it bounced off the walls and rang in her ears. Silence was her only answer. No one came running.

"I told you so," Quincy said mildly. "Sorry about the wrist and ankle restraints. But after that little episode outside, something tells me I won't be able to trust you to remain lying on that bed. Will I?"

Instead of answering, Kate stared at him in mutinous silence.

He laughed. "Still the same old stubborn Kate, I see."

"Where are we?"

"In an old warehouse. It hasn't been used in years, but structurally it's still sound. I thought I'd tell you, just in case you were worried."

"Is this where you did your drug dealing?"

His smile faded. Though his body blocked the flickering candle and cast a huge shadow over the room, she could still see the light of fanaticism that rekindled in his eyes. "That's none of your concern."

"I thought you were in jail."

"I was, until this morning."

"I can't believe they just let you walk away."

"They didn't."

He pushed off the desk and brushed the dust from the back of his pants. A second later, he let loose a string of curses. When his head twisted back to peer over his shoulder, he turned his body at such an angle that she could see he was looking at a rip in the back of his pants.

Kate felt a surge of irritation. There he stood, having kidnapped her and planning to do goodness knows what to her, and he was all upset about a stupid rip in his pants?

"If they didn't let you walk away, how'd you get out?" she asked.

As she'd intended, the question seemed to distract him

from the examination of his pants. "Again, that's none of your concern. As you can see, I'm here. That's all that matters."

Which meant he'd broken out of prison and had managed to get a new pair of clothes and a gun. She didn't want to think of the resources he possessed that allowed him to accomplish that feat. Or of what those resources might still accomplish.

"You're my biggest fan, aren't you?"

He gave a low bow. "At your service."

"Who'd they arrest last night?"

When he straightened, she saw that his lips were curved mockingly. "My brother-in-law. He did my legwork for me. He'll do anything for money."

"Including going to jail for you?"

"Even that. I have some...leverage, shall we say, over him."

So he was blackmailing his own brother-in-law. "Why are you doing this?"

A look of disappointment crossed his face. "Haven't you figured it out yet? I thought you were smarter than that, Kate."

Yes, she'd figured it out. She'd known the truth the minute she'd seen him standing in her den. "You did this to get back at Steve."

"Good girl." He glanced at his watch. "He should be on his way here any minute. I left a note for him on your front door. It's a little cryptic, but he'll figure it out."

"Why use me as bait?" she asked, trying to buy time, to think of a way out. "Steve and I are divorced, remember?"

"He agreed to act as your bodyguard, didn't he?"

"That's because I hired him. It's what he does for a living. But now that he knows who's behind all the threats and why, what makes you think he'll come here to save me? Maybe he'll send someone else."

"He'll come," Quincy stated confidently, "because he

loves you. He's always loved you. The way you love him. Everyone seemed to know it but you two.''

Kate didn't want to think about her love for Steve, a love that he deemed hopeless. If she did, despite the danger confronting her, the ache in her heart would surely overtake the throbbing in her jaw. She'd become lost in memories and self-pity. Then what good would she be? She'd certainly never figure a way out of this mess.

''Why?'' she asked again. ''Why are you doing this, Quincy?''

He began pacing back and forth. ''Because of Steve,'' he spat, glaring at her, ''I lost everything. *Everything*. My wife. My kids. My job. My freedom. He has to pay for that, Kate.''

''Steve didn't make you jump into bed with those drug dealers,'' she felt compelled to point out. ''He didn't force you to accept their blood money.''

Quincy's face darkened with fury, and she shrank back against the mattress. ''He never should have turned me in,'' he shouted. ''A cop doesn't turn on his own.''

How did one fight such crazy logic? It was impossible. To try to reason with someone like Quincy would be a waste of breath. He was incapable of understanding. And he wasn't about to accept responsibility for his actions at this late date.

''You're going to kill him, aren't you?'' Quincy would never know what it cost her to utter those words.

''The thought of hearing him beg for mercy is the only thing that's kept me going these past months. First, though, I want to make him suffer. I want to make him lose everything that is precious to him the way I did. That means you, Kate.''

Which meant he planned to kill her, too. ''You'll never get away with it.''

''Won't I?'' His smile sent a chill up her spine. ''I'm out of prison, aren't I? Don't worry about me, Kate. Once I kill Steve, I have enough money stashed away to get me out of the country. I'll do just fine. My only regret is that I have to kill you, too.'' He shrugged. ''Just think of it as being in the wrong place at the wrong time.''

He was insane, she realized. Completely insane. Somewhere, during his time in prison, or maybe even before, he'd gone over the edge. Instead of being afraid for herself, she was terrified for Steve and what awaited him when he arrived. She had to do something to help him.

Quincy stopped his pacing and blew out the candle. ''Much as I'm enjoying our little discussion, I have to leave you now. There are a few things I have to do before your ex-hubby arrives. Don't worry. I'll be back. In the meantime, why don't you take a nap? You look a little…stressed.''

When the door closed, the room was plunged into a blackness so complete Kate felt she'd been imprisoned in a cave. The fear that had laid claim to her when Quincy blew out the candle increased a hundredfold at the turning of a key in the lock. She was well and truly trapped.

Taking deep breaths, Kate fought against the panic that threatened to overwhelm her. She couldn't let her fears take control. She had to keep her wits about her.

Where was the cavalry when you needed them? she wondered in despair, before smiling grimly in the darkness. Here she was, Miss Independence personified, and all she could think about was getting rescued. The truth was, she was going to have to rescue herself. Because if she didn't, something terrible was going to happen to Steve.

Her first order of business was to untie the rope around her wrists and ankles. Once that was accomplished, she'd think of what to do next.

Kate rolled onto her side and wrinkled her nose at the odor wafting up from the dirty mattress. When she tried to touch the knot at her wrists, her fingers wouldn't reach. No matter how she twisted and strained, the goal remained stubbornly elusive. If anything, her efforts served to tighten the knot.

When she stopped struggling, she could feel perspiration pouring down her face. She was getting nowhere fast, she decided. Since she wasn't going to be able to untie the rope, or twist her way out of it, she'd have to find another way to loosen it. But how?

The tear in Quincy's pants, she thought suddenly. Was it possible that something on the desk had caused it, that he hadn't just discovered it when he stood up to brush off his pants? There was only one way to find out.

She wasted precious seconds struggling to a sitting position, but finally she found herself on the edge of the bed, her feet flat on the floor. She stood carefully and began hopping toward the desk. At least, she hoped she was heading toward the desk. It was impossible to tell in the blackness that surrounded her.

A few seconds later, she collided with something big and square. Turning her back to the desk, she felt her way along the top until she reached the corner. Apparently, a piece of the chrome that had originally covered it had broken away, leaving a sharp, jagged angle. Her fingers traced over it. If she was very, very lucky, it just might do the trick.

How much time did she have before Quincy returned, before Steve walked into the trap Quincy was setting for him? Minutes? Seconds? Quincy had said that Steve would be arriving shortly. Surely that meant that whatever time she had left, it was of the essence.

Frantically Kate began sawing the rope back and forth against the jagged metal. The tender skin of her wrists was quickly rubbed raw. *Think of Steve,* she told herself to take her mind off the pain. *Think of Steve.*

Funny, how she could see things with such clarity now that everything might be lost. She was as much to blame for the breakup of her marriage as he was. Before Steve, she'd never wanted to need anyone, had gone out of her way *not* to need anyone. When she'd discovered how vital he'd been to her, how much she'd actually depended on him, it had scared her silly.

The truth was, she'd let him walk away all those times, because to beg him to stay would be to admit her need for him. And, while he might not have uttered the three little words she'd longed to hear from him, she hadn't played fast and loose with them, either.

It shamed her to realize that, when they were married, he'd done all the giving, and she'd done all the taking. When had she ever offered him the comfort he needed and was too proud to ask for? Never.

No wonder he hadn't been able to open up to her. She'd been so busy trying to stand on her own two feet, she hadn't been able to see she was driving Steve away. Now, when it was probably too late, she finally understood that being independent didn't mean that she couldn't confide her problems and concerns. To need someone was not a show of weakness. It was simply human.

And, oh, how she needed Steve. He was as essential to her as breathing.

If she managed to live through this, Kate vowed she wouldn't make the same mistakes again. Every day of their lives—together, if she could talk him into it—she'd show Steve how much she loved him and needed him. And if he couldn't get past his fear of harming her? She wouldn't let that be an obstacle.

She'd been a fool to think her love wasn't enough. It was. With time and patience, Steve would see that he was no threat to her. Then, and only then, would he be able to give his emotions free rein.

Kate almost sobbed with relief when the rope gave way and fell from her sore wrists. As quickly as she could, she untied her ankles. Now that she was free, she needed to find a weapon.

Unfortunately, the desk had no chair that could be smashed over the head of an unsuspecting Quincy. And, for some unknown reason, the desk drawers had been locked. Ditto the filing cabinet drawers. No matter how hard she tugged, she couldn't get one drawer to pull free. That left the mattress—which was too unwieldy for her to lift, let alone swing at anyone—and the candle, which was so insubstantial it might as well be dust.

''There has to be something I can use,'' Kate said out loud. ''There just has to.''

Even though she couldn't see a thing, she closed her eyes and concentrated. Going very still inside, she used her memory to visualize every inch of the small room. It was a trick Steve had taught her to recall things she had forgotten. In the past, she'd used it quite successfully to find her car keys and other small items she'd mislaid.

No matter how many times she pictured the room, however, she saw nothing that would work as a weapon. Nothing, that is, except that blasted candle. And her own two hands and feet.

She would have to attack Quincy herself. The minute he opened the door. The odds weren't good that she would succeed, but she had no choice. Hopefully, the element of surprise would work in her favor.

Out of sheer frustration and fear, Kate batted an arm in the direction where she knew the candle to stand. When she made contact with the thin tube of wax, it toppled over. And made a thunk. A loud thunk.

Kate slowly felt her way across the rear of the desk. To her delight, she discovered the candle had been anchored into a chipped glass ashtray. Somehow—most likely because Quincy had blocked her view of it a great part of the time— it had passed her notice.

Kate pulled the candle from the ashtray and lifted the glass to get a sense of its heft. It felt heavy enough to accomplish its task. Positioning herself behind the locked door, she settled down to the chore of waiting. And building her courage.

What seemed a lifetime later, she heard footsteps echoing up the metal stairs. A moment after that, someone paused outside the door. The sound of a key scratched in the lock.

Holding her breath, and hoping that the rapid beating of her heart wasn't audible to anyone but herself, Kate raised the ashtray and mentally prepared herself to strike. When the door started to creak open, she was assailed by second thoughts. What if it was Steve? Or someone else who had come to her rescue?

The door opened wider, and she banished the thoughts. This was no time for cold feet. She had to act. She had no choice. She might not get another chance.

Stepping out from behind the door and squeezing her eyes tightly shut so she wouldn't be blinded by the light, Kate brought the ashtray down with all her strength. The contact nearly wrenched her arm out of her socket. She heard the sickening sound of glass meeting flesh, the thunk of a gun as it hit the floor, and the thud of something big and solid at her feet. When her eyes adjusted to the light, she saw with relief that it was Quincy. He was out cold.

"Quincy?" she said, nudging him with her toe, just to be sure. "Quincy?"

The body on the floor didn't move. Kneeling by his side, she raised one arm and checked for a pulse. When she felt its steady rhythm, she let go of his hand. She had to get out of there before he regained consciousness.

Even though she knew it was hopeless, she found herself screaming at the top of her lungs as she stumbled from the room. "Help!" she cried. "Help! Can anybody hear me?"

She was at the top of the stairs when she heard someone shout her name. Leaning over the railing, she saw Steve step out of the shadows. Never in her life had a sight been more welcome.

"Steve!" she cried. "Up here!"

"Kate!" he cried back, his gaze flying to hers. "Are you okay?"

She gave him a wide smile. "I am now."

"Don't move. I'll be right there."

He took the stairs three at a time, and then she was in his arms. His wonderful, strong arms. He held her so tightly she couldn't breathe, and rained her face with kisses. She didn't complain. She was where she wanted to be, where she wanted to stay forever.

"I thought I was too late, that I'd lost you forever," he said between kisses.

Kate's heart swelled with love and need. "You'll never lose me, Steve. Haven't you realized that yet?"

He looked around them. "Where's Quincy?"

She nodded over her shoulder at the open doorway. "In there. I knocked him cold with an ashtray."

"Good girl." He ran his gaze over her. "He didn't hurt you, did he?"

Kate thought of her jaw, which miraculously didn't bother her at all, now that Steve was here. "No," she said. "He didn't hurt me."

Along with his cell phone, Steve pulled a pair of handcuffs from his pocket. After handing the cuffs to Kate, he placed a quick call.

"We'd better restrain him before he wakes up," he said when he disconnected. "The police will be here any minute."

"What's going to happen to him?" she asked.

Steve gazed at her with understanding. "He'll never be able to hurt us again. Not only won't his brother-in-law be free to do his bidding, but this time he'll be guarded around the clock while he awaits trial. Trust me, Kate, Quincy Ellis will never walk the streets again."

"That's what you think," Quincy growled.

Too late, Kate sensed movement from the open doorway. "Steve!" she screamed as Quincy launched himself at them.

Steve thrust Kate out of the way, leaving her to watch helplessly while he grappled with Quincy on the narrow walkway. While Steve was in much better physical shape than Quincy, Quincy had desperation on his side. He had nothing to lose, which gave him a strength that far surpassed his normal abilities.

Kate inched her way to the open doorway. She couldn't just stand there and hope that Steve would be able to subdue Quincy. She had to help. Somewhere, inside that dark room, there was a gun. And she was going to find it.

Sobbing with worry and terror, she inched around on the filthy floor. She finally found the gun against the wall under the narrow bed. When she reached the doorway, the sight that greeted her eyes took her breath away. Steve was bent backwards over the narrow railing, and Quincy had his fingers around Steve's throat.

She raised the gun. "Don't move, or I'll shoot," she commanded in a voice that was surprisingly strong considering how terrified she was. If Steve fell…

Fingers still around Steve's throat, Quincy turned his head. When he saw the way the gun wavered, he laughed.

"You going to shoot me, Kate? Your hand's shaking so bad, you couldn't hit the side of a barn."

"You willing to take that chance?" she challenged. Through sheer effort of will, her hand steadied. The gun now pointed directly at Quincy's head.

"You willing to hit your lover here?" he taunted.

His words almost made her lower the weapon. She didn't know the first thing about shooting a gun. What if she hit Steve by mistake?

Mercifully the question went unanswered, because Steve took advantage of Quincy's distraction to attack. With a roar of rage he brought his feet up and kicked Quincy in the midsection. While Quincy went flying against the wall, Steve fell to the floor, coughing.

"The gun, Steve!" she cried, tossing it in the air as Quincy found his feet. Steve deftly caught it, and charged his former best friend.

The battle ended a minute later, with Quincy facedown on the floor. Steve straddled his back and held the gun to his head.

"This is the last time you'll ever threaten her," he vowed in a voice of raw fury. "Do you hear me?"

"The only way to make sure is to finish me off," Quincy said. "Do it. End it here, now. Otherwise you'll be forever looking over your back."

Heart thumping, Kate held her breath. *No, Steve,* she begged silently. *Don't do it. Please don't do it.*

For what seemed hours, but was probably only seconds, Steve sat motionless. A dozen emotions flitted across his face as he stared down at the man he had once called friend. Fury. Hatred. Confusion. Resignation.

"No," he finally said, shaking his head forcefully. "No."

Relief surging through her, Kate scrambled to his side and placed the handcuffs around Quincy's wrists. They used the rope Quincy had bound Kate with to secure his legs. Then, leaving him where he lay, they strolled hand in hand outside and into the sunlight.

Kate didn't realize that tears were streaming down her cheeks until she saw the worried look on Steve's face.

"What is it?" he asked. "Are you hurt? Why are you crying?"

"It's just...I'm so happy. You stopped. You *stopped,* Steve. If you couldn't bring yourself to harm the man who was threatening both our lives, you'll never hurt me. Surely you can see that now."

And, suddenly, she knew that he did see. The wonder in his eyes filled her heart with joy and love. To Kate it was like watching the sun appear over the horizon for the first time.

"I stopped," he repeated, his voice filled with awe. "I really stopped."

"Yes," she said. "You did."

His gaze met hers. "I'll never hurt you, or anyone else."

"No, Steve, you won't."

He pulled her so close that she lost all sense of where she ended and he began. "I love you, Kate."

"I love you, too."

"You sure you want to hook up with me again?"

She tightened her arms around his neck. "I've never been more sure of anything in my life."

Neither of them paid any attention to the wailing sirens

that hailed the arrival of the police. Inside the abandoned warehouse lay a man whose life, by his own choice, was essentially over. But theirs had a new beginning. A wonderful new beginning.

# *Epilogue*

"What is it that you ask for this child?" the priest said.

Kate looked down at the sleeping infant in her arms, and a wave of love washed over her. "Baptism," she and Steve answered in unison.

They were surrounded by those they loved most. Kate's father had traveled up from Florida with his new bride to attend the momentous event. Mrs. Edmund and Clara Mae Edgington beamed at them from the front pew.

To Kate's right, Martha stood, her joy at being selected godmother written all over her face. And to Steve's left stood all six of her brothers.

Kate supposed it was rather unconventional for one small child to have six godfathers. The one thing she'd learned from her experience with Quincy, however, was the importance of showing those you love how you feel. When it came down to it, she hadn't been able to choose which of her six brothers on whom to bestow the honor of being godfather. So she'd chosen them all. One thing was for certain. Her daughter was going to grow up showered with love from her father and all six of her overprotective uncles.

And she'd probably rebel just the way Kate had. Such was life.

"Happy?" Steve asked when the ceremony was over and they walked out of the church together. As always, the love shining in his eyes made Kate's heart turn over.

"I'm so happy it should be illegal."

"Me, too."

So much had happened in the two years since she and Steve had remarried. He'd sold his grandparents' home, and they now resided in the house she'd bought. Quincy had never gone to trial. The night before he was to be tried, he'd used a sheet to hang himself in his cell. While Kate was saddened by the waste of his life, in a way she was also relieved. Never would she or Steve have to look over their shoulders and wonder if Quincy would once again try to get even.

As for Steve's fear of confrontations, things hadn't changed overnight. In the beginning, he'd still had the tendency to try to walk away whenever things had gotten tense. But, little by little, with the passage of time and Kate's patient persistence, he'd learned to air his feelings. Each time he had done so without the worst happening, his confidence had grown. Now it was simply routine for him to blow off steam whenever things got to be too much. The bottle of antacid that had been his constant companion was history.

And now this wonderful child, this beautiful little girl they'd named Sarah Elizabeth, had entered their lives. Things couldn't be more perfect.

"I should have fought for you, Kate," Steve said as he helped settle the baby into her car seat. Since their remarriage, it was almost uncanny how he always seemed to read her thoughts without her saying a word. "Back when we were first married, I mean. I know that now. I warn you, if you ever try to leave me again, you'll be in for the battle of your life."

Kate turned to her husband and kissed him on the lips. "Trust me," she said with a smile. "That's one battle you will never have to fight."

\* \* \* \* \*

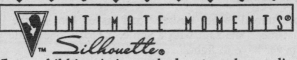

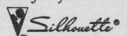

If you enjoyed what you just read,
then we've got an offer you can't resist!

# Take 2 bestselling love stories FREE!

# Plus get a FREE surprise gift!

## INTIMATE MOMENTS®

### ™ Silhouette®

and

# DOREEN ROBERTS

invite you to the wonderful world of

# RODEO MEN

A secret father, a passionate protector,
a make-believe groom—these cowboys are
husbands waiting to happen....

**HOME IS WHERE THE COWBOY IS**
IM #909, February 1999

**A FOREVER KIND OF COWBOY**
IM #927, May 1999

**THE MAVERICK'S BRIDE**
IM #945, August 1999

Don't miss a single one!

Available at your favorite retail outlet.

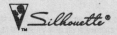

Look us up on-line at: http://www.romance.net          SIMRM

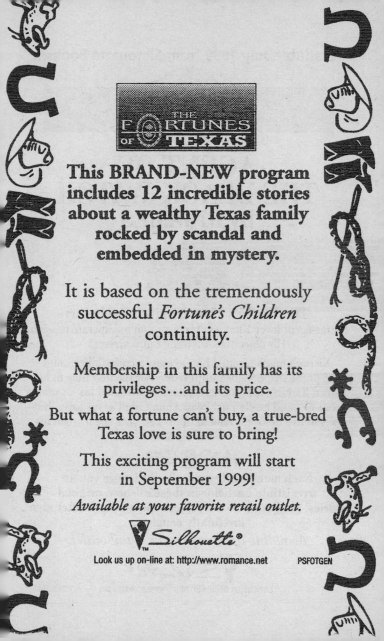

# THE FORTUNES OF TEXAS

This **BRAND-NEW** program includes 12 incredible stories about a wealthy Texas family rocked by scandal and embedded in mystery.

It is based on the tremendously successful *Fortune's Children* continuity.

Membership in this family has its privileges...and its price.

But what a fortune can't buy, a true-bred Texas love is sure to bring!

This exciting program will start in September 1999!

*Available at your favorite retail outlet.*

**Silhouette®**

Look us up on-line at: http://www.romance.net          PSFOTGEN

**Available July 1999 from Silhouette Books...**

# AGENT OF THE BLACK WATCH
## by BJ JAMES

### The World's Most Eligible Bachelor:
Secret-agent lover Kieran O'Hara was on a desperate mission.
His objective: Anything but marriage!

Kieran's mission pitted him against a crafty killer...and
the prime suspect's beautiful sister. For the first time in his
career, Kieran's instincts as a man overwhelmed his lawman's
control...and he claimed Beau Anna Cahill as his lover. But
would this innocent remain in his bed once she learned his
secret agenda?

**Each month, Silhouette Books brings you an
irresistible bachelor in these all-new, original
stories. Find out how the sexiest, most-sought-after men
are finally caught....**
*Available at your favorite retail outlet.*

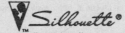

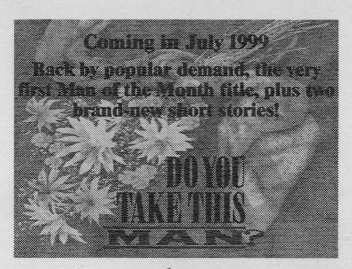
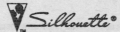

# THE MACGREGORS OF OLD...

**#1 *New York Times* bestselling author**

# NORA ROBERTS

has won readers' hearts with her enormously popular
MacGregor family saga. Now read about the MacGregors'
proud and passionate Scottish forebears in this
romantic, tempestuous tale set against the bloody
background of the historic battle of Culloden.

*Coming in July 1999*

# REBELLION

One look at the ravishing red-haired beauty and Brigham
Langston was captivated. But though Serena MacGregor
had the face of an angel, she was a wildcat who spurned
his advances with a rapier-sharp tongue. To hot-tempered
Serena, Brigham was just another Englishman to be
despised. But in the arms of the dashing and dangerous
English lord, the proud Scottish beauty felt her hatred
melting with the heat of their passion.

*Available at your favorite retail outlet.*

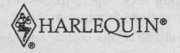